A Promise
of Forever

BOOKS BY SHERYL LISTER

A Perfect Pairing

A Table for Two

A Promise *of* Forever

SHERYL LISTER

FOREVER

New York Boston

This book is a work of fiction. Names, characters, places, and incidents are the product of the author's imagination or are used fictitiously. Any resemblance to actual events, locales, or persons, living or dead, is coincidental.

Copyright © 2025 by Grand Central Publishing

Cover design by Susan Zucker. Cover image by ISTOCK. Cover copyright © 2025 by Hachette Book Group, Inc.

Hachette Book Group supports the right to free expression and the value of copyright. The purpose of copyright is to encourage writers and artists to produce the creative works that enrich our culture.

The scanning, uploading, and distribution of this book without permission is a theft of the author's intellectual property. If you would like permission to use material from the book (other than for review purposes), please contact permissions@hbgusa.com. Thank you for your support of the author's rights.

Forever
Hachette Book Group
1290 Avenue of the Americas, New York, NY 10104
read-forever.com
@readforeverpub

First Edition: August 2025

Forever is an imprint of Grand Central Publishing. The Forever name and logo are registered trademarks of Hachette Book Group, Inc.

The publisher is not responsible for websites (or their content) that are not owned by the publisher.

The Hachette Speakers Bureau provides a wide range of authors for speaking events. To find out more, go to hachettespeakersbureau.com or email HachetteSpeakers@hbgusa.com.

Forever books may be purchased in bulk for business, educational, or promotional use. For information, please contact your local bookseller or the Hachette Book Group Special Markets Department at special.markets@hbgusa.com.

Library of Congress Cataloging-in-Publication Data

Names: Lister, Sheryl, author.
Title: A promise of forever / Sheryl Lister.
Description: First edition. | New York : Forever, 2025. | Series: Firefly Lake
Identifiers: LCCN 2025008723 | ISBN 9781538755310 (trade paperback) |
    ISBN 9781538704646 (ebook)
Subjects: LCGFT: Romance fiction. | Novels.
Classification: LCC PS3612.I863 P76 2025 | DDC 813/.6—dc23/eng/20250227
LC record available at https://lccn.loc.gov/2025008723

ISBNs: 978-1-5387-5531-0 (trade pbk.), 978-1-5387-0464-6 (ebook)

Printed in the United States of America

LSC-C

Printing 1, 2025

In memory of Georgia "Mother Rose" West, a true champion of authors and literature. Forever in my heart...

A Promise *of* Forever

CHAPTER 1

I'm losing him. The three words sliced through Terri Rhodes's heart. And she couldn't let that happen. Seated across the dinner table from her husband, Jonathan, who had his head buried in his iPad and was typing away, she noted that they'd become virtual strangers, neither of them speaking, and barely eating. Terri took a moment to study him. With his walnut-colored skin, dark brown eyes framed by lashes a woman would kill for, and neatly barbered goatee, she thought he was even more handsome than the day they met. And even the dress shirt he wore couldn't hide the hard, muscular planes of his chest and arms. The chest and arms that used to hold her close when he whispered, *I love you.* It had been weeks...or had it been months since she'd felt his nearness? And when was the last time he'd told her he loved her?

Sighing softly, she took a sip of her lemonade and wished she had wine instead. "So, how was your day?" she asked, attempting to fill the awkward silence.

Jonathan glanced up briefly and shrugged. "Fine. Busy. Just like every other day." He forked up some mashed potatoes, shoved them into his mouth, and resumed typing.

Terri toyed with the roasted chicken on her plate, her appetite steadily waning. "I was hoping we could talk," she said, trying once again to engage him in conversation.

His head came up again and he frowned. "Did something happen at the hospital?"

"No. I just wanted us to do like we used to." When he didn't reply, she ate a bite of her now lukewarm mashed potatoes. "There was a time when we talked about anything and everything. Now, I can barely get two words from you most days. Is there something going on that I should know about?"

"No," Jon answered without looking up.

She sighed. "Do you even want to still be in this marriage?" Terri held her breath, not sure she really wanted the answer. She seemed to be the only one trying to keep the relationship together these days.

This time when he looked up, concern lined his features. "Of course. I don't want anyone else but you, Terri. And if you're talking about divorce, that's *definitely* not something I want."

She slumped against the chair in relief. It wasn't something she wanted to entertain, either. "I'm glad we can agree on that, but things can't continue like they've been these past several months, Jon. Maybe we should try counseling or something."

Jon set the iPad on the table, picked up his glass, and drained half the contents. "We don't need counseling. Every married couple has their ups and downs. It'll work itself out."

Terri stared at him incredulously. "You're a lawyer, Jon, and you know better. Don't insult my intelligence." She stood, picked up her plate and glass, and carried them to the sink.

"Terri—"

"When you're ready to have a conversation based in truth, let me know." With nothing more to say, she pivoted on her heel and retreated to the back deck. Dropping down into one of the cushioned chairs that faced the mountains and a distant lake, she drew in a deep breath and let it out slowly in hopes it would cool her anger. She repeated the process a few more times, then trained her eyes on her beautiful surroundings as the sun dipped below the horizon. From the moment they saw the house, she'd fallen in love with the view and knew it would be her favorite place. It had also become her solace. Tears stung her eyes, and she blinked them back.

When she had proposed them having dinner tonight, she had hoped it would remind Jon of the times when they had promised to eat together at least three nights a week, despite their busy schedules. Obviously her husband hadn't gotten the same memo, because over the past two years their time together had steadily dwindled and she could count on one hand how many evenings they'd sat down to have dinner. Jon had taken on more cases at the law firm where he served as a senior partner and arrived home later and later as the months passed. Not wanting to come home to an empty house, she'd begun to take more nursing shifts in the emergency room. They'd moved from Los Angeles to Firefly Lake almost four years ago, hoping to put their year-old whirlwind marriage back on track. It had worked for a short time. But now? Terri had no idea how to make it better, since she had yet to figure out a way to get Jon to even acknowledge they had problems.

Terri had done everything she could think of to put the spark back in her marriage, from leaving sweet notes to planning intimate dinners, but nothing seemed to be working. She startled when her cell buzzed in her pants pocket. Digging it out, she smiled when she saw her friend Serenity Cunningham's name on the display.

"Hey, girl," she said when she connected.

"Hey. How did dinner go?"

"It didn't. Jon had his face buried in his iPad the whole time, and I couldn't even engage him in a simple conversation."

Serenity's heavy sigh came through the line. "I'm so sorry, Terri. I thought for sure that since he agreed to be home for dinner, you two would be able to talk about your problems."

"According to him, we don't have any." She told Serenity what Jon said about their issues working themselves out and her leaving him at the table.

"Okay. Wait. What does he mean they'll work themselves out? Girl, please tell me he didn't say something that ludicrous."

"I wish I could, but yeah, he said it. I don't know what to do, Serenity. He said he doesn't want a divorce, and I absolutely don't want it, either." She sighed, leaned her head back, and closed her eyes. "But I feel like I'm all out of options."

"There has to be something left to do, especially since neither of you wants to end the marriage. I have to say I'm really glad to hear that, because I truly believe you two belong together. Let's discuss it next Saturday at supper club."

Terri smiled. One of the best things about her move had been the friendship with Serenity and their two other friends

Natasha Hayes, who'd reconnected with and married her high school sweetheart a couple of months ago, and Dana Stephens. Because of Serenity's love of cooking, the women had started what they lovingly called Serenity's Supper Club. They got together at least twice a month and caught up over great food, wine, music, and lots of laughter. "Do you think you should still be doing all this cooking with the baby coming soon?"

"Girl, please. This child isn't due for almost five weeks, so I'm fine, especially now that I've stopped working." Serenity worked as a nurse in the town's doctor's office. "Besides, you know Gabriel is more than happy to help me out."

"I just bet he is," Terri said with a chuckle. Gabriel's sister, Andrea, had been the fifth member of their supper club until she relocated due to a job promotion and asked Serenity to help her brother get acclimated to small-town living. She couldn't help remembering all the tension between Serenity and Gabriel when he moved in next door to Serenity. However, with them both being foodies, the two had worked out their differences and were now happily married and awaiting the birth of their first child.

"With Thanksgiving being a little over three weeks away, I figure I'll keep it easy. I'm thinking bacon-wrapped filet medallions because the guys are always talking about needing something more filling. Hmm, maybe I'll add crab-stuffed shrimp. They can be wrapped in the bacon, too. And because you and Natasha keep raving about them, I'll make the bruschetta—chicken, bacon, and ranch, and beef tenderloin with caramelized onions—along with two or three kinds of salads. Gabriel said he'd fry some chicken wings for us. And before you say anything, no, I'm not cooking for Thanksgiving. Nana and Gabriel will handle everything this year."

Terri laughed. "Mmm, you know me well. My mouth is already watering thinking about that bruschetta, and *oooh*, that man can make some fried chicken." A brisk breeze kicked up and Terri shivered. She reached for the purple hand-crocheted blanket she'd made at one of their supper club meet-ups earlier in the year and wrapped it around her. "Do you need me to help with anything?"

"Nope. Is Jon coming?"

She sighed. "I don't know. He said he was when I asked yesterday, but after tonight..."

"Well, don't worry. I'll have Gabriel or Antonio talk to him." Serenity paused, then said, "For what it's worth, I do believe Jon loves you. I see him watching you sometimes when he doesn't think anyone's looking. I hope you two can get past this."

"I do, too." Terri didn't want to consider the alternative.

* * *

Friday afternoon, Jon stood in his office staring out the window. He should be going over notes for at least two cases, but his mind was everywhere except work. It had been two days since the disastrous dinner with his wife, and he hadn't been able to concentrate on anything since. They walked on eggshells around each other, only communicating when necessary. Jon had been more than a little shocked when she asked about divorce, but he was thankful that neither of them wanted it. He loved his wife with every beat of his heart and hated the distance, but had no idea how to bridge the steadily widening gap between them. Terri had wanted to talk, but he had never been good at sharing his feelings. When Jon was growing up, his father had drilled into his head that only a weak man allowed others to see his *feelings*. Now, Jon had buried his emotions so deep, he didn't have a clue how to dig them out and open himself up.

Maybe he should've been more receptive to her suggestion of counseling. As quickly as the notion entered his mind, he heard his father's booming voice: *The last thing you need to ever do is sit in some stranger's office and tell him about all your business. Nobody should know what goes on behind your closed doors except the folks in your house.* Jon scrubbed a hand down his face and blew out a long breath.

Turning away from the window, he glanced at his watch and went back to his desk. If he planned to leave no later than six, he had two hours to get some work done. Lately, he rarely made it home before eight or nine—another point of contention between them. Four years ago, he'd been given an opportunity afforded to very few younger attorneys when his boss decided to open a small firm a few miles outside of Firefly Lake. Drake Hodges had felt it would be more cost-effective to have a dedicated office to handle cases in the area, instead of flying back and forth from LA. The job had come with a promotion to junior partner and promise of a senior partnership within three years. Since its opening, Hodges, Smith, Wildes and Rhodes had expanded to include two administrative assistants, a paralegal, and three associate attorneys, including a new woman who had joined the firm two weeks ago. Now as one of two senior partners, Jon felt like he had a responsibility to ensure everything ran well, which required more than the usual forty hours per week.

His head came up at the sound of a knock on his partially closed door.

"Got a minute?"

"Sure. Come on in, Selena."

Selena Bailey crossed the space and took a seat in one of the chairs opposite Jon's desk. "I wanted to let you know that Mr. Nelson's attorney is requesting a twenty-five-thousand-dollar settlement, but I found something you might find interesting."

"What's that?"

"He's filed similar lawsuits against at least twenty-seven other wineries, as well."

Jon leaned back in his chair. "You have got to be kidding me." Nelson had sued the winery over website accessibility issues due to his visual impairment, citing that the small, family-owned vineyard had violated the Americans with Disabilities Act by denying him full use and enjoyment of the site.

She slid a folder across the table. "See for yourself." As Jon opened the file and flipped through the pages, she said, "A few of the wineries have already settled because they felt it would be cheaper than trying to go to trial."

"I can see that," he murmured, still reading. Significant billable hours and court costs could add up quickly. "Something about this just doesn't sit well with me. All twenty-seven lawsuits read almost verbatim, and it feels like some kind of shakedown. Almost predatory."

Selena lifted a brow. "You think Nelson is doing this just for money?"

"It wouldn't be the first time someone's done something like this for the sake of money." Jon reached for his notes on the Henley Estates Winery case and scanned them. "I don't see anything here that indicates they were notified about fixing the site before filing. In fact, it's not mentioned in any of the other cases, either."

"I spoke with Jeff Henley yesterday, and he said that never happened, because they would've jumped on it immediately."

"Interesting. And all these lawsuits are being handled by one firm." Something was definitely up. "I know we were considering settling, as well, but I'm wondering if we should think about going to trial. Nelson will have to prove that he's suffered an injury because of the website's accessibility issues, as well as prove he's an actual customer. Did he attempt to purchase any wine or schedule a tour?"

She looked through her notes. "I don't think he did. The first contact Henley received was when they were blindsided with the lawsuit. I'll see about getting phone records as well as finding out whether we can trace Nelson's internet footprints."

Closing the file, Jon slid it back across the desk. "Sounds good."

Selena peeked at her watch, then stood and picked up the file. "Since it's almost five, I'm taking off on time for a change." She walked to the door and turned back. "You should do the same. I've only been here a short time, but I know you put in way too many hours, Jon. Go home and take that beautiful wife of yours out on a date." She gestured to the photo on Jon's desk. "Have a good weekend, boss."

"You do the same." After she walked out, his gaze strayed to the picture. It was one of his favorite shots of them. It had been taken the day they moved into their new home here in Firefly Lake. Terri had insisted that they *needed* to take a selfie from their amazing deck with the mountains and lake as a backdrop. Jon studied the face of the woman he loved. Her dark brown eyes sparkled in her beautiful honey-colored face, and the wide, teasing smile she wore was the same one that had captured him from the first. She'd been so happy. What he wouldn't give to go back to that time.

His cell chimed with an incoming call, interrupting his trip down memory lane. Jon frowned when he saw Gabriel Cunningham's name on the display. After Gabriel had moved to town last year, they'd become pretty good friends, and they might have been better ones if Jon had reached out more. They typically texted, so Jon's heart rate kicked up as he wondered if something had happened. "Hey, Gabe. Everything okay?" he asked when he picked up.

Gabriel's laughter came through the line. "Yeah, man. I figured I'd call this time to make sure you'll be at the supper club dinner tomorrow."

Jon dragged a hand down his face, his heart slowing. "I—"

"You've missed the last couple. And before you give me some crap about working, it's a *Saturday*, Jon. Man, you've got to take some time to chill. I can tell you're close to burnout, along with some other things. And I know Terri would love to have you there," he added.

Burnout didn't come close to describing all the things

swirling in his gut, and yeah, he knew his wife wanted him there. He recalled the look of hurt in her eyes each time he'd canceled. "I'll be there."

"Great. Then Antonio and I won't have to come and drag your butt to the house."

He chuckled. "That won't be necessary." Jon had not only canceled on his wife often, but had also canceled on getting together with Gabriel and Antonio.

"I'll hold you to it. Later, my brother."

"Later." He disconnected and stared at the photo again. If he didn't do something, he was going to lose his wife, despite her not wanting a divorce. And that was one thing he could *not* handle.

CHAPTER 2

"Are you almost ready?"

Terri glanced up from where she sat buckling her ankle boots and stared at Jon. "Just about." She'd been on pins and needles all week waiting for him to find one excuse or another to skip out on the supper club dinner, but he hadn't, and she was finally starting to relax. She buckled the other boot, stood, and reached for her jacket. The temperatures had dropped over the past couple of days and barely reached sixty degrees.

"Here, let me help you."

He took the jacket and held it for her. His fingers brushed the nape of her neck when he moved her shoulder-length hair and his touch sent a flurry of sensations through her. She shivered.

"Cold?" he asked, turning her to face him and rubbing up and down her arms.

She looked up at him. "No, I'm good." He continued to stare at her, as if he wanted to say something. After a long moment, Terri said, "Are we leaving?"

Jon nodded, then stroked a finger down her cheek. "I know things aren't good between us, but no matter what, I love you, Terri."

Hearing him say the words put a sheen of tears in her eyes. "I love you, too."

He smiled faintly, then placed a soft kiss on her lips. "We'd better go."

The sweetness of the kiss poured over her like molasses. Her heart was so full, she could only nod. He gestured her forward, and they went out to the car. Terri sat silently in the car for the short drive, trying to process Jon's show of affection and feeling a small measure of hope. After parking, he came around, extended his hand, and gently pulled her to her feet. He continued to hold her hand as they made their way up the steps leading to Gabriel and Serenity's home.

The door opened seconds after Jon rang the bell, and Gabriel smiled. "Come on in." He kissed Terri's cheek and pulled Jon in for a one-arm hug. "Glad you made it, my brother."

Jon laughed. "I figure I didn't want to find out whether you'd make good on that threat."

Terri divided a questioning glance between the two men, but neither said anything. "What threat?"

"Nothing," Jon and Gabriel chorused.

She really wanted to know, but left it alone. Whatever Gabriel had said to get Jon here worked for her. Smiling, she rubbed her hands together. "Ooh, I smell fried chicken." They followed Gabriel to the kitchen, where Serenity stood at the counter dicing chicken and bacon. "Hey, girl." She hugged Serenity's shoulders. Terri shrugged out of her jacket.

"Hey, Terri. Hi, Jon. I'm so glad you could make it tonight," Serenity said.

Jon greeted Serenity with a kiss on her upturned cheek. "Looks and smells good."

"It'll taste good, too."

"I have no doubt because it always does. I'm going to see if Gabe needs some help with the setup."

"I'll wash my hands and help you, Serenity." Terri followed Jon's departure, then washed her hands in the kitchen sink and dried them on a paper towel.

Serenity shook her head. "You don't need to help. I'm just about done. All I have to do is assemble everything and pop the dishes into the oven."

"Good. Then *we* can assemble them and get it done faster, so you can sit your little pregnant behind down."

"Whatever," she said with a roll of her eyes and a smile.

"Okay, what do you want me to do first?"

"You can stuff the shrimp with the crab mixture, wrap them in the bacon, and place them on that cookie sheet." Serenity pointed.

Terri moved the pan within easy reach and picked up the first shrimp. She chuckled.

"What?"

"You know, there sure is a lot of bacon on this menu. *Bacon*-wrapped stuffed shrimp. *Bacon*-wrapped beef tenderloin. Chicken, *bacon*, and ranch bruschetta." She waved a hand over the waiting appetizers. "I guess Gabriel was right about bacon making everything better," she said with a grin, referring to the time shortly after Gabriel and Serenity had met and gotten off on the wrong foot.

Serenity's mouth fell open, and she shot Terri a mock glare. "I can't believe you're bringing up old stuff," she muttered.

Terri playfully bumped her friend's shoulder. "I couldn't resist. I'm just happy the two of you worked out your differences."

"Yeah, so am I. And he's been so amazing throughout this pregnancy."

A brief pang of envy and sadness rose, but she forced it back down and concentrated on her task.

Serenity finished assembling the bruschetta and washed her hands. "Enough about me. Any—" The doorbell sounded. "That's probably Natasha and Antonio. Be right back." She started toward the front.

"I got it, babe," Gabriel said, intercepting Serenity and placing a quick kiss on her brow.

She came back to the counter. "I might as well wait for Tasha before asking my question so you'll only have to answer once. Too bad Dana won't be here this time, otherwise we'd wait for her, too."

Terri and Serenity shared a smile. "Did Dana say when she'd be back?" Although Dana worked as the town's mechanic, she had been gone for the past two weeks playing piano with a symphony orchestra.

"Sometime next week. She wasn't sure which day, but this will be her last series for the year."

"I'm here!" Natasha came into the kitchen with her arms spread, hugging both Serenity and Terri.

"Oh, my goodness. You look so good," Terri said. "That LA trip must have been more than just work."

Natasha glanced over her shoulder at her husband, Antonio. "Much more." The women all screamed with laughter. "But I did work my butt off during the week getting the color schemes for each apartment done." She had secured a corporate interior design project in Los Angeles and had been traveling back and forth for the past few months.

"Hey, ladies," Antonio said, kissing both Terri's and Serenity's cheeks. "Looks like we're having a feast...as usual. Need any help?"

"No, but thanks for the offer," Serenity said. "You just go hang out with the guys, so we can have some girl talk."

Antonio glanced at Gabriel and Jon, who laughed. "I guess I'm getting kicked out of the kitchen."

Gabriel said, "Grab a drink and follow me."

The women waited until the men left, then Serenity turned to Terri. "Okay, what's been going on with you and Jon?"

Terri wrapped the last piece of shrimp in bacon, sealed it with a toothpick, and put it on the pan before answering. "Nothing since we talked last week." She went over to the sink to wash her hands. "We've pretty much only been communicating when necessary, but that's it." She shrugged.

Serenity placed the pans in both ovens and set the timer.

"Wait, what did I miss?" Natasha asked, filling a glass with wine.

Terri shared the details of the failed dinner. "I got tired of trying to engage him in conversation, so I got up and left him sitting there."

"Oh, I'm so sorry, Terri. You don't think counseling will help?"

"Not if your husband believes the problems will work themselves out and doesn't think counseling is necessary." Serenity and Natasha gave Terri a sympathetic look. It was getting harder and harder to attend the supper clubs and see the love so visible between her friends and their husbands. She didn't begrudge their happiness, but she wished things could go back to the way they were when she and Jon had first married. A soft smile curved her lips at the memory of her husband pulling her into his arms for an impromptu dance whenever and wherever, music or not. She longed for those days again.

"There has to be something you two can do to get back on track...maybe a weekend getaway, favorite dinner spot. What kinds of things did you do before you moved here?"

"Have weekly date nights—dinner, a movie, a walk on the beach—and we made a concerted effort to have dinner together at least three times a week." She shrugged. "It was our first year of marriage, so I guess you could say we were still in the honeymoon phase." Until their lives were shattered.

"Dinner almost done?" Gabriel asked as he came into the kitchen with Jon and Antonio trailing him.

Serenity leaned over to check the timer. "There's about three minutes left on the timer, so you can start putting the salads and other things on the table."

He lovingly caressed Serenity's belly, then led her over to a chair. "You have a seat and we'll take care of the rest. You've been on your feet long enough."

Natasha hopped up from the stool she'd claimed. "Let me set the table real quick." She took another sip of her wine, then picked up the tote she had carried in. "Are we eating at the kitchen table or the in the dining room?"

Serenity angled her head thoughtfully. "Since it's close to the holidays, let's do the dining room."

"Okay. It'll only take me a minute."

Antonio wrapped his arm around Natasha's waist and kissed her lips. "I'll help you, sweetheart." The two shared a smile and disappeared around the corner.

Terri caught Jon's gaze. She'd noticed him watching Gabriel and Antonio, but his face was unreadable. He made no attempt to approach her, and she sighed inwardly. Pasting a smile on her face, she turned to face Gabriel. "I'll help you, Gabe." She didn't know how much more she could take.

* * *

Throughout dinner, Jon couldn't help but notice how open and loving Gabriel and Antonio were with their wives. If his wife's tight features were any indication, she'd noticed it, too. As if she'd read his thoughts, Terri glanced his way, a mixture of sadness, hurt, and longing in her eyes, before she turned away and refocused on her food. He sighed inwardly. She had asked him to talk last week, and maybe they should.

As soon as the notion crossed his mind, once again, he heard his father's voice ringing in his head: *Don't* ever *show your emotions in front of a woman. She'll think you're weak, and a man should never show weakness. To anyone.* That conversation had taken place at a family gathering when Jon was fifteen. An uncle or distant cousin—he couldn't recall which—had mentioned attending therapy sessions for his depression and marital problems. Jon distinctly remembered his father scoffing at the concept and telling Jon therapy was for losers, something his own father had drilled into his son. As a result, Jon had grown up pretty much keeping his emotions on lockdown. After so many years, he wasn't sure whether he even knew how to explain that to his wife.

Yet, as he studied the two men seated around, neither seemed to be weak, and they had no problems wearing their hearts on their sleeves. If anything, Gabriel and Antonio appeared stronger. Jon had canceled going to the last three meet-ups they'd invited him to because he'd never had what could be considered close male friendships—another casualty of his upbringing. In LA, with everything and everyone moving at warp speed, surface friendships worked just fine. But here in Firefly Lake, things were different. Maybe it was time for him to do something different, starting with accepting the next invitation.

"Is the food okay, Jon?" Serenity asked, interrupting his musings. "You're not eating."

"Everything is great, as usual." And it was. The steak and seafood bites, as well as the fried chicken, had been seasoned and cooked to perfection.

Gabriel chuckled. "You looked like you were a million miles away. I hope you're not thinking about work."

Every pair of eyes turned his way, but the ones that held

his attention most were his wife's, as if she was wondering the same thing. For once, work hadn't crossed his mind. His marriage dominated the space in his brain, but he couldn't very well say that. Instead, he said, "I was just thinking about how cool it is getting together." It wasn't a lie, because he did enjoy himself whenever he made the time to come.

"Does that mean you won't be canceling on us anymore?" Antonio asked with a raised eyebrow.

Jon noted the hint of amusement on his and Gabriel's faces, curiosity on Serenity's and Natasha's, and hope on Terri's. He knew his absence at the gatherings bothered his wife, probably more than she'd voiced. *I have to do better.* "Yeah. I'll be here."

Antonio and Gabriel let out loud whoops, then both stood and started clapping. The women laughed.

Jon shook his head. "Shut up and eat your food," he said with a laugh.

Antonio snatched up his wineglass. "Nah, bro. This calls for a toast." He waited for everyone to lift their glasses. "Here's to Jon becoming a full-fledged member of the couples supper club."

"Amen," Gabriel said.

Still chuckling at their antics, Jon shifted his gaze to Terri. Her relieved smile met his. Once everyone settled down, they continued to laugh and talk throughout the remainder of the meal. At the conclusion, plates and serving dishes were cleared from the table.

"Tasha, are your parents still visiting for Thanksgiving?" Serenity asked as the group stood around the kitchen's bar.

"They are. Mom's been calling me every day talking

about all the things she needs to do and all the people she has to visit while here. She's acting like she didn't just spend two weeks here when she came for the wedding. It was only a couple of months ago," she added with a roll of her eyes, which brought on more laughter.

It brought to Jon's mind the fact that he and Terri hadn't made any concrete plans for the holidays. They'd gone home to LA for Thanksgiving last year, but after having to endure endless questions and comments about their lack of children, he had no desire to go through the same thing again, especially from his mother. He loved her, but the woman didn't know when to leave well enough alone. Thinking back, things had gotten worse between him and Terri after that visit. Yeah, he'd definitely be skipping it this year. Tuning back in to the conversation, he heard Gabriel mention the men serving dessert. "What are we having? Although, I know whatever it is will taste amazing." He'd never had a single bad thing from Serenity's kitchen. If she ever wanted to give up her nursing job, she'd have no problem opening a catering business. "I'm partial to anything chocolate."

"Same," Terri said. "Please say there are brownies or those little chocolate cups somewhere."

"I...*ohhh*." Serenity clutched her stomach and doubled over. "I think...y'all...are going to...have to start...dessert... without me."

Jon watched as his wife rushed to Serenity's side, and a frisson of fear crawled up his spine. His heart started pounding, he struggled to draw in a breath, and perspiration broke out on his forehead.

"Come on over here and sit," Terri said as Gabriel led Serenity to the chair Terri indicated. "Is this the first contraction?"

Serenity shot a look Gabriel's way before answering. "No. They started about forty-five minutes ago," she said sheepishly.

"Forty-five minutes ago?" Gabriel asked, glaring at her. "Why didn't you say something? How far apart are they?" When she hesitated, he threw up his hands. "I'll get the bag."

Terri shook her head. "Girl, please tell me those contractions are more than ten minutes apart."

"More like five to six," Serenity mumbled. "I didn't want to miss dinner."

Natasha came over and rubbed Serenity's back. "I don't know what we're going to do with you. Out here about to have my godchild born on the kitchen floor."

As the women continued to huddle around Serenity, Antonio sidled up next to Jon. "You okay, man?" When Jon didn't answer immediately, he clapped Jon on the shoulder and said, "We're all friends here, and if there's anything you need me or Gabe to do to help you and Terri, let us know."

Jon could only nod.

Gabriel returned with an overnight bag and jacket. "Come on, baby. I already called the doctor, and she said she'd meet us at the hospital." He eased her to her feet and helped her into her jacket. "Sorry the supper club is being cut short."

Natasha waved him off. "Just take care of our girl. We'll clean up everything and lock up. I still have my key."

"Thanks. I'll keep you all posted."

As soon as the door closed, Terri came over and slid her hand into Jon's. "They're going to be okay."

Jon didn't know who she was trying to convince more, him or her, but his heart was still beating in fear and a sense of déjà vu washed over him. He did something he hadn't done in a long time. He prayed.

CHAPTER 3

Monday morning, Terri took a quick break and went up to maternity to see Serenity. "Knock, knock," she said, standing in the open doorway.

Serenity's tired face lit up. "Hey, girl. Come on in. I was wondering if you were on duty today."

She came and hugged her friend. "How are you feeling?"

"Still tired as all get-out, but excited about this new journey called motherhood." She smiled down at the small bundle in her arms and stroked her cheek. "As soon as I held her, I forgot all about those twelve hours of labor with little Miss Giana playing cat and mouse, having my contractions slowing and speeding up at random."

Terri laughed softly. "Well, she's beautiful, and with Gabriel's hazel eyes, she's going to give the boys fits."

Serenity groaned. "I don't even want to think about that. Come hold your goddaughter." She carefully transferred the baby to Terri.

She choked back the emotions engulfing her and smiled at the little girl staring up at her curiously. This was what she wanted, what she longed for. "Are they letting you out of here today?"

"Yes, as soon as Gabriel gets back. He went home to shower and meet with Darius and Brent about one of their programs. He said he'd be back around noon." Gabriel co-owned a software development company with his two friends, who still lived in his hometown of Atlanta.

Terri rocked Giana, and the baby's eyes drifted closed. "As much as I'd love to sit here and hold her all day, I should get back down to the ER. I seriously need to think about a job change." She stood and handed the baby back to Serenity.

"The new memory care center is going to open sometime near the beginning of the year. You should apply for a position there. I'm sure it would be less stressful."

"That's a great idea. I can't believe how fast the Hunters got that building up." The Sacramento-based company was owned by friends of Antonio's, and the guys had worked overtime to get the facility up and running. "I know they've already hired Dr. Adams as the medical director." In his late forties, the man had a reputation for getting things done, but also had a great personality and bedside manner.

"And since you worked with him for those two years he headed the ER, and he was always singing your praises, you'd be a shoo-in. I'd lobby for one of those eight-hour day shifts with weekends off, if I were you. I can't tell you how much that helped my stress levels."

"I'm sold." Hopefully, it would help her marriage as well. "Okay, let me get going. I can bring dinner over tonight, so you and Gabriel can rest."

"I appreciate it, but Nana's got it covered."

"Sounds good. I'll talk to Natasha, and we'll see about rotating to help you guys out if need be." Terri went to the door, then paused. "I almost forgot. I talked to Dana last night. She said congratulations and she couldn't believe you had the baby before she got back."

Serenity laughed. "That definitely wasn't the plan. I'll text her when I get settled at home. And I'll let you know if we need something."

Terri threw up a wave and went back downstairs. As soon as she walked through the doors, a nurse let her know she was needed in one of the rooms. Terri rushed off. *Back to the madhouse.*

By the end of the day, Terri was beyond tired. She trudged down the hallway to give her report to the incoming staff. As they finished the staff change, one of the nurses approached.

"You look whipped, Terri."

She gave Hazel a tired smile. "Girl, you have no idea. It seems like flu season is in full effect." The emergency room had been packed with patients old and young with fevers, strep throat, and all manner of viruses. Thankfully, she'd gotten her flu shot a few weeks ago.

Hazel groaned. "Great. It's starting much earlier this year. Usually, we don't get them until after Thanksgiving. Well, let's get this party started. Have a good evening, and I'll see you tomorrow."

"Later, girlfriend." Terri went to the staff lounge and changed out of her scrubs, then headed to her car.

"Ah, Terri. Just the person I was looking for." Dr. Adams fell in step with her.

"Should I be worried?"

He laughed. "Not in the least. I wanted to talk to you about a position at the new memory care center. The concept is genius, and I can't wait for it to be up and running. But I need a competent staff to offer the best to our seniors."

She smiled inwardly. "Your ears must have been burning, because I just mentioned to a friend that I wanted to ask you about it. What position are you offering?" They exited to the employee lot.

"I'd like you to consider the director of nursing position," Dr. Adams said.

Terri stopped in her tracks. "What did you say?" Her heart started pounding.

A grin spread across his handsome mahogany face. "I assume that was a rhetorical question. I know you have your doctorate and a geriatric certification, so your expertise would be invaluable."

It took her a moment to find her voice. "Would this be a Monday through Friday, eight-hour shift?"

"Yes. I'd also like to have a night supervisor, as well. Why don't you think about it and let me know by the end of the week?"

I don't need to think about it. The answer is a resounding yes, she wanted to shout, but kept her cool. "I'll do that. I appreciate the opportunity."

Dr. Adams nodded. "Have a good evening."

"You, too." She continued to her car.

"Oh, and did I mention it comes with a big pay increase?" he called over his shoulder, smiling.

Terri heard him chuckle at what she knew was a stunned

look on her face. It took everything in her not to break out in a happy dance as she nearly skipped to her car. When she went straight into her doctorate after getting her bachelor's degree, everyone thought she'd been out of her mind trying to complete her schooling while working. Even more so when she'd added the certificate in geriatric nursing. Now, her hard work was finally paying off. She couldn't wait to get home and tell Jon. Her smile faded. He'd been even more distant since the supper club dinner, and she wished he would talk to her about it. Pushing the melancholy thoughts aside, she got into the car and sat for a moment. Terri didn't feel like cooking, so she took a few minutes to call in an order from Ms. Ida's Home Cooking. The family-style restaurant served everything from breakfast staples like pancakes and waffles to sandwiches and comfort foods, including chicken and dumplings and beef stew. She toyed with ordering something for Jon, but she wasn't sure whether he'd even be home to eat it, so she settled for just getting a salad for herself.

After making a quick stop to pick up her dinner, Terri drove home. As she suspected, her husband wasn't there, even though it was close to six. He rarely left his office at the normal five o'clock closing time, and at least three days last week, he hadn't made it home until almost eight. Swallowing her disappointment, she left her food on the kitchen counter, dropped her bag with her scrubs in the laundry room, and went to the bedroom. Terri sat on the side of the bed to remove her shoes and send a text to her girlfriends about the offer, including the hours and that there would be no weekends and came with a pay increase. It wasn't until a message popped up immediately from Serenity that she remembered she'd sent it in their regular group chat. She knew her friend was getting settled at home and adjusted to her new life as a mother and didn't want to disturb her.

Serenity: *Yes, girl, YES! You'd better take it. I just did a little squeal and Giana gave me the side eye, lol!*

Smiling, Terri replied: *Ha! You're going to be in trouble with that little one! I've all but decided to take it. I just want to talk to Jon about it.*

Serenity: *Sounds good. I can't see him having an issue.*

Terri: *Me, either.*

Natasha: *Hallelujah! Doing a happy dance for you. Hopefully, this will give you and Jon more time together.*

Terri: *Same here.*

Dana: *Girl, I let out a whoop and have these folks looking at me. I'm so happy for you, and I'm doing that dance with Tasha. Celebration and drinks when I get home next week!*

Terri: *Can't wait. Love y'all!*

Tears misted Terri's eyes. She didn't know what she'd do without her sister-friends. Back in LA, she'd had a few friends, and one whom she considered her bestie, until the woman showed her true colors by trying to badmouth Terri in order to secure a promotion. But here, she didn't have to worry about that kind of foolishness. These women had shown her what true friendship meant.

She headed back to the kitchen with her iPad, washed her hands, and sat at the table to eat her salad and read the romantic suspense novel she'd started weeks ago but hadn't had time to finish. After the first bite, she didn't know what she enjoyed more, the perfectly seasoned shrimp atop the

Caesar salad or the still-warm baguette with Ms. Ida's honey butter. A low moan of pleasure escaped.

"That good?"

Terri gasped and spun around in her chair, clutching her chest. "Oh, my goodness, Jon. You scared me to death. I didn't hear you come in." She took a deep breath and let it out slowly in an effort to calm her pounding heart.

"I guess not." Jon came over to the table, took the chair across from her, and eyed the salad.

"Um, I didn't know what time you were coming home, so I didn't get you anything. You're welcome to have some of my salad. There's enough to share."

He shook his head. "I'm good. I'll get something a little later."

They sat in awkward silence for a lengthy moment before she asked, "Long day?"

A faint smile curved his lips. "Pretty much. Yours?"

"It was busy, but not as much as on the weekends." She forked up another bite of her food. "I did get another job offer, though."

Jon lifted a brow. "In another department?"

"No." Terri placed her fork on the plate. "It's for the new memory care center that will be opening at the beginning of the year. I ran into Dr. Adams as I was leaving today."

"The doctor that used to head up the emergency department?"

She nodded. "He's been appointed as medical director, and he offered me the director of nursing position. Instead of my current ten-forty schedule, this one will be Monday through Friday, eight to five. No weekends."

His face lit up. "That's great. Congratulations."

"I haven't accepted it yet." Terri measured her next words. "I plan to, and I'm hoping it will give us more time together to work on our marriage."

Just like that, the smile faded from his face. "Terri—"

She held up a hand. "Our marriage isn't going to fix itself, Jon. Only we can do that. We don't talk, go out on dates, or take long walks by the lake and hold hands like we used to do. You've been even more closed off since Saturday night, and I know why."

Jon lowered his head and gritted out, "Don't."

"Don't what? When are we going to talk about Amara? When are we going to talk about our little girl, Jon? Don't you think talking about her and grieving together would help us both?"

"Just leave it be, Terri. I don't want to talk about it."

"It's been four years, Jonathan. When are you going to be able to talk about it?" she pressed, her anger, sadness, and loss rising.

"I can't do this right now," he whispered, the pain they both were feeling evident in his voice.

Pushing away from the table, she stood. "Neither can I." She needed some time away to think about whether her marriage would survive. Maybe they both did. She loved her husband, but would it be enough to keep them together?

CHAPTER 4

After another long day at the office, Jon trudged into the house Thursday evening from the garage and found the kitchen dark, as was the front of the house. Between having to explain to a client for the umpteenth time to provide only the requested information and not folders of "research" to "help" them, and reminding another one of their agreement after doing something completely different that could negatively impact the case, he was beyond exhausted. He stretched his neck to relieve some of the stiffness. His entire body ached like it did back when he'd played football in college. As a running back, he'd endured tackles game after game, and he'd be sore from head to toe. Much like his muscles felt tonight. Except, he hadn't played one down in more than a decade.

He placed his briefcase on the table and grabbed a bottle of water from the refrigerator. As he drank, he sifted through the mail Terri had left on the counter, then started for their bedroom. Jon stopped in his tracks when he found his wife stuffing clothes into a small overnight bag that sat on the bed. His heart started pounding in his chest. "Terri?"

Terri briefly glimpsed over her shoulder at him, then went back to what she was doing. "Hey."

"What are you doing?" he asked, crossing the room to where she stood.

"Packing. What does it look like?"

He sighed. "*Why* are you packing, and where are you going?"

"I need some time away to think, and I'm not going too far. If something comes up, you can reach me on my cell." She walked around him, went into the bathroom, and came back with her toiletry bag.

Jon turned, trying to keep up with her movements. "Hold on a minute and talk to me."

She glared at him. "Oh, *now* you want to talk," she said with a bitter chuckle. "I've been asking you to talk for months, and you shut me out every time."

She had a point, but he didn't have to like it. And he didn't want her to leave. Yes, a lot of their issues could be laid at his feet, but he didn't know how to explain that he wasn't *supposed* to share his feelings, or the fear that she might think him less of a man if he did. But he didn't want to lose her, either. Jon ran a weary hand down his face. "Just give me—"

He reached for her, but Terri shook her head and held up a hand. "I need to go." She slung her purse on one shoulder, the overnight bag on the other. "I have to do this. For me," she added softly with tears in her eyes as she rushed from the room.

Jon never could stand her tears, and knowing that he put them there sent a searing pain through his heart. He followed her out to the garage and watched her load her bags into the car. "Where are you going to stay?" When she didn't answer, he said, "Then will you at least call to let me know you arrived safely?" He couldn't take it if she got hurt. "You haven't even said how long you'll be gone."

She came up on tiptoe and pressed a soft kiss on his lips. "I'll let you know when I get there, and I'll be back in a couple of days."

He stood there as she got into the car and backed out. His feet stayed rooted to the spot as the garage door slowly came down and until it closed completely. Inside again, he paced the floor in their bedroom, then dropped down on the bed and buried his head in his hands. *When are we going to talk about Amara? When are we going to talk about our little girl, Jon?* The words came back, unbidden. The loss of their baby had broken him in ways he couldn't explain, and he didn't know if he'd ever be whole again. Just the memory made a knot form in the pit of his stomach, and he could feel his emotions rising. Though she still wanted children, the possibility of it happening again kept him from hoping. He considered calling his father, but nixed the idea as quickly as it entered his mind, recalling the last time he'd gone to the man for advice. The emotional beating Jon had taken negated any chance of him asking again.

Jon jumped up and started pacing again. He checked his watch. She'd been gone for only fifteen minutes, but it felt like a lifetime. He stripped and, after grabbing his phone, went to shower. He leaned his head against the marble wall and let the warm water run over his head, wishing it could wash away the turmoil in his life. After another minute, he washed up, got out, dried off, and wrapped the towel loosely around his waist. He immediately checked the phone. *Thirty-five minutes and still no call. Where did she go?* A minute later, it buzzed. Jon snatched it up and read the text: *I'm here and safe. Goodnight.*

"Dammit!" he muttered. It was going to be a long night.

The next morning, Jon's alarm blared at five. He shut it off and rolled over, expecting to see Terri, but remembered he was alone. Groaning, he dragged himself out of bed. He'd lain awake for much of the night and tossed and turned the rest of the time. In the nearly five years they'd been married, he and Terri had rarely spent a night apart, and never for this reason. For the first time in his career, he wanted to call out sick. However, he had three back-to-back meetings and cases to oversee, so the fantasy would have to wait.

Jon made it to the office at six, and as usual, he was the first to arrive. He savored the early morning quiet, which gave him a couple of hours to catch up on emails, return calls, and do some legal research for his cases. Jon booted up his computer, then went to the break room to make coffee because he would need at least two cups of it—strong and black—to get his brain functioning. While waiting for it to brew, he headed back to his office and leafed through the messages on his desk, prioritizing the ones that required some action on his part. Once the coffee was ready, he poured a cup and sipped the dark brew while answering emails.

By his second cup, the fog clouding his brain finally cleared. Yet, he still had difficulty concentrating on the papers in front of him. His mind kept straying to his wife and where she might be. Since it took less than an hour for her to reach her destination, he assumed she'd gone somewhere in wine country. Jon's gaze strayed to the photo of them on his desk. He picked it up and, once again, studied the joy radiating from her. He missed her smile, her laugh. He missed *her*. And them.

"Morning, boss."

He set the photo back in its place when he saw his administrative assistant, Gail, in the doorway. "Morning."

She came in and placed a stack of folders on his desk and handed him three messages. "I'll let you know when Mr. Jones gets here."

"Thanks," he said as he read through the messages. As she walked out, he heard voices, signaling that the office was open. Jon glanced down at his notepad, which had less than a paragraph written, and sighed. *So much for getting any work done.* Tossing it aside, he picked up one of the folders.

Though he stayed busy the entire day, Terri was never far from his mind. He'd sent her a text earlier, but she hadn't responded yet. He needed to know if she was okay. *If she was okay, she wouldn't have left*, an inner voice mocked, but he dismissed it. Jon glanced up at the wall clock. Almost five. Maybe he'd leave on time for a change. Then again, maybe not. He had no desire to go home to an empty house. Even with them not talking much, he still savored his wife's presence. *I have to figure out a way to talk to her.*

Jon's cell buzzed, and he went still when he saw his mother's number on the screen. "Hey, Mom. Everything okay with you and Dad?" he asked as soon as he answered.

Her laughter came through the line. "Hello, son. Everything is great. So great, in fact, your father and I decided we're coming to spend the weekend with you and Terri. We haven't seen you since Christmas, and it's almost the holidays again. And you haven't called me in weeks, so I need to see for myself how you're doing."

He muttered a curse. This was the last thing he needed. Deborah Rhodes had a habit of trying to "fix" everything, and during every call he'd received from her since their last visit to LA, she always had some suggestion as to how he and Terri could revive the spark in their marriage. Somehow, it *always* revolved around them having children. For the past few years, he found himself growing more and more distant from his parents, and being on the other side of the state helped keep the relationship somewhat cordial. But today, Jon didn't have the time or inclination to cross verbal swords with her. Scrubbing a hand down his face, he asked, "When are you flying in?" He accepted a message from his assistant.

"Oh, we're already here."

"Wait. What?" He shot to his feet.

"Alan and I drove to San Francisco on Monday. We've had a marvelous time in the Bay and in Napa for the past couple of days. With us being this close, it makes no sense not to visit. We're going to get some dinner first, and we should be there in a couple of hours. I don't want Terri to have to worry about cooking when I know she's been on her feet all day in that emergency room."

Jon dropped back down into his chair, put the phone on speaker, and sent a text to Terri letting her know that his parents were in Napa and decided to spend the weekend with them. He knew she'd planned to be away for a couple of days, but if his mother showed up with Terri gone, it would give her more ammunition and, in her mind, more justification as to why they needed her marital advice. "Okay. I need to finish up a few things so I can get out of here. See you guys when you get here." They spoke a moment longer, then he disconnected and tossed the phone on the desk. Of all weekends, why this one? Jon only hoped his wife would return.

* * *

Friday morning, Terri lay in bed until nine. She'd tossed and turned all night, thinking about the state of her marriage, and felt no more rested than she did last night. Getting up, she dressed, grabbed her book, and headed to a little café she'd visited on one of the day trips she'd taken with her supper club sisters. Terri really didn't have an appetite, but knew she had to put something in her stomach since she hadn't been able to eat much at dinner yesterday.

She tried focusing on the story line in her book while eating her toast, fruit, and bacon, but after reading the same page three times, she gave up. Her phone buzzed as she sipped her tea.

She sighed heavily when she saw a text from her mother-in-law. "Just great," she muttered. The last thing she wanted or needed right now was to hear anything from that woman.

Deborah: *Terri, I just saw an advertisement for a couples retreat that would be perfect for you and Jon. You two really need to do something to put the spark back in your marriage. I know something's going on and this would be perfect. You can thank me later! I've included a link to the conference.*

Not bothering to look at the link or respond, Terri tossed the phone on the table and picked up her mug again. It was the second text in as many weeks with some new thing or event she and Jon needed to try. *She needs to mind her business and work on her own damn marriage.* While her own parents could still be found laughing, holding hands, and stealing kisses, she didn't remember seeing the same with her in-laws. Jon had been just the opposite... until last year. Not wanting to dwell on it any longer, she finished her food. Thinking that she probably wouldn't want to leave the hotel again for lunch, she ordered a sandwich to go. After Terri paid the bill, she took a leisurely stroll down the block, stopping in a few quaint shops before going back to her car. On the way to the hotel, she spotted a steakhouse and decided that she'd treat herself to dinner later.

Two hours later, she still couldn't concentrate on the book, so she surfed through the television channels for something to watch. When her phone buzzed again, she went still. "If this woman is texting me again...," she muttered. Snatching up the phone, Terri relaxed, but only marginally. This time it was Jon. *I love you. Please let me know if you're okay.*

Tears stung her eyes. No, she wasn't okay, because *they* weren't okay. Instead of responding, she called her mother for some advice.

"I have no idea what to do, Mom." Terri sat on the small balcony off her hotel room and stared at a couple walking through the courtyard holding hands and smiling at each other. That used to be her and Jon.

"Are you thinking about divorce?" Her mother's voice was full of concern.

"No, but we can't keep going this way. We're barely talking, and when I suggested counseling, Jon said we didn't need to talk to anyone and that our problems would work themselves out."

Her mom chuckled. "If problems worked themselves out, there wouldn't be a divorced couple in the world. Jon always impressed me as being so level-headed, and I wonder what's gotten into him. It just doesn't sound like something he would say. I don't doubt he loves you. When you two were here last year for the holidays, I caught him on more than one occasion staring at you like you were his favorite dessert, even though you'd mentioned having some issues in your marriage."

"At least that's something," she mumbled. That he still thought her desirable was good to hear, but it didn't salve her troubled heart.

"You don't think he's cheating, do you?"

Terri thought for a moment. Even with all their drama, she'd never felt that he might be seeing another woman. "No." She debated whether to tell her mother about the last conversation. Regina McCall had always been her confidante, so she decided it couldn't hurt. "He's been more closed off since Serenity and Gabriel had their baby, and I figured it had something to do with why he'd become more closed off. I asked him when we could talk about Amara, and he completely shut down. I know losing her hurt him just as it hurt me, but I haven't once been able to get him to talk about how he feels."

"Ah. Well, honey, you can't make him talk, although I agree that it would probably help you both. Men tend to be pretty closed-mouthed about their emotions. It took your father years to be able to open up to me when something was bothering him."

Years? Terri sighed. That was *not* what she wanted to hear. "I don't know if I can take this for years. What should I do?"

"I can't tell you what to do, baby. You and Jon have to figure that out."

"Really, Mom. You don't have one little piece of advice?"

She laughed. "Nope. I told you at the beginning that I wouldn't be interfering in your marriage. A marriage is between three people—God, the husband, and the wife—no one else."

"I know," Terri grumbled. "But you can't offer *anything*?" Her phone buzzed in her hand, and she saw another text from her husband. She opened it and read: *Terri, I know you didn't plan to come home until tomorrow, but my mother just called and said since she and my father were in the Bay Area, they decided to visit us for the weekend. Please come home. You know my mom. Not sure you want to deal with her questions if you're not here.* She groaned. Yes, she did know his busybody mother.

"What's the matter?"

"Jon just texted me and said his parents decided they were coming for the weekend. Apparently, they're in the Bay Area and since they're so close..." She let the sentence hang.

"I like Deborah, but that woman needs to keep her nose out of other people's business. I had to check her when they came for Thanksgiving a couple of years ago."

"What? You didn't tell me that." Terri could imagine how that conversation went. Her mother didn't bite her tongue.

"There was no need to ruin your holiday. I can't even remember how we got on the subject, but she tried to tell me all the things I needed to do to spice up my marriage because it seemed like your father and I were in a rut. I politely told her my marriage was fine and that she should be more concerned with her own husband and stay out of grown folks' business."

She laughed. While Terri got along reasonably well with her mother-in-law, the woman often tried sticking her nose in places where it didn't belong.

"I'd better let you get back to work then so you can get ready for Ms. Nosy."

"Actually, I'm in Napa. I needed a couple of days away and left last night. I'd planned to go home tomorrow, but Jon just asked me to come back."

"Oh, Terri, I'm sorry, honey. Are you going home?"

"Probably. The last thing I need is her blowing up my phone with all her advice." Like earlier. Last year, when they'd gone home for Thanksgiving, the woman had sensed the tension between Terri and Jon and spent the entire two days telling them what they should be doing. Then she'd had the nerve to call and text Terri for a good two or three weeks, asking whether Terri had taken any of her advice. She blew out a long breath. She was not in the mood to deal with her in-laws this weekend or to pretend all was well.

"Well, if you need me, just send up a bat signal. Your dad and I will be there."

"Thanks, Mom. I love you."

"Love you more, sweetheart. Call me next week and let me know how the visit went."

"Will do. I guess I'll go pack." Terri stood and went back inside. She and her mother spoke a few minutes longer, then disconnected. She sent a text to Jon: *I'll be home in a while.*

Almost immediately, his reply popped up: *Thank you! Drive safely.*

He'd ended the message with a heart emoji, which surprised her. Tossing the phone aside, she went into the bathroom to gather up her toiletries, then added them to her overnight bag. Because she had only planned to be there for a couple of days, she didn't have much to pack. However, Terri wasn't happy about losing the cost of one night in the hotel.

After taking one last look around to make sure she hadn't left anything, she sighed softly and headed to the front desk to check out. She only hoped she'd be able to pull off the façade well enough to keep her mother-in-law satisfied that all was well. Or well enough for her to keep her advice to herself.

CHAPTER 5

When Terri pulled into the driveway forty-five minutes later and opened the garage, Jon's car was already there. She couldn't recall the last time he'd been home before six. She got out and retrieved her bag from the back seat and startled upon seeing Jon standing next to her. "So, are you into scaring me these days?" It was the second time this week that he'd come upon her so silently. Apparently, he'd been home a few minutes, because he had changed into a pair of well-worn jeans and long-sleeved tee.

"Sorry. Just came to help you with your bag." Jon eased it from her hand, shut the car door, and gestured for her to go first. He followed her to the bedroom and set the bag down on a chair. They stood in awkward silence for a few seconds before he asked, "Was the drive okay?"

She nodded. "Fine. A little traffic, but that's typical for a Friday afternoon. What time are your parents coming?"

"She said they should be here by seven."

Terri glanced down at her watch. That gave her an hour to figure out something for dinner and put a good face on. "I'll go find something for dinner." She made a move to pass him, but he placed a staying hand on her arm. The warmth of his touch flowed through her and reminded her how much she missed it.

"You don't have to cook. They're stopping to get something first."

"Okay. I'm going to find something to eat before they get here." One more thing she'd had to cancel. She'd gone ahead and made a dinner reservation at the steakhouse. Terri started toward the kitchen, and this time when she passed him, he didn't try to stop her.

"I picked up something from Ms. Ida's," he said, trailing her.

She spun around and lifted a brow. "Oh?"

Jon shrugged. "I figured since my parents ruined your weekend, it was the least I could do. I'll also pay for your room since—" He cut himself off and busied himself with removing the containers from a bag on the counter.

Terri really wanted to know what he'd planned to say. Was he offering to pay for the room since he was the reason she'd left in the first place? Putting it out of her mind, she wandered over to the counter. The delicious smells drifted to her nose and made her stomach growl.

"I guess you're hungry. I know you like the fried catfish, so I got that with mac and cheese and green beans. Is that okay?"

She smiled. "It's more than okay." He got a plate from the cabinet and handed it to her. "Um... did you already eat?"

Jon hesitated briefly. "No. I wanted to wait for you."

Part of Terri wanted to ask why. The last time they'd eaten together, she might as well have been at the table alone with the way he kept his head buried in his iPad and phone.

Apparently, he read her questioning expression because he added quietly, "It won't be like the last time."

She didn't say anything, just added portions of the food on her plate and carried it to the table.

He fixed his own plate and joined her at the table, then went back to the refrigerator for the drinks he'd also purchased.

"Thanks." She bowed her head, recited a short blessing, and scooped up some of the mac and cheese. The meal was one of her favorites on the menu. That Jon had remembered warmed her heart.

"Did you call Dr. Adams to accept the position yet?"

"Yes. I called him this morning. I can't wait to leave the ER behind."

Jon's brows knitted together. "I thought you loved working there."

"I do, but I'm ready for a change. I think I'm feeling a little burned out with the frantic pace and can't wait for the new center to open."

He nodded as he forked up some green beans. "I hear you. I can't believe how fast they got that building up. Seems like I remember them saying it would take almost a year, and it's only been six months."

"Surprised me, too, but I think the Hunters and Antonio were anxious to get the place open. I drove by the other day and it looks beautiful. You can't tell it's a medical facility." It had been designed like a small community with apartment-style rooms, paved streets, a grocery store, and a restaurant. The medical personnel would run the store and restaurant and dress in street clothes instead of uniforms. After wearing scrubs for more than a decade, she was looking forward to being able to pull out all the clothes she'd purchased but rarely had an opportunity to wear. The conversation tapered off as they continued eating. Both seemed to be purposely keeping the conversation in neutral territory. Neither wanted to greet his parents angry, which was just as well with Terri. No need to give her mother-in-law ammunition before she got in the door good. They finished eating while talking about everything except themselves.

Afterward, Terri went to ready the guest room. She'd just finished replacing the pillows on the bed when she heard the doorbell ring. Butterflies took flight in her belly. She drew in a deep, calming breath, pasted a smile that she hoped passed as genuine on her face, and went out front.

"There she is!" Deborah Rhodes grabbed Terri up in a crushing hug. "How's my Florence Nightingale?"

Chuckling at the nickname, she returned the hug. "Busy, as always." She repeated the gesture with his father. "How are you, Dad?"

"Still here, so that's a good thing. Deb had me running all over San Francisco and Napa, and I feel like I need another week to recover from this vacation."

Terri was glad she hadn't run into them while in Napa. No way would she be able to explain being there without Jon.

"Come on in and get comfortable," Jon said. They all made their way into the family room at the back of the house.

"I can't get over this view," Jon's mother said. "The comfortable deck, the mountains and lake—so gorgeous, I could stare at them all day. Makes me want to move here."

Terri and Jon shared a panicked look, but before either of them could comment, Jon's father said, "Deb, you say that every time we visit. We aren't selling the house and moving anywhere. You wouldn't last two weeks here without your gossiping friends, those weekly trips to the hairdresser you've been going to for forty years who you said is the only person you'd allow to touch your hair, and your doctor, who's supposedly the only real one in the state of California. So, sit down and relax."

Jon shook his head. "So, how was San Francisco?"

"Fine," his father answered.

Mama Deb came and sat next to her husband. "Oh, Al, you know you enjoyed yourself. Weren't you the one who wanted to do the Golden Gate Bridge cruise twice and who bought all that chocolate from the Ghirardelli store?"

Apparently busted, he hung his head.

"Have you two taken the cruise?" She divided a look between Terri and Jon.

"Not yet," Terri said. It was one more thing that had gotten canceled in the last year, along with dinners and movie dates.

"Well, what are you waiting for? You've been here for a good four years, and it's not that far."

Here we go. She sensed the woman was gearing up for one of her lengthy speeches on relationships, and part of Terri wished she had stayed in her quiet little hotel room with her book and a glass of wine.

"You two don't think I know something's going on with you? It's nothing that a few good dates can't cure. Or a little baby," she added with a grin.

Scratch the wine. What Terri needed was a shot of tequila, whiskey, bourbon, or anything that would mute the woman. One look at Jon's face told her he was close to exploding. The mention of her name pulled her back into the conversation.

"You don't wait too long, Terri, because you're getting close to being in the high-risk category. And Jon, you don't want to be so old you can't play with your son or daughter. I've been waiting a long time for grandchildren. Yes, the last—"

"Mom, that's enough," Jon said, cutting off her tirade.

"I'm just trying to help." She turned to Terri. "Did you get my text earlier, Terri?"

He held up his hand. "We're both adults, and whatever decisions we make are ours and ours alone. We don't need your help or interference. You have to stop trying to fix everything. And what text are you talking about?"

"I sent her a link to a couples retreat. You should really think about going. It could be just what you need. Oh, and I saw something else about a procreation retreat."

"*Mom!* Just. Stop. We're fine."

When the woman turned Terri's way, Terri said, "As Jon said, we're fine." She stood and left the room. A complete lie, but it was better than sitting and listening to her go on and on about their loss or trying to bully them into going to some retreat. No denying she wanted to have the conversation, but only with Jon. The look on Mama Deb's face said she wasn't satisfied with their answers, and Terri knew the woman wouldn't let it go. *It's going to be a long weekend.*

***

Jon had never been so eager for his parents to leave. For the past two days, his mother had taken every opportunity to point out some little thing he and Terri should be doing to help their relationship, from weekend getaways and candlelight dinners to advice about what they should be doing in the bedroom. With every dig, he'd watched his wife retreat more and more; instead of helping, his mom's interference had made things worse. Much worse. He'd waited for his father to jump in like he used to when Jon lived at home, but this time Alan Rhodes didn't utter one word outside of his initial comment about them moving to Firefly Lake. They had initially planned to be on the road early Sunday morning, but changed their timetable and would be leaving after breakfast, which blessedly was almost done.

"Thanks for breakfast, Terri," his father said.

"You're welcome. I'm glad you enjoyed it."

His mother stood with her empty plate. "I'll help you clean up before we leave."

"That's okay," Terri said at the same time Jon said, "You don't have to worry about it."

Jon added, "Just leave your plates on the table. I'll take them to the kitchen. Are you planning to do more sightseeing before heading home?"

"No," his father said emphatically. "Since we're leaving so late, we'll probably run into traffic, and I'm not trying to be on the road until midnight."

He whipped out his phone and hit the maps app. "Looks

like it should take about seven and a half hours. There are a couple of road closures on I-5 and some traffic."

His mother said, "Then we should probably get on the road. The way LA is these days, that could turn into eight or nine quickly."

Jon helped his father load the bags into the trunk of their small SUV.

"Whatever problems you and Terri are having, remember what I always taught you." His father pointed a finger Jon's way. "You're the man in the relationship, and men are strong. Always."

"How has that worked with you and Mom?" Thinking back, he recalled very few times when his parents were openly affectionate.

His father waved a hand. "I just tell her what she wants to hear, then send her to one of those little day spa places. Maybe you should consider doing the same to keep her off your back." He frowned. "I hope you're not thinking about doing those retreats. I told you, no one should know what goes on in your house. You don't need a bunch of strangers in your business." Pointing at Jon, he added, "Oh, and you'd better not be thinking about seeing a therapist. Only a weak man goes crying to a shrink about his problems. Man up and take charge of your marriage."

Rather than say something disrespectful like telling his father to mind his own damn business, he remained silent. He turned as his mother and Terri came out the door and headed toward him. He hugged his mother. "You guys be careful."

"We will. Are you coming home for Thanksgiving?"

Jon shared a look with Terri. "We're most likely going to hang out here this year, but if that changes, we'll let you know." While they hadn't discussed it, he already knew his wife wouldn't want to be subjected to another round of his mother's "help," and definitely not so soon. Neither did he. It would be even worse because all his aunts would jump on the bandwagon, and he had no desire to deal with their antics, either. After rounds of goodbyes, his father backed the car down the driveway and pulled off. He threw up a last wave. "Well, that was fun," he said sarcastically.

"Yeah. And you're right, I'm not going anywhere near LA for the holidays, especially if it means spending one more minute listening to your mother." Terri spun on her heel and strode back into the house.

He sighed wearily and slowly followed. Inside, he found her clearing the kitchen table. Without a word, he brought the rest of the dishes to the sink, rinsed them, and placed them into the dishwasher. The thick tension between them hung in the air and threatened to suffocate him. Jon wanted to say something, anything, but had no idea what. When they finished, she left the kitchen and went to sit on the deck. Although the sun shone, the temperatures hovered in the low sixties, and she pulled a blanket around her shoulders.

He took a step, intending to go sit with her, something they both used to enjoy doing, but then his cell buzzed. Jon groaned, thinking it was his mother again. He pulled the phone out of his pocket and relaxed when he saw a message from Antonio: *Serenity is allowing Gabriel to come out to play for a couple of hours. We're headed to the high school in about half an hour to shoot around on the basketball court. You're welcome to join us.*

Jon had declined their offers in the past, but today he needed to get out of the house, so he replied: *I'll be there.* He stepped out onto the deck and took the chair next to Terri. "I'm going to go with Antonio and Gabriel to the high school to shoot hoops for a little while."

"Fine." She never looked his way.

When she didn't say anything else, he stood and went back inside to change. Yeah, he needed to get out for a minute.

CHAPTER 6

When Jon arrived at the school, Antonio and Gabriel were already there.

"Well, look who decided to show up today," Gabriel teased. "Man, we thought you'd never stop working long enough to have some downtime."

"I wasn't working this weekend. My parents called and showed up unexpectedly."

There must have been something in his tone, because Antonio asked, "Was it that bad?" He sank a three-point shot, then tossed the ball to Jon.

He replayed every uncomfortable moment of the weekend in his mind. "Worse." He shot the ball. It went around the rim a couple of times, then went in.

Gabriel retrieved the ball, dribbled a couple of times, then made his shot. "So what's up with you and Terri? And don't even bother to say it's nothing. I've noticed it since I moved here."

Jon's gaze went first to Gabriel, then Antonio. He figured they would ask, but didn't think it would be two minutes after they hit the court. Both men had paused the game and were staring at him. He envied the ease with which they had developed a friendship, and he wanted the same for a change. His father's parting words rose, but he forced them down. "We're having some issues."

Antonio chuckled. "Tell us something we don't know. Have you talked about it with Terri?" When Jon didn't answer, he said, "Man, you have to talk to your wife. Communication goes a long way in clearing up misunderstandings. I had to do that with Tasha."

"I almost lost Serenity because I hadn't opened up to her," Gabriel said. "Have you guys thought about going to counseling?"

"Terri mentioned it a few times, but..." Jon ran a hand over his head. "It's not that easy, especially when you've grown up your entire life with a father who drilled into your head that showing emotions means weakness, especially to a woman."

Antonio was about to take a shot but spun around. "What? Are you kidding me?"

"No. As far as the whole counseling thing—"

"That's not something *men* do," Gabriel finished.

He nodded.

Antonio shook his head. "That had to be rough. It's bad enough that there's a perception that therapy or counseling isn't something Black folks do—what happens in the family, stays in the family—but to hear it from your own father makes it even harder to overcome."

"I agree. But you're going to have to decide what's more important—what your father said or saving your marriage. Unless that's not what you want."

"I love Terri, and I don't want out." But her leaving the other night meant she might be thinking about it, a realization that didn't sit well.

"Then maybe now's the time for you to put that love into action." Antonio tossed him the ball.

"I don't even know how to do what you're suggesting."

"Start with the crux of your problems. Find the thing that caused the rift in the first place."

Jon already knew the cause. Him. He felt a tightness in his chest, and the words stuck in his throat. He hadn't said the words since that day four and a half years ago. He lowered his head as the pain surfaced as if it had just happened. "Before we moved here, we lost our little girl when Terri was five months pregnant," he finally choked out. Saying the words out loud only magnified the pain, and he had to fight the urge to leave. He gripped the basketball tighter and took a deep breath, fighting to control his emotions.

Gabriel must have sensed Jon's torment, because he laid a hand on Jon's shoulder. "I'm sorry, bro. It was good that you two didn't have to go through it alone."

Only they had. Not because of her, but because of him. He hadn't been able to tell her how heartbroken he'd been, how helpless he'd felt, how he wished he could take away her pain—*their* pain—and wipe away her tears. He hadn't done any of that, and now his marriage was on life support. "I wasn't there for her like I should've been," he whispered brokenly.

"Then be there for her now, Jon," Antonio said. "There's no shame in showing your vulnerability to your wife. And there's definitely none in admitting you need to talk to someone. When Tasha and I broke up in college, I was so upset and distracted, my grades started to suffer and my game was off. I ended up having to talk to a psychologist to help me work through my issues. Trust me, it will help. But I also had my brother."

"You can't do life alone, my brother. I tried it," Gabriel said. "If it hadn't been for my buddies kicking my butt into gear, I might have missed out on my biggest blessing because of my past relationships. We've got your back, Jon, but you really should consider talking to someone who can help you unpack all this baggage you've been carrying around."

"Thanks." That they hadn't judged or belittled him eased the pressure in his chest and let Jon know he'd done the right thing in confiding in them.

"Oh, and what happens on the court stays on the court," Antonio said with a wide grin.

Gabriel extended his hand for a fist bump. "Amen, my brother."

"I appreciate that." Of course, talking to his wife wouldn't be this easy.

* * *

"I'm so glad you all are here," Serenity said, adjusting herself on the chaise lounge.

Terri placed a sleeping Giana in her bassinet, then took a seat on the sofa next to Natasha. "Me, too. After the crazy weekend with my in-laws, I need some sister love."

Dana, who had returned from her trip, passed out cups of warm apple cider. "What happened?"

She took a tentative sip of the fragrant drink with cinnamon and hints of orange before answering. "This is good, Dana. But to answer your question, my mother-in-law called Jon on Friday and announced that they were nearby and were coming to stay for the weekend."

Natasha held up a hand. "Stop. I know you're not saying she called out of the blue, no planning, no are-you-available-for-a-visit-next-weekend, just, *bam*, 'We're on the way.'"

"That's exactly what I'm saying." The mention of Mama Deb made her blood pressure rise again.

"As excited as my parents are about Giana's birth, they wouldn't ever just show up." Serenity rolled her eyes. "And then you had to come home from a long day of working in the ER to try to cook and take care of them."

She bit her lip and hesitated for a moment. "Actually, I'd taken the day off. I left Thursday night and had planned to spend the weekend in Napa. I needed some time away to think. The only reason I came back when Jon texted me was because I knew had I not been there, it would've given her more reasons to harass us about our marriage. That woman makes me so damn mad, sometimes." The calls and texts had started a few months before they moved, but had ramped up over the past two years.

"Oh, Terri," Natasha said with a touch on Terri's arm. "I'm so sorry things aren't getting better. What did Jon say?"

"He told her to stop trying to fix everything, but it just wasn't enough for me. Not after years of her doing the same thing, and him basically just letting it happen. I mean, he tells her to back off, but he hasn't really put his foot down. I was two seconds away from cussing her out and telling her to leave."

"Maybe you two should think about going to counseling."

Dana hadn't been there when Terri shared what happened after the counseling suggestion to Jon, so Terri took a moment to fill her in about him saying their problems would take care of themselves. She shrugged. "Not sure what else to do at this point."

Dana shook her head. "Girl, what is wrong with these men thinking there's something wrong with going to counseling?"

"I have no idea." He hadn't shared his aversion to therapy with her; he had only said that it wasn't an option. His staunch refusal had given her pause and made her wonder, more than once, why.

Serenity waved a hand. "Dana, you know men always get criticized if they even mention *therapy*, so it's not so far-fetched." She shifted her gaze to Terri. "Is there one thing you can point to that may be an underlying cause of your problems?"

Terri knew exactly when their troubles started, and even after being friends with these women for the past several years, had never given them the full details. However, with all the support they'd given her, she felt it was time for them to hear the full story. "Six months before we moved here, I lost my baby when she was born at twenty-six weeks. We were both so devastated," she said on a broken sob. And still were. "Our baby girl fought and fought, but was gone in less than a day." She'd prayed and prayed, holding out hope that Amara would survive. There were miracle babies who did every day. But for them, it didn't happen. Terri experienced every emotion—grief, anger, resentment—seemingly all at once.

A chorus of gasps sounded in the room, and Natasha placed a comforting arm around Terri's shoulders. "Oh, sis, I am so very sorry for your loss. I can't even imagine your pain."

Tears pooled in the corners of her eyes. "Thanks," she whispered. "It was the worst night of my life and *so* hard, and Jon never wanted to talk about it. By the time I got home from the hospital, he'd boxed up everything we'd bought and put it in the garage." The only thing she had left was the remembrance photo that the hospital had provided of her and Jon holding Amara while she kissed her cheek, and Jon kissed her forehead. She would never forget the tenderness, love, and tears she'd seen in her husband's eyes that evening. The next day it seemed like a switch had been flipped and Jon had turned his emotions off completely. He'd held and comforted her for the first few days, but never said another word. The easygoing, loving man she'd married disappeared. In his place was a man who rarely smiled and had buried himself in work, leaving her to grieve alone. She swiped at the tears running down her cheeks. "After a few months, between our friends and coworkers all trying to urge us to get over it, the stress had taken a toll on us. When Jon's law firm decided to open an office near here to handle a couple of large cases, we both saw it as an opportunity to start fresh. It worked well for the first couple of years."

"Oh, no." Serenity brought her hand to her mouth. "I wish you had said something. No way would I have—"

"Don't even think it, Serenity. No way would I have stayed away. You having a healthy baby is a blessing, and I would never be resentful of that, especially since I'm one of Giana's godmothers," Terri added, trying to lighten the mood. She didn't want her friend to feel one ounce of guilt for something that wasn't anyone's fault. "Besides, the doctor said she didn't see any reason for us not to try again." Except it was one more thing Jon wouldn't discuss. "At this point, though, I feel like we need some time apart." All three women stared. "We're barely talking and we're walking on eggshells around each other, so perhaps a short separation would give us both time to decide if this relationship is what we really want. I love him, and he says he loves me and doesn't want a divorce—neither do I—but something has to give. I just have to find a place to stay. Too bad those condos aren't finished yet." The town was in the process of building a small condo complex, but they wouldn't be available for another six months or so.

"If you need a place to stay, you can use our house next door," Serenity said. "Gabriel won't mind. As much as I hate the idea of you two not being together temporarily, maybe this separation will be the wake-up call Jon needs to get his butt in gear." They had kept the home that Gabriel lived in for family and friends who came to visit.

"Thank you. I think I'll take you up on your offer." She didn't see Jon agreeing with her decision, but that couldn't be helped. After so many sleepless nights worrying about their relationship, she needed to do this for her. For them.

Serenity eased up from the lounger. "Okay, this calls for a sister group hug." She beckoned them.

They gathered in a circle, and the strength of the women's arms around her made a fresh set of tears cascade down Terri's cheeks. Aside from her parents and a close cousin, who had remained at her side those first weeks, no one else had been there to offer comfort. She met their teary gazes. "I love y'all."

"We love you, too, girl," they chorused.

This was the balm she needed, and she regretted waiting so long to share her story with these amazing women. After the emotional moments, they finished their cider and chatted about the upcoming Thanksgiving holiday and whether Terri and Jon would be going to LA. She answered with an emphatic *"No!"* that brought on a round of laughter.

The sound woke up Giana, and Serenity quickly scooped her up and kissed her brow. "We're sorry, sweetie. When you get older and have your besties, you'll understand." They all smiled.

They chatted a little longer before Terri stood. "I'm going to go. I'll call you to let you know when I'm ready to move in."

Serenity gave her another sisterly hug. "Sounds good. I hope this puts you two back on the path to healing your relationship and each other."

"So do I."

Dana and Natasha followed suit, and Natasha said, "Yeah, we'd better do the same so you and this little cutie can rest."

Serenity said, "I appreciate you all coming over so I can have a mini supper club. I'm still a little salty about not being able to be in the kitchen yet."

Terri waved her off. "Girl, you'll be back in there soon enough. At least you won't starve, because Gabriel can throw down. Natasha, you don't have to worry, either, with Antonio. If I'm ever laid up, I'll have to rely on Ms. Ida's, because you know Jon is lost in the kitchen."

"Well, we'll be starving together," Dana said. "Y'all know I hate cooking."

Natasha lifted a brow. "You hate it, but you can still cook."

"Barely."

"Whatever, girl. Come on. Serenity, don't bother to walk us out. We'll see you later." She hugged Serenity.

The three women headed to the front, and Natasha locked the door behind them. In the driveway, Terri hugged her two friends. "Thank you so much for your support. I don't know what I'd do without you ladies."

"I know what you mean," Dana said. "If you need anything, let us know. We've got you, sis."

"Same goes for me," Natasha said. "You know, our conversation when we found out that Serenity was pregnant makes so much sense now. I just wish you had shared this with us a long time ago so we could have been there for you."

When Serenity had shared her good news, Terri had become emotional and confessed to Natasha that it was because she wanted her own children. That had been only partially true. "I wish I had, too. Better late than never, though. I'll see you later."

Natasha snapped her fingers. "Oh, since you and Jon are staying in town, you're more than welcome to join us for Thanksgiving, that is if you're... you know, still going to do the holidays together. We're going to host it in our new home." Antonio and his construction crew had done the restoration of the grand home that held fond childhood memories for Natasha and gifted it to her as a wedding present.

"Thanks for the invite. I'll check with Jon to see what he wants to do and let you know." He might not want to once she shared her plans.

"Sounds good."

The three women got into their cars and went their separate ways. When Terri arrived home, Jon's car was parked in the garage. After the weekend with his parents and baring her soul to her friends, she was emotionally exhausted and in no mood to go another round with her husband. She hoped they could get through the evening without another blowup.

The house was silent when she walked in. Heading down the hallway toward their bedroom, she saw movement out the corner of her eye on the deck and slowed her steps. Jon was standing at the rail on the deck with his hands shoved in his shorts pockets, seemingly staring at nothing. For a moment, she studied his tense features as he dropped his head, and she wondered what was on his mind. As if sensing her presence, he turned her way, and their eyes held. In his, she saw what looked like regret, sorrow, and something else, but she didn't have the energy to find out. Today, she had to put her well-being first. Tearing her gaze away, she continued to the bedroom. Terri really wanted to start packing, but the next four days were workdays, and after the ten-hour shifts, she wouldn't feel like doing much more than coming home and putting her feet up. Instead, she'd have to settle for doing it next weekend. *Now, I just have to tell Jon I'm leaving.*

CHAPTER 7

Thursday afternoon, Jon paced the length of the deck, stopped, and paced again. The breeze kicked up, but he ignored the chill. It had taken him the better part of the week to get the courage to open up to Terri, although she hadn't had much to say to him since returning home on Sunday. All his attempts at making conversation had been basically ignored, which made him feel more guilty, since he'd pretty much been doing the same thing to her. Another sin on his ever-growing list.

He hadn't been this nervous on his wedding day, but then what he'd felt was excitement and anticipation. This time, his emotions vacillated between fear and apprehension of how she would perceive him. He closed his eyes and tried to drown out the negative voices in his head telling him he was making a mistake. Jon glanced down at his watch. *Four fifteen.* Terri would be home soon, and once again, the nervous jitters hit him. This was uncharted territory for him and he hoped he didn't mess it up.

Jon went back inside, stopped in the kitchen for a bottle of water, then made his way to the bedroom, unbuttoning his dress shirt as he went. Once there, he tossed it in the laundry basket, grabbed a T-shirt from the drawer, and pulled it on over his head. After kicking off his shoes, he exchanged his slacks for a pair of sweatpants. He took a long drink of the cool beverage. He paused mid-drink when he heard the garage door opening. A few minutes later, Terri appeared. "Hey."

"Hi." Terri placed her tote on the chair, then sat on the side of the bed to remove her shoes. "We need to talk."

"We do." Jon opened up his mouth to speak, but she held up a hand.

"This past year and a half has been harder than the first few months after we lost Amara. In all the ways that matter, you haven't been there for me."

"I know, and I'm sorry."

"I am, too. And I think we need some time apart to decide if this marriage is something we both want."

It took a couple of seconds for his brain to register her words. When it did, his heart started pounding in alarm. "What do you mean, time apart?"

She stood and crossed the room to the closet, from where she carried out a large suitcase and placed it on the bed. "Exactly what I said." She opened it and began placing clothes inside.

He felt like he was trapped in a déjà vu loop. One week ago, she'd been packing to leave him. "Terri, I already know what I want. *Who* I want. I want you and *us*. We can't work on our relationship if you're not here."

Apparently, that was absolutely the wrong thing to say if

the speed at which her head snapped around and her dark brown eyes flashed in anger were any indication.

"That's real rich coming from the man who told me that our problems would miraculously work themselves out," Terri said with a bitter chuckle.

Jon held up a hand. "Can you just stop for a minute so we can talk? I know what I said, and I was wrong."

"Glad you finally figured it out, but it doesn't change anything." She continued filling the suitcase and when it couldn't hold one more piece of clothing, she zipped it closed, placed it on the floor, and started on a second bag.

How long was she planning to be gone? By the amount of clothing she was packing, she intended to be gone for more than just a couple of days. "I don't want you to leave."

"Why not? It's not like you talk to me when I'm here. I can barely get you to engage in a simple conversation. We've been tiptoeing around each other for *weeks*. So if I have to be alone, I may as well *be* alone. And I'm angry, Jon. Angry that you shut me out when I needed you. Angry that, in all the ways that matter, you left me. We're supposed to have each other's backs, but that hasn't happened in a long time. You won't even let me have yours, and I don't know why."

Okay, she had a point, but this was so not the way he envisioned the conversation going. She wouldn't let him get a word in so he could attempt to apologize and explain. "Baby—"

"I'm not done. You work ungodly hours every week, including the weekends. I can't remember the last time we went out on a date, because you find every reason to cancel them. I can't help but wonder if you really love me the way you say."

He sighed with exasperation. "I do love you, and if you'd just give me five seconds—"

She pointed a finger his way, cutting him off again. "And don't get me started on your mother. For *years*, she's tap-danced on my last nerve, butting into our relationship, and you've let it happen."

"Wait a minute. That's not true. Sunday, I told her to stop trying to fix everything." Now Jon was getting angry.

"Yes, you did, but it's not enough. I'm not telling you to disrespect her—although, she has one more time to come at me, and I'm going to cuss her out—but you need to figure out a way to let her know that what she's doing is unacceptable and it has to stop. *Immediately.* I'm your wife, and you're supposed to stand up for me. I'd do the same for you if it were my parents." Terri spun around and finished adding the last pieces to her bag.

Jon dragged a frustrated hand down his face. "I know Mom isn't the easiest person to reason with, and I'll do my best to get her to back off." When she raised a skeptical brow, he added, "I promise." He grasped her hands. "You don't have to leave, Terri," he pleaded. He didn't even know where she was going. Again. Or how long she planned to be gone. It couldn't be anywhere far since she still had to work. But would she tell him this time? And how was he supposed to work on their relationship if she left?

"Yes, I do. For me. For us," she whispered, tears standing in her eyes.

Jon's heart clenched. He could never stand to see her cry.

"Where are you going to stay?" The Firefly Lake Inn was a possibility, but a costly one, depending on the length of time.

"Gabriel and Serenity are letting me stay in their guesthouse."

He should have known her friends would help her out. He didn't know whether to be relieved that she'd be close enough for him to see her often or angry that Gabriel—after all his talk about friendship and brotherhood—hadn't let him in on this little bombshell. Jon decided he felt both at the moment.

"I need to get going so I can get settled before it's too late." Terri rushed over to the closet, took down two coats, and slung them over her arm.

Jon's heart was breaking, and he didn't know how to stop her from leaving. Admittedly, he'd screwed up big-time, but he was ready to put his marriage first. To put his *wife* first again, where she should have always been. He closed the distance between them and cradled her face in his hands. "I love you, and I'm not going to give you up."

"Then prove it."

He threw up his hands. "That's what I've been trying to tell you, but how am I supposed to prove anything if you leave? Stay. I know I have a lot to make up for, and I want to do that."

"I can't. And if you're serious about us, you'll find a way."

Antonio's words echoed in his head. *Then maybe now's the time for you to put that love into action.* "I plan to." He donned a pair of running shoes, grabbed his keys off the dresser, and picked up her bags. As much as he didn't want her to go, he wasn't going to let her leave alone. "I'll give you the space you asked for, but I'm not going to stop fighting for us." *Not now, or ever.*

* * *

Friday afternoon, Terri put the last of her groceries away. It felt odd living alone again after so many years, and the peace she thought she'd have didn't come last night. She had the red, puffy eyes to prove it. Jon had shocked her when he followed her to the house to make sure she was safe, and it gave her a small measure of assurance that she had done the right thing. If it took them separating to open his eyes, then Terri was all for it.

She sliced an apple, placed it on a plate, added diced cheese cubes and a few grapes and almonds, and called it charcuterie. The house had a small deck in the backyard, but it lacked the view she had at home—something she already missed. However, the cool weather negated the possibility of sitting outside, so she grabbed her plate and the glass of wine she'd poured and took them to the den. Terri made herself comfortable on the double chaise lounge and picked up the book she'd been trying to finish. Two pages in, her cell rang. Letting out a soft growl, she retrieved it from the end table. Her frown faded and a smile lit her face when she saw her cousin's name on the display.

"Candace! Oh, my goodness. I haven't talked to you in ages," Terri said when she connected.

Candace laughed. "Hey, girl. And it's been less than a month. What's up in Smallestville? I talked to Aunt Gina, and she said you and Mr. Sexy were still having issues."

She shook her head at her cousin's nickname for Firefly Lake. On her first visit, Candace had taken one look at the town and called it Smallestville, comparing it to the fictional town in the television show *Smallville*, but claiming it was even tinier. "Quit hating on my little town. And yes, we are. I haven't called Mom yet to tell her, but I decided Jon and I needed to separate for a while."

"Hold up, cousin. That's a drastic move. Did he cheat on you? Because if he did, I'm taking the next flight out to kick his butt." At two years older, Candace had always been protective of Terri, and the two were as close as sisters. However, now that Candace had moved to New York, they didn't get to see each other often.

"No, he's not cheating." As she'd told her mother, she still didn't think he was seeing another woman. "I'm just tired of coming home to a silent house." She shared the same things with Candace that she had with her supper club sisters. "We can't keep going this way. I know something is bothering him and has been for a long time, but I can't get him to open up and talk about it."

"He still hasn't shared his feelings about losing the baby?"

"Not one word." And it was killing her. "I asked him again a couple of weeks ago, and he shut me down cold. I don't understand why, and it's so frustrating." She popped a cheese cube into her mouth. "I just want him to talk to me. I know he was as devastated as I was, but—" She sighed and set the plate aside.

"A lot of men have a hard time sharing their feelings, Terri. I'm not trying to make an excuse for Jon, but you know society celebrates alpha males, and if they even hint at exposing their emotions, folks are quick to call them punks."

"That's so ridiculous." But Terri knew her cousin was right. It was the same thing Serenity had said. She searched her memory for any instance when her husband had shown his vulnerability and couldn't come up with one. Had she not been so caught up in the whirlwind romance, maybe she would have noticed something. "Do you think I moved too fast in marrying Jon?" she blurted.

"Um... where did that come from?"

"I was just thinking about what you said, and that maybe I didn't take enough time in dating him to find out important stuff like him not wanting to share."

"Terri, don't second-guess yourself. Are you saying you don't love him anymore?"

"I still love him, more than I ever thought I would, which is why I'm so frustrated."

"I'm glad to hear it, and I believe he loves you, too. I have to admit, I was a little jealous about you finding a great guy, falling in love, and marrying him in less than three months. Not in a bad way, though. I thought y'all were cute, like one of those sappy fairy tales that make you go *aww*. And there's no timetable on falling in love. You know Grandma and Grandpa met and married in less time than that, and they were together for over sixty years before he died. If you recall, I dated my ex-husband for almost two years before we married, and look how *that* turned out." Her voice softened. "Hang in there, T. I truly believe you and Jon will be able to get through this."

"I hope so. I don't want to lose my husband," she whispered.

"And I *know* he doesn't want to lose you, either."

"Thanks, Candace. I can always count on you to talk me off the ledge." Terri prayed that her cousin was right, that they would be able to scale this hurdle.

"I do have a question, though. How did he react when you said you were leaving?"

She should have known her cousin would ask that question. "He said he loved me, that he didn't want me to leave, and that he wanted to work on our marriage. And he followed me over to the house to make sure I was safe," she added softly.

Her cousin's happy scream came through the line. "Ha! I *knew* it. I may have to make a trip out there to see how this makeup-reconciliation-courtship is going to go. I'm bringing some popcorn and wine for the show."

"I can't stand you sometimes," Terri mumbled.

"Aw, girl, you know you love me. And Jon loves *you*. Mark my words. The brother is going to come around. I saw the way he was looking at you last year at Christmas. If my ex had *ever* looked at me with that kind of fire in his eyes, we'd still be married."

She opened her mouth to say something, but was interrupted by the doorbell ringing. Standing, she made her way to the front to tell Serenity, again, she was fine. Her friend had come over once and called twice since Terri arrived. "Whatever you say," she said to Candace. "He said he loved me, and I told him to prove it. Hang on a minute. I think

Serenity is at the door." She opened the door. "Girl, you don't—*Jon*. What are you doing here?"

"I came for you."

Obviously, he had come straight from work because he still wore his suit. "It's only four o'clock. You're never off this early." She heard a scream and realized it was coming from Candace, who Terri had forgotten was on the phone.

A grin kicked up on the corner of his mouth. "Is everything okay?"

"Um, yeah. Come in." Terri stepped back for him to enter. "Give me a minute to get Candace off the phone."

Jon nodded. "Tell her I said hello."

"Candace, I'll call you later."

"Checkmate, my sweet cousin. I told you," Candace said in singsong. "Oh, and tell Jon I said hi, too. Bye."

A beep sounded, and she looked at the display. Candace had disconnected. *That girl!* When she glanced up, Jon was staring at her. "I'm back here." She spun around, went back to the family room, and reclaimed her chair. Jon took a seat on the sofa.

For a moment, he sat with his arms braced on his knees, his hands clasped together and his head bowed. Finally, he asked, "How are you?"

"Okay." *Liar!* her inner voice screamed. "And you?"

"Miserable as hell without you."

Her surprised gaze flew to his. It was the last thing she expected him to say.

He slid off the sofa and hunkered down next to her. "I owe you an apology, Terri." He took her hands and pressed a kiss on her knuckles.

"For?"

"First, for my mother and her meddling. And for not protecting you like I should have." He used one hand to tilt her chin. "And second, for not living up to the promises I made to you the day we married. I'm so sorry, baby. So sorry."

His heartfelt apology touched her deeply and opened the floodgates. Jon rose, scooped her up, turned, and sat on the lounger. She cried in his arms the way she had wanted to all those years ago. As she did, he held her close and told her how much he loved her. She didn't know how much time passed, but Jon continued to hold her and whisper tender endearments until her tears stopped. "I love you, too, and I want us to be okay," she said.

Jon used the pad of his thumbs to gently wipe away her lingering tears. "I want that, too, but I have a lot of demons to get rid of first." At her questioning look, he added, "I promise we'll talk."

She moved off his lap and back onto the lounger, so as not to get caught up in the moment and have Jon make the assumption that everything was all good now that he'd apologized. They still had a whole mountain to scale. "So what happens now? If you're saying all this just so I will come home—"

He silenced her with a kiss. "No, sweetheart. I'm not. As much as I don't like it—and it's killing me—this time apart might be what we need. I did some thinking last night, and I realized that we met and married in a short period of time, then jumped right back into our busy careers."

Terri didn't know if she liked where the conversation was headed. Did he now have some misgivings? "So, you're saying you have regrets now?"

"Absolutely not. If I had to do it all again, I wouldn't change anything, except us spending more time with each other *after* the wedding."

She relaxed. As she listened to his explanation, she agreed that he had a good point. At the large law firm where Jon worked, he often had to put in at least sixty hours a week, just to keep up. And while the slower pace of the ER here in Firefly Lake allowed her a few minutes to catch her breath some days, the same couldn't be said about the hospital where she worked in LA. In all her eight years of working there, she could count on one hand the days she actually had a full lunch and breaks. Not a great start for newlyweds. "You're right, but that still doesn't have anything to do with us not communicating."

A shadow crossed his face. "It doesn't. That's on me."

Terri really wanted to shout, *Tell me now!* Then again, she was almost afraid of what he might say. "So where do we go from here, Jon? I don't want us to do some quick fix and throw a bandage on it, only to have it ripped off again."

"That's not what I want, either. I think we should do what we should have done in the beginning. What *I* should have done."

She eyed him. "And that would be?"

"Date. Do all of the things that couples do when they're getting to know each other." Jon shifted to face her. "I want to get to know you all over again, and I want you to know me. *All* of me. I want to do all of those things that I know you love, like walking near the lake, going to the movies, or going out to dinner. I want to take weekend getaways, just us two, where I satisfy your every desire. And I'm going to work on *me*."

The intense way he stared at her with that fire and passion Candace had mentioned made her want to throw caution to the wind and tell him to take her home. They'd never had a problem in the bedroom. The man knew his way around her body as if he'd been created just to please her. But she needed more. And they still hadn't addressed the proverbial elephant in the room.

"I'd better go." He rose to his feet and extended his hand to help her up, then led her to the front.

"Before I forget, Natasha invited us to their house for Thanksgiving, but if you'd rather not go, that's okay." It would be awkward at best, and she didn't want either of them to be uncomfortable—not that Natasha and Antonio wouldn't go out of their way to make sure she and Jon were good.

"No, I'd like to go, unless it would make you uncomfortable," he added as if he'd read her mind.

"I'll be fine." Or she hoped she'd be fine.

At the door, he stood there a lengthy moment, as if he didn't want to leave. Dipping his head, he placed a lingering kiss on her lips. "I'll call you." Then he was gone.

Terri leaned her head against the door. Despite all the difficulties facing them, for the first time in a long while, hope bloomed in her heart.

CHAPTER 8

Saturday, Jon drove to Seaside Meadows Park. With its tranquil lake, tree-lined trails, and blooming flowers, it was a beautiful and peaceful area, and he could see why it had become one of Terri's favorite places. When they first moved here, he remembered them coming nearly every weekend. He zipped his jacket to ward off the brisk breeze and cold air, stuck his hands in his pockets, and stared out over the water. How had he lost sight of the most important things in his life? No other woman had ever made him feel like his wife did, as if he were her world. She was his, but as of late, he'd done a poor job of showing her. That had to change.

He knew what he needed to do, but breaking through everything that had been ingrained from the time he could comprehend was proving to be the hardest thing he'd ever faced, including passing the bar. Once again, the guilt and grief rose up and almost choked him. Would he be able to live up to the promises he made to her on their wedding day? Could he figure out a way to slay the demons that had kept him in this cycle of fear and share himself the way she always did with him? As he sauntered down the path, Jon thought about the time with Terri last night. It had been the longest conversation they'd had in a long while, and though their relationship was a long way from being on solid footing, he'd enjoyed those few minutes.

Jon got to the end of the path, then retraced his steps to his car and drove home. Inside, the quiet was magnified. His cell chimed, and he dug it out of his pocket. He groaned when he saw his mother had sent a text reminding him that he still hadn't let her know whether they were coming home for the holiday. He typed: *Plans haven't changed. We'll be spending the holiday here.*

Mom: *That's a shame. I think it would be better for both of you to be around family that love you and can help you.*

Jon: *Again, we don't need help. Let it go, Mom.*

He tossed the phone on the bar and hoped that would be the end of it. At some point, he was going to have to have a heart-to-heart with his parents, and he could only imagine how that discussion would go. But he had something else he had to do that he'd been putting off for a long time. He booted up his laptop and drummed his fingers on the granite surface while it loaded. Once it did, he searched for psychologists.

An hour later, after reading bios, credentials, and services, which included individual and couples therapy, Jon had bookmarked half of the eight professionals available. *That was the easy part. Now I just have to make the appointment.* He'd attempted to make an appointment with one before moving from LA, but chickened out because his father had been in his ear constantly. This time he was ready. Ready to save his marriage. And himself. Shutting everything down, he took out the fixings for a sandwich. He'd just taken the first bite when the doorbell rang. Wiping his hands on a napkin, he placed his food back on the plate and went to answer the door.

"What's up, Antonio?"

"I'm here on behalf of the Separated and Shut-In Committee doing a wellness check," Antonio said without cracking a smile.

"Man, I don't even know how you said that with a straight face. Come in."

He burst out laughing and entered the house, towering over Jon's six-foot frame by a good four or five inches. "It wasn't easy. Trust me. I had to practice all the way over here."

"I bet. I'm having a sandwich. You're welcome to join me if you want." They entered the kitchen.

"Nah, I'm good." Antonio took the stool at the far end of the bar. "Seriously, though, I did want to see how you're doing. Gabe said he'll text you later."

He shrugged. "I'd like to say I'm okay, but it would be a lie. I want my wife home, and that's not happening, either."

"It will. You already took the first step by moving her in and going by to see her yesterday. And since no one heard any yelling, we figured you two are moving in the right direction."

Jon froze with his sandwich halfway to his mouth. "Right now, I really hate living in a small town. Y'all need to get a life."

He chuckled. "Look on the bright side: It was only Gabe and Serenity, unlike the time I kissed Tasha on the *cheek* in Ms. Ida's, and by the time I dropped my grandmother off ten minutes later, it was all over town that we'd engaged in a serious lip lock and had gotten back together. So it could've been worse." Antonio grinned. "Welcome to the Firefly Lake tabloids."

"Whatever." He recalled that incident and the one where one of Serenity's older neighbors told Gabriel's grandmother that Gabriel had spent the night at Serenity's house. He'd seen and heard the antics of the nosy townsfolk since moving here, but until now had never been part of it—and he wanted to keep it that way.

"Did Terri say how long she planned to be gone?"

"No." From their conversation, he got the sense that it wouldn't be an overnight fix. As he told her, he was willing to take things slow. He just hoped their definitions of *slow* were the same, like a week or two.

"Hopefully, it won't be long," Antonio said, mirroring Jon's thoughts. "Tasha mentioned you guys are coming to Thanksgiving dinner. Our families will be there, but you know we'll make sure to keep all this on the low."

"I appreciate that."

"What's your plan to get your wife back?"

One thing Jon had learned about Antonio and Gabriel was that they both were direct. "Date her and do what you suggested—put the love into action."

"That's what I'm talking about. If you need help with anything, let me or Gabe know."

He could probably handle everything he wanted to do, except for one piece. "Actually, there is this one thing you can help me with."

"Name it."

"I want to prepare dinner for her. I can run the courtroom, but I'm lost in the kitchen." His claim to fame included being able to make toast, cooking scrambled eggs that were just edible, and throwing hamburgers and hot dogs on the grill.

Antonio rubbed his hands together. "When Gabe and I get done, you'll be an ace in the kitchen."

Jon raised a skeptical brow. "I'll settle for the food being fit for consumption and my kitchen to be still standing when it's over."

Antonio threw his head back and roared with laughter. Once calm, he said, "I promise it'll be better than fit for consumption. It'll be *good*. Decide what you want to make and when you want to have the dinner, and we'll help you get what you need from the store."

"I'll probably wait until after Thanksgiving, since it's this week. Maybe three Saturdays from now."

Antonio whipped out his phone. "Okay. I don't have anything big going on, and that should give us enough time to practice." His fingers flew across the phone's keyboard. "Does she have a favorite meal?"

"She loves seafood, steak."

"I can work with that." His phone buzzed and he read for a second. "Gabe says he's good, too."

"Thanks, man."

Antonio gestured toward the sandwich. "And if you get tired of sandwiches, I got you. I'll let you in on a little secret. Women love a man who can cook."

Jon chuckled. "I completely missed that gene and until now never worried about it." With his wife gone, he'd be relying on those fresh prep meals he'd purchased from the grocery store and Ms. Ida's for the foreseeable future.

"With those big lawyer bucks you're making, I can see why," he said, coming to his feet. "Some of us can't afford to dine out every day."

"Shut up. Not sure how being a hotshot investment manager and now owning a construction company qualifies as being in the poorhouse." They broke out in laughter. Then Jon said, "Oh, and how were you and Gabe not going to tell me Terri was planning to move out? What happened to all that brotherhood and friendship stuff?"

Antonio sobered. "Wasn't our place. The women made that decision, and we're staying out of it. But rest assured, they're pulling for you two to get it together, and I guarantee they'll be in her ear about all the reasons she shouldn't give up on the relationship." A smile curved his mouth. "So we'll just have to do a little matchmaking of our own."

Jon grinned. *Things are looking up.*

* * *

Terri stood at the counter in Natasha's kitchen dicing the celery, bell peppers, and onions that would be used in the dressing for tomorrow's Thanksgiving dinner.

"How are things with you and Jon?" Natasha asked, prepping the mac and cheese. "And how are you handling being apart?"

She paused. "It's hard being away from him. With all our problems, I didn't think I'd miss him the way I do." Somehow, she'd mistakenly believed that because she spent so much time alone, with him being away from home and working long hours, moving out would be virtually the same thing. But she'd been proven wrong in spades, and she hadn't slept well in the week they'd been separated. She had awakened more times than she could count reaching for him, only to encounter a cold, empty space.

"Of course you'd miss him. You guys have been married almost five years and have never really spent nights away from each other. It's completely understandable, and hopefully, that means you won't want to keep things this way for long."

"As much as I'd love to be back in my own home, there's no way I'm going to do it without some changes." Terri added the vegetables to a bowl and went to the sink to wash the knife and cutting board.

Natasha propped a hip against the counter. "Exactly how long are you planning for this separation to last, Terri?"

"I have no idea. I didn't really think about any of that. I just knew we couldn't keep going the same way."

"I get that, but what's going to be the deciding factor for you going back? What are you waiting for Jon to do before this is resolved? Is there some kind of list you're checking off?"

Terri hadn't considered any of what her friend was asking, and she didn't have a clue of what she would deem "enough." "There's no list or anything," she said with frustration, throwing up her hands. "I guess I'll just know."

"I'm not trying to upset you, sis. I'm just giving you something to think about."

"I know, and I appreciate everything you, Serenity, and Dana are doing for me. It's just...I don't know." She knew she wanted them to communicate more, and for him to open up to her about his feelings, but did she unconsciously have some mental list she was waiting for him to fulfill?

"Have you two talked at all?"

"Yes. He came by the day after I moved, apologized, and said he's willing to put in the work. Yesterday, he sent roses to the hospital and a note letting me know he was thinking about me." The sweet gesture had taken her by surprise, and she wanted to think it wasn't a ploy just to get her back, only to stop and never happen again.

"Aww, sookie sookie now," Natasha said with a little shimmy. "Jon is doing a little old-school courting. I can't wait to hear what he does next."

Old-school courting? "Oh, hush. He's not courting me." But Terri was smiling. "I mean, he did tell me he wants to date. We got married fast, and our jobs kept us so busy that we didn't do a lot of that in the beginning."

"Like I said, *courting*."

"Who's courting who?" Antonio asked, coming into the kitchen.

"Jon is courting Terri. He sent her flowers."

He smiled. "Yep. That's part of courting."

Terri narrowed her eyes at her two friends. "What are you two up to? Did you put him up to that?"

Antonio held up his hands in mock surrender. "I had nothing to do with it. I didn't even know he'd sent them until now. I'm just here to support the both of you in any way you need. Other than that, I'm minding my own business."

"I didn't know, either," Natasha said with a laugh. "Can't promise that I'll be minding my own business, though."

"Mm-hmm. I'm watching y'all." Terri pointed back and forth between hers, Antonio's, and Natasha's eyes. The three burst out in laughter.

"Somebody's phone is ringing," Antonio said, pulling out his. "Not me."

Terri retrieved hers from the kitchen table. "It's me." Her mother was calling. "Hey, Mom," she said as she headed to the family room.

"Hello, daughter of mine. I've been waiting on that promised call. Not that little message letting me know you and Jon weren't coming home."

She hadn't called her mother because she wasn't ready to confess what she'd done. "I was going to wait until after Thanksgiving because I know you have a lot to do."

"More like you're worried about what I'm going say in response to whatever decisions you've made."

Terri took the phone from her ear and stared at it for a moment. *How does she do that?* Her mother had always been able to read her—and everybody else—for as long as she could remember.

"That silence tells me everything I need to know. What did you do?"

"I moved out," she mumbled.

"Oh, honey. I'm so sorry. I was really hoping it wouldn't come to that. Hopefully, the separation won't last too long and you two can work through your troubles."

Surprised, Terri said, "That's all you're going to say?"

Her mother laughed. "What did you think I was going to say? You're a grown woman, Terri, and what happens in your marriage is between you and Jon. No one else. Now, you know I'm here to listen, but I will not be telling you what to do."

She wished Jon's mother had the same philosophy. The woman had texted her a couple of days ago, trying to convince Terri to change her mind about coming home. "Thanks, Mom."

"Hey, that's what moms are for."

So grateful to have this woman in her life, she shared everything that had happened: Jon's apology and him sending flowers and calling to check on her every day.

"Well, it seems like he's putting in the effort, and that's good. The only thing I'm going to say is to meet him halfway. He's not perfect, and neither are you. How long this separation lasts is up to you and him. Of course, I'm pulling for the both of you. I believe that you belong together, and I know you'll figure it out."

"I love you so much, Mom." Her words were like a balm for her soul.

"I know, and I love you. Your dad says hello."

"Tell him I said hi and I love him. I'll call you guys tomorrow."

"Sounds good, baby."

Terri disconnected and held the phone against her chest, her emotions rising. *Meet him halfway.* "I can do that." Wiping the moisture from her eyes, she smiled and went back to the kitchen.

CHAPTER 9

Thursday, Jon felt about as nervous as he did the day he asked Terri to marry him. He parked in front of the guesthouse, got out, and went to ring the doorbell. While waiting, he debated whether to ask her out to dinner. He didn't think he'd be able to handle it if she turned him down. Then again, they couldn't work out their problems if she said no. Thinking back to a few weeks ago when he'd told her things would take care of themselves, he wished he could go back in time and slap a hand over his mouth before he let those stupid words out.

"Jon?"

He spun around at the sound of Terri's voice. Lost in his musings, he hadn't even heard the door open. "Hi. You look beautiful." Working in the hospital for so many hours, she rarely had the opportunity to dress up, but whenever she did, the woman took his breath away. *Then maybe you should give her a reason to dress up more often*, a mocking voice said. Yeah, he'd already acknowledged his shortcomings and pledged to do better. The dark purple jumpsuit dipped low enough in the front to give a glimpse of her full breasts and lovingly hugged every inch of her curvy body. His arousal was instant. He'd give anything to be able to strip it off her slowly and make love to her until they were both satisfied and unable to move. His growing erection stretched in silent agreement.

"Thanks. You look good, too. Come on in. I just need to grab my jacket."

Jon followed her inside and his gaze followed the enticing sway of her hips as she walked over to the sofa. Rushing over, he eased the garment from her hand and helped her into it. He didn't miss her slight tremble when his hands brushed against her nape. "Ready?"

"Ready as I'll ever be."

He wanted to ask what she meant, but he realized he had a good idea what she was thinking. He'd spent a big part of last night worrying whether someone would notice the rift between them. However, Antonio had assured him they would keep the secret. Yet, the way gossip flourished in the small town of fewer than two thousand residents, he had no doubt they'd be the subject of the next round of chatter. Taking Terri's hand, he escorted her out to his car, pleased that she hadn't pulled away.

When they arrived at Antonio and Natasha's house, he couldn't help but admire the fully renovated two-story, four-bedroom, three-bathroom home with its wide wraparound porch.

"I love this porch," Terri said, mirroring his thoughts. "I wish we had one at ho—" Her gaze flew to his.

That she still considered their house "home" made his heart leap. He *had* to find a way to bring her back. The door opened as their feet touched the bottom step.

"Are you two going to stand out there all day staring at each other, or are you coming inside?" Antonio said with a huge grin on his face. "Then again, if you need a little more time before facing the masses, I can slip you the key to Tasha's she shed." He tossed them a bold wink.

"So much for minding your own business," Terri said, rolling her eyes and climbing the steps.

Antonio affected an innocent expression and placed a hand on his heart. "What? I am minding my business. I was only making the offer just in case."

"Mm-hmm."

Chuckling, he kissed Terri's cheek and gestured her forward. "The ladies are in the kitchen." She started in that direction, and he clapped Jon on the shoulder. "I was serious about you two using the shed if you need a few minutes of privacy. Just let me know, and I'll slip you the key."

"I take it this is part of your matchmaking," Jon said, though he wouldn't mind having his wife to himself for a short while. "I'll let you know." He could hear the laughter before they entered the family room. Jon had met Antonio's parents, his brother and his family, as well as his grandparents. He was surprised to see Antonio's grandfather, who resided in a memory care facility in Napa due to his Alzheimer's diagnosis. "It's good to see Mr. Hayes."

"I'm glad he's still with us, and will be able to take advantage of the new center when it opens at the beginning of the year," Antonio said emotionally. His grandparents had been married for sixty years, and being so far apart, especially with Mr. Hayes slipping every day, had been the catalyst for Antonio to have a center built in town. "That's why we changed dinner to one o'clock. His memory gets worse later in the day. One of us will take him back shortly after dinner."

As much as his parents got on his nerves, Jon loved them and didn't know what he'd do if faced with the same thing. After rounds of greetings, he grabbed a soda from one of the coolers and took a seat on the sofa to watch the football game. Minutes later, Antonio's niece climbed up next to him with what looked like an iPad that had some animated show playing.

"Hi. I'm Noelle, and I'm four. Are you my uncle Tony's friend?"

He smiled, even as his heart ached. His little girl would have been around the same age. "Hello, Noelle. Yes, I am your uncle's friend. What are you watching?"

Noelle held it up so he could see. "It's *Encanto*. My favorite. Do you know the song 'Bruno'?"

Jon shook his head. "I don't have a little girl to sing it for me."

"You don't?" she asked sadly. "Do you even have a niece?"

Her big brown eyes held so much concern, he felt his emotions rise. "No," he answered around the lump in his throat.

"Well, that's okay. I can be your niece, and you can be my uncle," she announced. "Okay, Uncle... what's your name?"

"Jon."

She gave him a bright smile. "Uncle Jon." Shifting to her knees, she wrapped her small arms around him and hugged him tight.

Jon clung to her, a heartbeat away from breaking down.

"I have to go tell my mommy that I have a new uncle. Yay!" Noelle bounded off the sofa and took off at a run.

He stood and quickly made his way to the outside deck at the back of the house, hoping no one had noticed. Tears stung the back of his eyes, and he gulped in air, trying to ease the tightness in his chest. Why had life dealt him such a cruel blow? Why did his little girl have to die? He'd asked the question over and over, but would never have the answer. He could imagine Amara being as open and bubbly as Noelle and knew instinctively that the two would have been good friends. His cell rang and he groaned when he saw his mother's name on the display. "Hey, Mom."

"Happy Thanksgiving, son."

"Same to you."

"It would be happier if you were here."

Sighing inwardly, he said, "Don't start, Mom. We've already exhausted this conversation."

"I just don't understand why you two chose to stay there," she fussed. "This is a time for *family*, and you have no family in Firefly Lake."

But we have friends who stay out of our business, Jon wanted to say. "We're hanging out with friends, and I think they're ready to eat." He glanced inside and saw the guys still watching the game, and the women putting the finishing touches on dinner. As he started to turn around, Terri looked up. Their eyes held for a lengthy moment, then she resumed her task. His mother's voice brought him back to the conversation. She was still going on and on about all the reasons he and Terri should be in LA.

"You know, your marriage would probably be better by now if you two hadn't left LA."

That's it! Keeping his anger in check, he said, "Mom, I have to go. Tell the family hello."

His mother's heavy sigh came through the line. "Well, okay. I'll call you this weekend."

Jon quickly said his goodbyes, disconnected, and shoved the phone back into his pocket. His mother wasn't going to let up, and he understood his wife's concerns. The conversation he needed to have with his parents was going to happen sooner rather than later. He heard the slide of the patio door open and blinked back the tears.

"Are you okay?" Terri placed a comforting hand on his back.

"Fine. Just needed some air."

"Are you sure?" She stared up at him, seemingly unconvinced. "If you want to talk about it—"

"I'm fine, Terri. I'll be in shortly." He could see the hurt in her eyes, and he wanted to call back his curt words. "Really. I'm okay," Jon said softly, hugging her to him and placing a kiss on her temple. She nodded and went back inside. He turned back to the large backyard that offered a stunning view of Crystal Lake. A moment later, the door opened again. He turned to reassure his wife that he was fine, even if it wasn't exactly the truth. Except Mrs. Hayes, Antonio's grandmother, stepped out, instead. "Mrs. Hayes. How are you?"

"Oh, doing okay for an old woman." Nora Hayes tightened her jacket around her, then came and stood next to him at the railing. She smiled. "Velda and I had so many wonderful memories out here."

He assumed she was referencing the previous owner. According to Natasha, the woman had slipped into dementia, and her sons had moved her to be closer to them. She scanned the grounds, seemingly lost in her own thoughts.

"You know, I met Terri three years ago when we had to take my Fred to emergency one afternoon. She is such a sweet young woman."

It took Jon a moment to realize she had been talking to him.

"I found out that she left the emergency room and went to visit him every day while he was in the hospital."

He had no doubts about what she'd told him. Terri always went out of her way to try to lift someone's spirits. *She tried to do the same with you and you rejected her. Again.* Another pang of guilt hit him. He owed her more apologies than he could count.

She turned to face him. "She'll always have a special place in my heart for the way she cared for the man who holds my heart. And I want you two to experience the same kind of love I've had for over sixty years. How many years have you been married?"

"Almost five," he said, looking out over the lush grounds.

"I know all isn't well with you two."

Stunned, his gaze flew to hers. "What makes you say that?"

Mrs. Hayes patted his arm. "I may be getting on up there

in age, but there's nothing wrong with my eyesight. Until you let go of all the pain, you won't get there, sweetheart."

Jon thought he and Terri had done a good job hiding their turmoil. Apparently not. He didn't know how to reply, so he said nothing. Not that Mrs. Hayes needed him to comment, because she plunged on.

"And before you tell me you don't know what I'm talking about, if everything was okay between you, Terri would be residing with you instead of at Gabriel and Serenity's guesthouse." Mrs. Hayes shrugged. "Adele called to let me know. She thought since you and Antonio were friends, I'd have some information. Small-town living at its best or worst, depending on how you look at it. But don't worry, I didn't tell her anything. I love her like a sister, but that woman can't hold water," she added with a shake of her head.

Just great. Not only was he at odds with his wife, now he had to worry about the town's rumor mill. He recalled Ms. Adele doing the same thing when Gabriel and Serenity were dating. In LA, no one would blink at or, most times, even notice someone dealing with marital issues. But here...Jon ran a weary hand over his face. He didn't need this. *They* didn't need this.

"Do you see the green grass and beautiful flowers?"

The woman changed subjects on a dime. "Yes," he answered slowly, not sure where the conversation was going next and wishing he could figure out an escape.

"It takes a lot of work to keep it looking this good— watering, pruning, feeding it." She shifted to face him. "It's the same with marriage. You have to water and nurture it, or it will die. Oh, I know you two love each other," she said with a little laugh. "You watch each other with eyes of passion when you don't think the other notices. But I see the hurt and sadness there, too." Mrs. Hayes reached up and gave his cheek a grandmotherly caress. "We all have struggles and dark parts of our lives, but it's difficult to move forward if you hold on to those things that may have hurt you in the past. Don't be afraid to open yourself up and shine the light into those dark places. Let go, sweetheart, so you can be free to love your beautiful wife the way I know you want to do. We're always freed by the truth, no matter how painful the process may be. You don't have to carry this burden on your own. That's why the good Lord gave you Terri."

Once again, Jon had to fight to keep his emotions under control. His body trembled, and moisture filled his eyes. He felt as though this petite wise woman had reached down into his very soul and seen his heart. As if she knew he needed it, she wrapped her arms around him in a comforting hug.

"If you ever need someone to talk to, I'm a good listener. No judgment. Just love. Come on back inside when you're ready." She gave him a soft smile before leaving him alone.

Blowing out a long breath, he leaned against the railing with his head bowed. He stayed out a minute longer, then went inside and nearly ran into Terri. Jon brought his hands up to steady her. He loved this woman with every beat of his heart. He didn't have the words at the moment, so he placed a soft kiss on her lips and just held her in his arms, letting her familiar warmth surround him. At length, he eased back.

Terri gave him a curious look. "You okay?"

We're always freed by the truth, no matter how painful the process may be. You don't have to carry this burden on your own. That's why the good Lord gave you Terri. Mrs. Hayes's words sounded in his head. "I will be." Jon didn't know who was more surprised at the admission, her or him. But the words were true. He would be, no matter how uncomfortable he knew the process would be.

CHAPTER 10

Terri observed Jon throughout dinner. Although he said he was fine, she knew he'd lied. One minute he had been laughing with the guys while watching the football game, and the next he'd nearly sprinted outside like the house was on fire. She hadn't noticed anything out of the ordinary and couldn't put her finger on what changed in that short amount of time. Her pride was still a little stung from his dismissal. Sure, he had tried to soften the blow with the kiss and his reassurance, but the damage had already been done.

Had the change occurred after the phone call? Jon appeared to be upset by whatever had transpired during the conversation. Terri's stomach dropped, and a kernel of dread crawled up her spine. She tried to keep her mind from traveling down the dark road of suspicion but had a difficult time. The bite of turkey stuck in her throat, making it hard to swallow. When her mother had asked if Terri thought Jon was cheating, she'd said no. Now...she wasn't so sure. Antonio's mother calling her name cut into Terri's troubled thoughts.

"I'm so glad you were able to get the day off."

Smiling, she said, "So am I. I was really hoping to get the entire weekend, but no such luck. I'm back on the clock tomorrow bright and early." She also had to cover another nurse's shift on Saturday. Terri couldn't wait to start her new job and have the weekends to herself.

"Then it's a good thing we decided to have dinner early today, so you'll have plenty of time to rest tonight." Antonio saluted her with his glass.

"What you do is so important," Antonio's grandmother, Mama Nora, said. She gave her husband a soft smile.

Terri wondered if she and Jon would ever have the deep, loving relationship Mama Nora shared with her husband. The two had been married for sixty years, and even with his Alzheimer's diagnosis and inability to care for himself, resulting in him having to reside in a care facility, that love had never wavered. Terri studied the older woman as she patiently assisted him with his meal, and she envied the private smiles the two shared. She hazarded a glance at Jon, seated next to her, and found him doing the same. He turned her way briefly, his expression unreadable, then continued eating. Sighing inwardly, she picked up her fork.

The conversation turned to the new memory care center. Natasha's parents, who'd moved away some years ago, hadn't seen the building, and Natasha said, "You and Dad have to stop by to see it before you leave. It's gorgeous and I can't wait for it to open." She smiled at Antonio. "My hubby did a fabulous job with the design. I'm so proud of him."

Antonio winked at her. "Thanks, baby."

"Oh, and you have to see the new condos he designed, too."

"Sounds like you've been busy, Antonio," Natasha's father said.

He shook his head. "I haven't stopped going since I took over the business." Antonio's godfather had been the original owner. When Antonio moved back to town at the beginning of the year, Mr. Davenport had been ready to retire and offered him the business. According to Natasha, Antonio had worked for Davenport Family Construction during the summers and, despite having a career in finance, had kept up with his construction license.

"I'd rather be busy than bored every day," Antonio's father said. "Besides, hard work never hurt anybody. You *should* be busy."

"Says the man who's been retired for over a year," Antonio cracked, which brought on a round of laughter. "I'm not the only one who's busy. Jon is a senior partner at a law firm right outside of town, and he works as much as or more than I do."

Every eye around the table focused on Jon. He shrugged. "It's hard to work only forty hours a week when you have to make sure the firm is running smoothly."

"True," Mama Nora said. "But don't forget to take time for what's important in life. She happens to be sitting right next to you."

Grinning, Jon leaned over and placed a quick kiss on Terri's lips. "You're right."

Terri was torn between rolling her eyes and asking him "Since when?" But she just smiled as a chorus of "aww" and "that's so sweet" sounded around the table. Fortunately, the conversation shifted to Noelle, and everything she'd been doing in preschool.

After dinner and dessert, Terri helped Natasha clear the table.

"Looks like Jon is pulling out all the stops," Natasha said quietly as they went into the kitchen.

This time she did roll her eyes. "Girl, please. If I was so important, we wouldn't be living in separate houses." She placed the plates into the sink and waved a hand. "It was all for show." And that made it so much worse.

"Are you saying he hasn't made one romantic gesture since you guys have been separated?"

She couldn't say that at all.

"What about the flowers you mentioned yesterday?" Natasha raised a hand when Terri started to speak. "I'm not saying this means everything is all good now, just that he seems to be trying to do a little better. I heard he's been over to the house a few times and wearing a suit, like he came straight from work. *And* it was before six. So, again, my dear sister-friend, are you sure that kiss was for show?" A wide smile curved her lips, and she wiggled her eyebrows.

"What? You've been spying on us?" It had surprised her, too, but she decided to keep that to herself. And she had no intention of answering the last question.

"Nope. But apparently, Ms. Adele is back on her job. She called Mama Nora, fishing for information. But don't worry, Mama Nora doesn't spread everybody's business like that. Serenity said she saw him, too."

Terri rubbed her temples. "Great," she muttered. "All I need is to be part of the Firefly Lake rumor mill."

Natasha gave Terri's shoulders a quick squeeze and chuckled. "Now you can say you're a full-fledged member of the town. We've all been there. You remember that little peck on the cheek at Ms. Ida's that had morphed into a passionate kiss in less than twenty minutes. There was a room full of people who saw the whole thing, and they didn't even bother to correct it."

"I remember," she said with a little laugh. "I also remember you being mad enough to spit nails."

"Yeah, yeah. Well, I'm over it now."

"Mm-hmm."

Natasha folded her arms and leaned against the counter. "But seriously, how did it go today? We made sure to keep your business private. I don't think our families noticed anything."

"I'm not sure. One moment, I felt like we're making progress, then in the next, we're back to square one. Something is going on with him, and whatever it is, he refuses to talk about it. Earlier, I saw him go out to your deck, and he looked upset. I went out to check on him, and he nearly bit my head off, telling me he was okay, which wasn't the truth. I'm so frustrated with him, I could scream."

"Oh, Terri. I don't know what to say. I really thought you two were turning a corner. Jon seemed more relaxed today than I've seen in a while."

Terri had believed the same thing, but now didn't know what to think. She toyed with mentioning her suspicions about him possibly cheating, but changed her mind. If she didn't say anything, maybe it wouldn't be true. Besides, Jon should be the first person she asked the question, something she would do before the night ended.

"What are you doing, Terri?" Antonio asked, coming into the kitchen.

"Helping Natasha."

He shook his head. "You were here helping with all the prep last night, so you're officially off duty. We'll take care of all this later. I think Jon was looking for you."

As if on cue, Jon stuck his head in the kitchen. "You ready to head out?"

"Let me finish rinsing these last few dishes."

He nodded.

"I'm glad you guys came," Natasha said. "We have so much food left over, I'll fix you a to-go plate."

"You don't have to do that." Jon took up a position at the bar.

"I agree," Terri said. "Your parents are still going to be here for a few more days, so you should save that food for them."

"Please. My parents already have lunch and dinner invites with at least three people, so far. And my dad said he's definitely not leaving without a trip to Ms. Ida's."

"Which means there's even more reason to send some home with you," Antonio said, helping Natasha place the food in some divided bowls. "And don't worry about returning these containers. We bought them specifically for this reason."

Terri started to argue, but Natasha cut her off.

She shoved the container toward Terri. "Girl, just take this food and hush. You have to be on your feet for ten hours tomorrow. This way, you'll have one less thing to worry about when you get home."

"Okay, okay. You win. I appreciate y'all." After collecting their bags of food, and several rounds of goodbye, Terri and Jon headed out.

As they drove, Terri contemplated when to bring up her concerns. They hadn't said one word since leaving.

"Did you enjoy yourself?" Jon slanted her a quick glance before refocusing on the road and turning onto her street.

"Yes."

"I know you have to work tomorrow, but if you're off on Saturday, would you like to go out to dinner?"

"I am working on Saturday, but only half a shift, so dinner is fine."

"Seven a good time?"

"That works. Is it a woman?" she blurted. Okay, that wasn't how she'd planned to broach the subject.

He parked in the driveway, cut the engine, and shifted in his seat to face her. Frowning, he asked, "Is what a woman?"

"The reason you've been pulling away."

"No," he answered without hesitation. "There's no woman, Terri. Why would you think I'm seeing another woman when I told you I loved you?"

Terri stared out the window. It was almost dusk. "I don't know. It's just that earlier you seemed to be having a good time, and the next thing I see is you rushing outside. Then I saw you on the phone," she added softly.

"My going outside had nothing to do with another woman, and the phone call was from my mother."

"Oh. I guess that clears up the irritation you had on your

face." But it still didn't explain the reason he'd gone outside in the first place or justify his brusque tone to her.

Jon got out and came around to help her out. He didn't let go of her hand as they sauntered up the walkway. They'd held hands more in the past couple of weeks than they had in the last six months. *So, again, my dear sister-friend, are you sure that kiss was for show?* Natasha's words came back to her, forcing her to acknowledge that maybe his romantic overtures weren't for show.

Jon eased the key from her hand and unlocked the door. He stepped back and gestured for her to go first. After closing the door behind him, he leaned against it. "I need you to believe me when I tell you I'm not cheating on you," he said, picking up on their conversation. "I have *never* even thought about it."

"Then why can't you just tell me what's going on with you? Why won't you talk to me, Jon? Why do you keep pushing me away?" Her voice rose with each question. "You say you love me, but I don't see it. I don't feel it here!" She pointed to her heart.

"I...Terri..." He ran a hand over his head, then opened and closed his mouth again.

She threw up her hands. Leaving him standing there, she stalked out and went to her borrowed bedroom. Terri dropped down on the side of the bed and blinked back the tears filling her eyes. Her cell buzzed. She dug it out of her purse and saw a text from Natasha: *Apparently, Noelle decided Jon is going to be her new uncle because he doesn't have a niece. Nate mentioned she was really excited. Not sure how Jon feels about it, but wanted to let you know.*

Terri sent back a reply: *Thanks, sis!*

She'd seen Antonio and Natasha's niece approach Jon and say hello. Terri had been so engrossed in getting the food onto the table, she didn't think anything of it. Then it hit her. *Oh, no.* Jon had gone outside after that. Their daughter would have been around the same age, and interacting with Noelle most likely brought back painful memories. After meeting the little girl, even she had wondered if Amara would have been as outgoing and friendly, or if she would have asked a million questions like Noelle often did. Terri would bet those same questions had crossed her husband's mind. And sent him running.

She kicked off her shoes and headed back to the living room. Jon sat on the sofa with his arms braced on his knees, head buried in his hands. Terri lowered herself next to him. "Natasha sent me a text and told me what Noelle said to you." He didn't move. "Kind of hard not to wonder what Amara would have been like at that age." She placed a hand on his arm. "I've wondered a time or two myself, and it's not easy because I keep asking myself why. I hope you'll want to talk about her soon. I *need* to talk to you about her."

Without a word, he hugged her, then stood. "Maybe." Bending, he placed a lingering kiss on her lips. "I'm gonna go."

Terri didn't bother to stop him. He'd said "Maybe" this time, instead of shutting her down cold. *Progress.*

CHAPTER 11

Friday, Jon sat on the deck, sipping a cup of coffee. He'd made the decision to close the office the day after Thanksgiving—a first—and he lay in bed until nine. Another first. Truthfully, he couldn't say he'd slept in since he hadn't fallen asleep until well after five that morning. His conversation with Terri had played on a loop in his head all evening, and as a result, he'd tossed and turned, unable to shut his brain off.

Jon didn't realize that anyone other than his wife and Mama Nora had noticed his near sprint outside or his interaction with Noelle. Then again, the little girl had excitedly shared her plans to spread the word about their new bond. When she'd given him the bright smile and wrapped her small arms around his neck, he'd been torn between wanting to hold her and never let go and staying as far away from her as possible. In both cases, Jon hadn't expected the rush of emotions that had engulfed him. The sweetness and innocence of Noelle's kiss had gone straight to Jon's heart. Drawing in a deep breath, he let it out slowly and refocused on his surroundings. He'd begun spending time each day sitting here to think. Jon didn't know whether it was because of the beauty and peace, or because in some strange way it made him feel closer to his wife, as it had become her favorite place in their home.

When they first moved in, the two of them would sit together and watch the sunset at least twice a week. However, as the years passed, Terri continued the ritual daily, while he drifted away and couldn't recall the last time he had joined her. Now, with the weather change, it would soon be too cold to sit outside, even with the fire pit, something that saddened her. Terri had mentioned on more than one occasion her wish to be able to sit there year-round. Jon took a sip of his coffee and frowned. The dark brew had cooled significantly and he set it aside. Rising to his feet, he scanned the deck, which spanned the length of the house, and an idea came to him. He picked up his phone and sent a text to Antonio asking him to stop by when he had a moment, then went inside to dump the now cold coffee.

Several minutes later, Antonio replied: *Need some cooking lessons already... lol?*

Jon: *Ha, ha. No. Have a construction question.*

Antonio: *Since the office is closed, I can stop by around 11, if that works.*

Jon: *That works.*

It gave him an hour to do a little research and to make the call he'd been putting off. Jon rinsed his cup and put it in the dishwasher before powering up his laptop. While waiting for it to load, he thought about Antonio's comment. He would need to find some food soon. The two pieces of toast he'd eaten an hour ago were long gone. Before he could talk himself out of it again, he opened the file with the list of psychologists he'd compiled and called the one who seemed to be the best fit. A big part of him hoped that, like many other businesses, they had closed for the holiday.

"Healing Pathways Counseling Center, this is Autumn. How may I help you?"

So much for it being closed. The words stuck in Jon's throat. "I'd like to make an appointment with Dr. Walker," he finally said. The center had both male and female psychologists, but he preferred talking to a man.

"Okay." She paused for a few seconds. "I have next Wednesday at either two or three available."

"I'll take the one at three." Jon had figured it would be at least a month before he could get in to see someone, giving him more time to gather his courage. *Gotta love small-town living.* Had he still been in LA, the wait for specialty medical services would have most likely exceeded two months. He provided his name, number, and email address.

"I'll be sending you some preliminary forms to complete and send back before your appointment. We look forward to seeing you next week, Mr. Rhodes."

"Thanks." Making the appointment was the easy part. Actually going would be much harder. But the baggage he'd been carrying around for so many years was tearing his marriage apart, and he had to find a way to move past it or he was going to lose his wife. *Until you let go of all the pain, you won't get there, sweetheart.* Once again, Mama Nora's words came back to him. Jon had no idea how she'd seen so much in such a short time. Briefly, he wondered if it might be cheaper just to talk to her, since she seemed to be able to read him so well. She certainly knew how to keep a marriage together after sixty years.

Closing the file, he opened another window to search for sunrooms and enclosed porches. There were so many options, he had no clue where to begin. Jon got so engrossed in the different sizes and features, it took him a moment to realize someone had rung the doorbell. He made his way to the front, saw Antonio, and glanced at his watch. Had an hour passed already? "Come on in," he said, opening the door and stepping back for his friend to enter.

"How's it going?" Antonio asked, following Jon back to the kitchen.

Jon shrugged. "It's going."

"You said you had a construction question. Something going on with the house?"

He reclaimed his stool at the bar, while Antonio took the one next to him. "No. I want to add a small sunroom or glass-enclosed porch to the deck. Terri likes to sit out there every day, but can't during the colder months." He turned the laptop so Antonio could see. "I don't need anything complex. Just something simple and big enough to fit a couple of loungers with a small table between them." Jon scrolled through some of the designs he liked.

"Sounds like a great idea. I see you're getting the hang of this courting your wife thing, huh?"

"I don't know about the whole courting thing. I just hope she'll be back to actually enjoy it."

"She will," Antonio said confidently. "All right, let's see what will work best. I suggest you make it a little larger to accommodate a table and a couple of chairs in case you two want to have dinner out there."

Jon hadn't considered that, but liked the idea. "I'd like to have a gas fireplace, ceiling fan, lighting, maybe A/C. How long do you think it'll take to build?"

Antonio had pulled out his phone and started typing. "Anywhere from two to four weeks, depending on size, materials, customizations, and whether the deck you have can support an added structure. Sounds like you want an all-season room, so that means insulated windows and doors, an HVAC system to maintain more consistent temperatures year-round."

"That's exactly why I called you," Jon said with a laugh. "Not my lane." He just wanted a simple but elegant space for Terri to be able to enjoy the water and mountains.

Antonio chuckled. "I hear you. If I ever need some legal help, I'll let you know."

"I've got your back." They did a fist bump.

He stood. "Let me go take some measurements and check your deck foundation."

Jon followed suit, and they exited through the sliding glass door to the deck. Theirs was considered a ground-level deck with two small steps down to the grass. He stood off to the side as Antonio walked the length of the space, stopping every so often to check something. While waiting, he sent a text to Terri: *Morning, babe. Thinking about you and hoping the ER isn't so crazy busy today that you'll miss lunch.*

Antonio came back to the end where Jon stood, squatted down, and placed a handheld laser tape measure against the deck floor. "With the deck being thirty-four by eighteen, you definitely have the space for a fourteen-by-fourteen enclosure and still have plenty of space for the deck furniture you have out here now."

Jon nodded. Currently, they had two deck chairs with a small bistro table between them, a round table with seating for four, and a grill, which could easily be moved to one side. It reminded him that he'd have to transfer everything to the shed soon. "Will that be large enough for everything I want inside?"

"Yep. When I go into the office on Monday, I'll do a cost estimate. I assume you want it done pretty quickly," he added with a knowing smile.

"I do. I'm not sure when Terri is coming home, but it would be a nice surprise." And with Thanksgiving falling earlier in the month this year, it gave them an extra week in November. He refused to believe things would turn out any other way. His phone buzzed, and he read a text from Terri: *Hey. Much slower than last year, so when lunch comes around in an hour I'm going to dance down to the cafeteria. Hallelujah!* Jon chuckled.

"Save all the sexy texts to your wife for when I leave."

He laughed. "Nothing sexy. I was just seeing how her day was going." And it gave him an idea. "I think I'm going to take her lunch."

Antonio grinned. "That's what I'm talking about. Too bad Serenity is busy with the baby. Otherwise, I'd suggest you ask her to make you a couple of those chocolate-dipped strawberries."

"I think I can come up with some dessert. Oh, and I'd like to hold off on dinner lessons until the porch is finished."

"A new enclosed porch, cooking dinner...she might be home sooner than you think."

Jon smiled. *I'm counting on it.*

* * *

"I am so glad it's relatively slow today."

Terri glanced up from her charting and smiled at her colleague as the woman dropped down into a chair at the desk. "Same. I'm actually going to be able to get my full thirty-minute lunch today."

"I just got back and it was heavenly." She let out a satisfied sigh. "I brought some leftovers from my mom's, and they were even better the second day."

The previous year, they had been inundated with patients who'd overeaten or had turkey carving mishaps, along with those coming in with the usual colds and flu. "I figured it would be wild, like last year, so I didn't bring much to eat. I'll have to settle for whatever I can get from the cafeteria." She wasn't looking forward to institutional food. Natasha had given her enough leftovers to last a couple of days, and she couldn't wait to dig in when she got home. Alone. Terri didn't know how much longer she could hold out being away from Jon. After living with someone for almost five years, she found it hard adjusting to this new arrangement—cooking for one, sleeping in a cold bed with no one to snuggle with, waiting for footsteps that never came. A smile curved her lips when she thought about the text he'd sent a while ago. It was almost like when they first got together. He'd send sweet texts and leave sexy messages on her voicemail. How she missed those days.

Turning her attention back to the chart, she finished up and left to check on the few patients once more before leaving for lunch. On her way back, Sheila waved her over.

"These came for you. Girl, this is the second time in what...two, three weeks?"

"Something like that." A huge grin spread across her face as she accepted the vase of red roses. First the text, now this. A small card sat in the center and she plucked it off to read away from prying eyes. Terri carried them over to her station, opened the envelope, and read the note: *You, and only you, are my heart. J*

Tears misted her eyes. She loved Jon so much. *We have to make it.* She locked the card in the drawer with her purse and headed for the cafeteria.

"Terri, the receptionist called and said she needs to see you out front," Sheila called out.

Terri sighed inwardly. She dearly hoped it wasn't anything serious, because her lunch would start in five minutes. "Okay. Thanks."

"Keeping my fingers crossed you'll still get that lunch."

"Girl, same." She made her way to the exit and headed toward the front desk. She froze when she saw Jon standing there. "Jon?" Then her heart started pounding. Was he okay, or had something happened? She forced her feet to move and rushed over. "Is everything okay? You aren't sick, are you?"

"No, baby. I'm fine." Jon bent and placed a kiss on her lips. "I thought I'd bring you some lunch."

She brought her hand to her chest and let out a sigh of relief, but she didn't see any bags.

"Are you still going to be able to take the time?"

"Yes."

"Then go grab your jacket and meet me out front."

Terri stared at him a long moment. "You're going to stay?"

"If that's okay. I thought we could eat together."

Her emotions nearly overwhelmed her. He'd never brought her lunch in all the years they'd lived here. "Yeah," she whispered. "It's okay. I'll be right back." She went back the way she'd come and retrieved her coat from her locker.

"Everything okay, Terri?" Sheila asked.

"Everything is fine. My husband surprised me with lunch."

"Whaaaat? I don't think I've ever seen your husband." She hopped up from her chair and latched on to Terri's arm and nearly dragged her to the front. "We were beginning to think he wasn't real because no one has met him."

Terri thought back and realized Sheila was right. Jon rarely came to the hospital and had missed all of the get-togethers hosted by some of the staff. "Well, he's real," she said as the doors electronically opened.

"If that's him, the brother is *definitely* real. Girl, I see why you keep him hidden. The man is fine, fine, fine!"

"Yes, he is, and he's all mine. See you in thirty." She smiled and threw up a little wave.

"Ready?" Jon asked when she reached him.

"More than ready. Where are we going?"

He let her precede him out the door. "Just around the

corner to the park. It's a little cold, so I figured we could have a little picnic in the car. I lucked out on a spot in front." He placed his hand in the small of her back and guided her to his late-model Audi parked a few feet away.

After he helped her into the car and got in on the other side, Terri said, "This is a nice surprise. And you took off work." She couldn't recall him ever leaving work in the middle of the day for anything.

Jon pulled out of the lot. "Actually, the office is closed today."

She whipped her head around. "Closed? Since when? You've never closed the office the day after Thanksgiving in all the years we've lived here." She tried not to be upset. Last year, she'd suggested they both ask for the day off and go away for the weekend, but he'd cited every reason in the book as to why he couldn't. "And why didn't you mention it?"

"You didn't give me a chance." And as if he'd heard her thoughts, he added, "I knew you had wanted us to get away for a weekend last year when we'd just gotten that class action case and I had to be here. With us hiring another attorney, I figured I could delegate anything that might come up this time and we could finally have some time together."

Just great. I messed up my chance at finally having that weekend. Had she been too hasty in her decision to leave? And would it have been the thing they needed to get their marriage back on track? Terri sighed inwardly.

He turned into the park's lot and found a spot facing the mountains. After turning off the engine, he covered her hand with his. "I didn't say all that to make you second-guess your decision, sweetheart. And we *will* get that trip in." Bringing her hand to his lips, he placed a sweet kiss on her knuckles. "You don't have a lot of time, so let's eat." Jon reached for the bag on the back seat. "I really wanted to get something from Ms. Ida's, but figured sandwiches might be a better choice this time."

Still contemplating his words, she unwrapped the sandwich he'd handed her, and her surprised gaze met his amused one. "Chicken salad on a croissant. My favorite."

"I remember, even if I haven't shown it lately." He dug into his roast beef.

"Thanks for this, Jon." The first bite almost made her moan, it was so good. He'd also gotten her a strawberry lemonade. Another favorite, earning him a few points. They ate in silence for a few minutes.

"I made dinner reservations for seven tomorrow night, so you'll have a little time to rest after getting off work. Is that okay?"

"It's perfect. Dressy or casual?"

"Dressy. We're going to By the Lake."

Another point. They'd only gone to the upscale restaurant a handful of times. "You mentioned the new attorney. How's it working out?"

Jon took a sip of his drink before answering. "Pretty well, so far. She's been an attorney for five years and doesn't need a lot of hand-holding, which makes it easier on Brian and me."

"Does that mean you'll be leaving the office earlier?"

"That's the plan. I'll still have to work late sometimes, but I'm going to do my best to be home earlier more often." His increasingly late hours had been another point of contention between them.

"Do you really mean it, Jon?"

"I do." Staring into her eyes, Jon said, "And hopefully, my wife will be there, too."

He also said he'd attend more of the supper club dinners. If he lived up to those promises and finally opened up to her—he'd said *maybe* instead of outright refusing as usual—she just might be there. Sooner rather than later.

CHAPTER 12

Saturday evening, Jon slipped into his suit coat and grabbed the long-stemmed rose from the refrigerator before leaving to pick up Terri. He felt a little worried about how tonight would go and didn't recall having this issue even on their first date. *You have more to lose now*, a mocking voice said. As much as he didn't want to give credence to the murmurings, he couldn't completely dismiss it. He'd already lost a piece of himself and couldn't deal with the possibility of losing any more.

While driving, his mind went to his upcoming appointment. He still had some reservations about sharing his innermost emotions with a complete stranger. However, he reminded himself for the hundredth time, until he could crush the generational curses of his childhood, nothing would ever get better. Not his marriage, and certainly not him. Jon supposed admitting to himself that he was a mess inside should be a good start.

He parked in the driveway and sat there for a moment. Pushing his troubling thoughts aside, he got out and headed up the walkway. Tonight, he only wanted to concentrate on his beautiful wife. When Terri answered the door wearing a long-sleeved sweater dress that stopped mid-calf and hugged every single one of her curves, desire hit him hard and fast. It was one more thing he missed more and more. They hadn't been intimate in weeks.

Terri smiled. "Hey. Come in," she said, stepping back so he could enter.

As Jon passed, he deliberately brushed his body against hers and heard her sharp intake of breath. *Good. At least I'm not the only one affected.* "You look gorgeous, as always." He handed her the rose and bent to kiss her.

"Thanks." She picked up her coat.

He moved closer and eased it from her hands. "Let me help you." He held it while she slid her arms into the sleeves. The soft, sweet perfume she wore drifted to his nose. The fragrance had always been one of his favorites on her. It took everything in him not to gently move her shoulder-length hair to the side and place fleeting kisses along her scented neck. Being so close to her continued to wreak havoc on his senses. Jon lingered a few seconds longer, then stepped back. "Ready?"

Terri faced him. "Yes." She slung her purse on her shoulder and preceded him out the door, locking it behind her.

Once in the car, he observed her staring out the window biting her lip, something she often did when nervous. At least he wasn't out there alone. "Is it warm enough?" he asked as he drove off.

"Perfect."

Jon hit a button on the console and the sounds of The Temptations' "Silent Night" filled the interior. He slanted her a glance, and they shared a smile. Every year, they kicked off the Christmas holiday with the song, and he hoped it reminded her of happier times. He wanted tonight to be a new beginning in their relationship. Admittedly, he was looking forward to actually "dating" his wife. From the start, he'd been so consumed with his career and being the provider like his father had always preached about that he had lost sight of all the reasons why he'd fallen in love with Terri in the first place.

"I see you've got all my favorite Christmas jams playing tonight," Terri said, snapping her fingers and dancing to TLC's "Sleigh Ride." "I can't believe you remembered."

"You'll be surprised by what I remember. Besides, the playlist wasn't that hard to do since you blast it throughout the house every year from Thanksgiving night until New Year's Day."

She burst out laughing. "Okay, you've got me there, but I still appreciate it all the same."

Jon reached for her hand. "I'm glad." They rode the rest of the short drive in companionable silence interspersed with Terri singing or humming softly. When they arrived at the restaurant, it took only a couple of minutes for them to be seated.

Terri opened her menu. "I'm shocked that you were able to get a reservation on such short notice. Usually, there's a good two- or three-week waitlist."

"So was I, but it's probably because everybody is still trying to finish all those Thanksgiving leftovers."

She chuckled. "Probably."

A server came to take their drink order. Both ordered a

late-harvest Riesling. Jon thanked the young man and went back to the menu. "What looks good?"

"Anything besides turkey."

Laughing, he said, "Agreed. I'm thinking about something along the lines of seafood."

"Ooh, you know that's my go-to, but I'm having a hard time deciding between the pan-seared sea scallops, jumbo lump crab cakes, and bacon-wrapped shrimp."

He smiled inwardly at her serious expression. His baby loved her seafood. "How about we share all three, add salad or soup, and a couple of sides?" The entire menu was à la carte, and the sides were large enough for two.

A huge grin spread across her lips. "I love that idea. I'm sold. Can we have the baked potato with the works? You can choose the other side."

"Sweetheart, this night is all for you. I want you to order whatever you want."

Terri lowered her head briefly, but he could see the slight sheen of tears in her eyes. "Thank you." She paused, then asked, "Will the sautéed spinach work?"

"Works perfectly." Seeing her emotions on full display made his own rise, and he vowed to do his best to make her smile more often. The server returned with their drinks and Jon gave the food order.

"This is nice, Jon. We haven't gotten dressed up and gone out in a long time."

"I know, and I'm sorry," he said quietly, forcing down that guilt that continued to plague him. He lifted his glass in a toast. "To starting again, and doing it better." She touched her glass to his. *Doing it more than better this time*, he assured himself as he sipped.

* * *

Terri couldn't get over the change in Jon. His attentiveness, the sweet endearments, and the sultry kisses had her more than a little conflicted. Part of her wanted to shout "Take me home with you!" Yet, the other, more cautious part argued that this was only one date, one night, and who's to say he wouldn't go back to doing the same old thing the next day or week. She also had to consider the fact that they still hadn't broached the conversation they needed to have before any permanent decisions could be made. She studied him across the table. While he still looked like his same sexy, handsome self, something had definitely changed. But she couldn't quite put her finger on what was different. While waiting for the food, they kept the topics general, as if neither wanted to shatter these fragile moments of peace. However, there was one thing that had been bugging her. She opened her mouth to ask, but closed it when their food arrived.

"You think we have enough?" Jon asked teasingly after the server departed.

Terri had to laugh. With the number of dishes covering the table, he had a point. Unlike most of the upscale restaurants they'd frequented in LA and other big cities that served tiny amounts of food and left three-quarters of the plate empty, By the Lake provided generous portions of their entrées. "Maybe we should've added an appetizer or two to make sure." They both laughed. It took a moment for them to calm before being able to fix their plates. The first bite of the flavorful scallop nearly melted in her mouth. "Oh, this is *so* good." Her eyes slid closed and she let out a little moan. When she opened them again, Jon was staring intently at her. "What?"

"You're killing me, Terri," Jon said, his voice strained. "I need you to eat without all the...the...vocalizations."

When they first started dating, he'd told her that watching her eat was like an aphrodisiac. Terri recalled with vivid clarity what had happened *after* a few of those times. As long as it had been, she wouldn't mind revisiting those sensual moments. "My bad."

"Yeah, *yo* bad."

She brought her hand to her mouth to stifle a giggle. Picking up her fork again, she scooped up some of the potato covered in butter, cheese, sour cream, and bacon and stuffed it into her mouth. This time she kept quiet. With everything between them still unsettled, they didn't need to add sex to the equation. *Speak for yourself*, her inner voice chimed. Her body pulsed in agreement. Terri thought it best to turn her thoughts elsewhere. "I know we talked about it briefly at lunch the other day, but when did you decide to close the office yesterday?" She'd been after him to take the day after Thanksgiving off since they moved here. "And what did you mean by me not giving you a chance to tell me?"

He paused with his fork halfway to his mouth and angled his head as if weighing his words. "I decided on it a couple of weeks ago. And I had planned to tell you the night you announced we needed time apart and you were moving out."

Just like that, tension descended over the table. *Great.* What a way to ruin a date.

They sat in awkward silence. Finally, Jon covered her hand with his. "It's okay. I don't want this to mess up our night. Just like I told you, there will be other holidays we can spend together. I promise," he added. "I don't want you to second-guess this decision, because regardless of how difficult it's been or how much I hate coming home to an empty house and being away from you, I understand. It's giving us time to work on some things. And I am working on them, and on me. But again, I'm not going to give up on us. I *can't.* I love you too much."

The passionate look in his eyes and deep conviction in his tone made her heart start pounding. It was the most transparent thing he'd said to her in years.

"Let's not worry about any of that tonight and go back to enjoying dinner. Okay?"

"Okay." Terri gave his hand a gentle squeeze.

After a couple of minutes, he asked, "Are you looking forward to starting your new job?"

She was grateful for the change in subject. "I am. Dr. Adams asked me to call him sometime next week to schedule a walk-through. I can't wait to see what the inside looks like."

"I know how much you love working with the patients, so I imagine this will be a big change, having to do primarily admin work."

She shrugged and took a sip of her wine. "It'll be a big change, but since we'll have a pretty small population, I may have some time to hang out with the patients."

"More like you're going to make time to hang out with them."

Terri smiled. "You know me so well." While she knew there would be far more paperwork involved, nothing would keep her away from interacting with those seniors who were navigating life with dementia, including Mr. Hayes.

"Have they said when the facility will open? I recall from the last town meeting that there are a couple of families waiting."

"No, but hopefully it won't be too much longer." Pushing away her plate, she leaned back. "I need to save room for dessert." They still had a decent amount of food left, and she figured they could split the remainder. As if on cue, the server returned. "Could we have a couple of to-go containers, please?"

"Sure. Would you like to see the dessert menu?"

"Please." He handed her and Jon the menus.

"I'll be back with the containers in a moment."

It only took her a moment to decide. "I'm getting the warm butter cake with vanilla ice cream and strawberries."

Jon set his menu aside. "I think I'll have the same."

As promised, the server returned with the two boxes and they gave the dessert order.

"Thank you," she said. "I figure we can split what's left and it'll save us both from worrying about dinner tomorrow." It felt weird to have them boxing the food separately after so many years.

"Sounds like a plan."

It didn't take long for the sweet treats to arrive. Terri watched as Jon took a bite. "How is it?"

"It's good, but your 7UP cake is much better."

She narrowed her eyes. "Are you lobbying for a cake?" She usually made it as part of her Christmas desserts each year, and he'd eat almost half of it within the first two days.

"Maybe. Does that mean you'll be making it?"

"Maybe," she said, throwing his word back at him. Smiling, they went back to the dessert. Afterward, Jon paid the bill and led her to the car. It had gotten much colder in the two hours they'd been inside, and she pulled her coat tighter around her.

Apparently, he'd seen her shiver, because he said, "The heat will be up in a minute."

With the short drive, it had just started to warm by the time he made it to the guesthouse. Sometimes, she still marveled at the fact that everything was so close and convenient. Inside, the house was warm and cozy. Terri looked up at Jon. "I had a really good time tonight."

Jon wrapped his arms around her waist and pulled her closer. "Me too, and I'm looking forward to doing it again."

"Just let me know when." He lowered his head and kissed her. It started gentle and sweet, but changed to hot and demanding in a nanosecond. "Jon," she whispered as sensations whipped through her.

"I know, baby." He rested his forehead against hers, his body trembling as if he were trying to maintain control. "I—we probably shouldn't be doing this right now, but it's been so long."

Terri placed a finger on his lips. "Don't talk. Just love me." She agreed on both accounts. No, they definitely shouldn't be doing anything to further complicate things.

But yes, oh yes, it had been far too long since he'd loved her this way. Maybe this *was* a bad idea, but she'd missed his kiss, his touch. She just missed *him*. As if that was all he needed to hear, his mouth locked on hers once more. The wicked things his tongue was doing to hers nearly melted her on the spot. Only his strong arm kept her from sliding to the floor. Fire surged through her veins. Gripping his shoulders, she tore her mouth away to take a much-needed breath. His breathing was as uneven as hers.

He placed light kisses on her forehead, eyelids, nose, and cheeks, before taking her mouth in another heated kiss. At the same time, he removed her coat. "I've missed kissing you this way, Terri." He reached behind her and lowered the zipper to her dress, all without breaking the seal of their mouths.

Dropping to his knees, he held the dress so she could step out of it, tossed it on the sofa, then caressed her legs. She shuddered as his heated gaze raked over her. She stood there wearing nothing but a black bra, matching bikini panties, and her shoes.

Standing again, he slid down the straps of her bra until her full breasts were bared. "So beautiful," he whispered, placing light kisses around them. He circled his tongue around the nipple until it hardened, and then suckled it. He moved to the other one, lavishing it with the same attention. His hand moved down beneath the waistband of her panties to touch her intimately.

"*Jon!*" Feeling the twin assaults on her body, she wasn't sure how much more she could take. He released her nipple and squatted down, taking her panties as he went. He placed kisses on her belly and on her inner thighs, then parted her legs and brought her forward. Terri screamed and her knees buckled at the first touch of his mouth on her core. She held on to his shoulders to keep from falling and felt him tighten his hold on her. Her legs quaked as he moved his tongue deeper inside her. The added feel of his fingers working in tandem was too much, and she shattered with the force of a tsunami. She screamed out his name and collapsed over his shoulder as waves of pleasure washed over her.

"You're mine, baby," Jon said, picking her up, carrying her down the hall to the bedroom, and placing her on the bed.

Terri didn't open her eyes. Then he started again, kissing his way from her mouth to her ankles, lingering here and there and making her feel like she was coming out of her skin. Moans spilled from her lips as he set her whole body on fire. He moved upward and cupped her breasts in his hands, kneading and massaging them. He took one pebbled nipple into his mouth, then the other, while his hand charted a path down her front to the softness between her thighs. Terri sucked in a sharp breath as he slid one, then two fingers inside her, slowly moving them in and out. He increased the pace and her thighs began to tremble. Without warning, another orgasm hit her and she cried out.

Jon stood and removed his clothes. The bed dipped as he climbed onto it and lowered his body on top of hers, being careful not to place all his weight on her. "I can't get enough of kissing you. I've missed being with you this way," he said softly.

Terri moaned as he parted her thighs and positioned his erection at her entrance. He pushed gently, slowly until he was buried deep. The play of passion on his face heightened her own desire. She understood it. She was there, too. No matter what other problems they had, this wasn't one of them. Their blended moans filled the room as he set a leisurely pace with long, deep strokes, while his hands continued to caress her hips, sides, and breasts. No man ever had touched her this way, and she knew no other man would. Soon, the pace increased, his thrusts deepened, and her body trembled. He thrust deep with rapid strokes, and she arched up to match his rhythm. A torrent of sensations coursed down her nerve endings, and she came in a blinding climax. Jon rode her hard, and moments later, he erupted with a hoarse cry of pleasure.

Shifting his weight, Jon rolled over onto his back, taking her with him. He traced a finger down her cheek and tilted her chin. "I love you." He placed a soft kiss on her lips and held her close.

Terri lay sprawled half on top of him with her head on his chest. The rapid pace of his heart matched hers. The conflicting emotions rushed through her almost immediately. How she wanted to lay with him this way every night. But she couldn't. Not yet. "Jon?"

"Hmm," he said, still idly running his hand up and down her spine.

"This wasn't about you trying to seduce me into coming home, was it?"

Jon chuckled. "No, baby. I'd be lying if I said I didn't want you to come home, but I wouldn't pressure you that way. Tonight was only about me loving you."

She closed her eyes, relieved. Despite the fact that nothing had been settled between them yet, had he asked, she wasn't sure the parts of her that missed this connection would've wanted to say no.

CHAPTER 13

Terri lay in bed Sunday morning, staring up at the ceiling and wondering how she'd lost control last night. Then she answered her own question—she missed the intimate connection with her husband: the dates, the laughter, and especially the sex. The man knew how to handle his business in the bedroom. Even now, she was tempted to throw her stuff in the car and go home. But that wouldn't solve their problems. They'd never had an issue when it came to intimacy, but a marriage needed more than just good—no, *amazing*—sex to survive.

She glanced over at the clock and couldn't remember the last time she'd stayed in bed past ten. Then again, since she hadn't gone to sleep until almost four, she was allowed... *regardless of how difficult it's been or how much I hate coming home to an empty house and being away from you, I understand. It's giving us time to work on some things. And I am working on them, and on me. But again, I'm not going to give up on us. I can't. I love you too much.* Jon's declaration filtered through her mind once again. He said he would fight for them, but what did that mean? Did he think promising to come home early from work some nights, having a few dates, and mouthing a few *I love you*s would be enough? Terri couldn't deny the fact that he had been more attentive, but in all the promises he'd made, the only one he hadn't even attempted to fulfill was opening up to her. She needed to know why he couldn't or wouldn't talk to her. She'd always shared her feelings with him, but looking back, she realized he'd never really done the same. Sighing deeply, she rolled onto her side. A minute later, her cell rang. *I hope it's not Jon.* She wasn't ready to talk to him just yet, not with all the emotions swirling around inside of her. Sitting up, she picked up the phone and let out a groan when she saw her cousin's name on the display.

"Hey, Candace."

There was a pause before Candace answered. "What's wrong with your voice?"

Terri cleared her voice. "Nothing." Other than all the screaming she'd done last night.

"Hmm. You sure?"

"Positive. What's going on? I just talked to you last week."

"I'm calling to see how it's going with you and Mr. Sexy and whether you've taken your butt back home."

"Of course you are, Ms. Nosy. It's going okay, I guess, and no, I haven't."

"How many hoops are you going to make him jump through, and how long are you planning for this separation to last, Terri?"

"I'm not trying to make him jump through any hoops, Candace, but I can*not* go back to the way it's been. Yes, he's been more attentive, and we went out to dinner last night, but he still doesn't open up to me. You know relationships can't survive without communication." Angry tears stung her eyes.

"Look, cuz, I'm not trying to upset you. I just want you to consider when what he does will be enough. And, yes, I agree that communication is important, but you can't be waiting for him to say some magic phrase."

Am I waiting for some magic phrase? She didn't know, but it was something she probably needed to think about. None of the things her cousin mentioned had never crossed Terri's mind, similar to the pointed questions Natasha had asked. Sighing heavily, she said, "I don't know if there's some magic phrase. I just want him to talk to me about what's going on with him. But I hear you."

"Good. Now back to this date. Where did y'all go? And please don't tell me it was that one little place with the woman's name. Um, Emma, Irma... I can't remember."

Terri laughed. "No, we did not go to Ms. *Ida's*, but it would've been fine, because the food is so good. The next time you visit and stay for more than five minutes, we'll go and you can taste for yourself."

Candace grunted. "Whatever. I hope it was somewhere with crystal and linen."

"I can't with you, girl. We went to a restaurant called By the Lake."

"Is that in San Francisco?"

"No, it's right here in Firefly Lake. It's an upscale steak and seafood place."

"Smallestville has an *upscale* restaurant? *Whaaat?*"

"Don't make me hang up on you."

"Okay, okay. I'm sorry."

"Liar." She shook her head at Candace's antics.

Candace broke out in a fit of laughter. "All right, I'll stop hating on your little town...*for now*. But only because I want all the juicy date details."

Terri filled her in on the dinner and the laughter. "It kind of felt like old times, but we did have one hiccup when I asked about him closing the law firm the day after Thanksgiving."

"Hold up. You mean he closed the office and didn't tell you?"

"Apparently, I didn't give him the opportunity. It was the day I left. But he was understanding about the whole thing and we went back to enjoying ourselves."

"And I bet there were some steamy kisses at the end, too," Candace said with a giggle.

"Hot kisses and—" She cut herself off and groaned inwardly.

"Oh, don't stop now. Did you slip up and indulge in a round of hot sex?"

"A slip-up would be one round, not three," Terri mumbled. After he'd told her he wouldn't pressure her to return home, the next she knew she had straddled him and rode him to another trip to ecstasy. The last round happened when he was leaving. They'd ended up against the living room door.

"Well, well." She started humming that song by Nelly, "Hot in Herre." "At least you can cross that off the list of problems. Oh, and now I understand why your voice sounds the way it does. You're out there getting your freak on."

Terri opened up her mouth to say something, but her

phone beeped. She held it away briefly to check the display. "Hang on, Candace. It's Serenity." She clicked over. "Hey, Serenity."

"Hey, Terri. Are you busy?"

"Nope. Just talking to my cousin. You need me to come over?"

"If you could."

She flipped the covers back and stood. "Okay. Give me about twenty minutes and I'll be there."

"Thanks, girl. See you soon."

Terri clicked back over, grateful to be getting off the hot seat. "I'm back. I need to go over and see what Serenity needs. She just had a baby."

"Okay. But don't think you're getting off the hook that easy."

"Of course not," she drawled. "I'll talk to you later." They spoke a moment longer, then said their goodbyes.

Since she'd showered earlier, it didn't take her long to dress in a pair of comfortable sweats and a long-sleeved tee. She toyed with grabbing a bite to eat, but decided to wait to see what Serenity wanted. If needed, Terri could always prepare a quick late breakfast for them.

After sticking her feet into her sneakers and donning her coat, she picked up her keys and went next door.

Serenity opened the door seconds after Terri rang the bell. "Hey, Terri." The women shared a hug, and Serenity waved Terri in. "Thanks for coming over," she said as they walked to the family room.

"Please. You know I'm here for whatever you need. Where's Gabriel?"

"He went to help Nana with some things around her house and will be back in a few hours. I'm enjoying this moment of peace while Giana is taking a nap."

Terri removed her jacket and rubbed her hands together. "What do you need me to do? I can fix you something to eat." The doorbell rang before they could sit.

"Let me get that. Have a seat and I'll be right back."

A moment later, Terri heard voices and laughter. Serenity came back with Dana and Natasha. Terri stood to greet her friends. "I didn't know you were coming, too. I feel like we're having a little mini impromptu supper club, except for food."

Natasha held up two bags. "We've got the food covered, courtesy of Ms. Ida's. So let's get our eat on."

"And you know I've taken care of the drinks." Dana wiggled her eyebrows. As they all made their way into the kitchen, she added, "I figured since it's close to Christmas, I'd do something cranberry. Full disclosure, y'all will be the test case on this little mocktail."

"Too bad I can't have a real cocktail," Serenity groused. "I miss the good stuff."

Terri smiled. "You'll be able to indulge soon." They all piled the eggs, bacon, sausage, fried potatoes with peppers and onions, and biscuits onto their plates while Dana poured her mixture into glasses. "Whatever it is, Dana, it looks so pretty," she said, holding the flute up.

"I hope it tastes as good." Dana lifted hers. "To sisterhood, supper club, and my besties who don't mind being guinea pigs for my drink creations. Bless y'all." Laughing, they touched glasses and sipped.

"Girl, I will volunteer to test anything you make. This is so good." Terri had drunk nearly half already.

"Agreed," Natasha and Serenity chorused. Serenity asked, "What's in here?"

"Cranberry juice, simple syrup, a little lemon juice, and the 7Up you saw me add. That's it. There's an alcoholic cranberry drink I love that has triple sec and champagne."

Serenity held up a hand. "Just stop teasing me. Anyway, let's get to business."

Terri lifted a brow. "What business?"

Grinning, she said, "The business of Jon leaving that house at almost four this morning."

Natasha and Dana, wearing huge smiles, whipped their heads in Terri's direction.

So much for being off the hot seat. "We just went out to dinner, and how do you know what time he left?"

"I was up with Giana and heard a noise, so I peeped out the window and saw him getting into the car." She leaned over. "And I must say, that suit looked a little wrinkled." The other two women screamed with laughter. "So, again, my dear sister-friend, spill *all* the tea." She raised her glass in a mock salute and sipped.

Terri shook her head, but repeated the information she'd shared with Candace. "And before you ask, no, we aren't any closer to resolving our issues."

Dana finished chewing a bite of bacon. "But it sounds like you two are moving closer to it."

She forked up a bite of the potatoes before responding. "I don't know. I mean, we've spent more time together in the past couple of weeks than we have in the last three months, but we've only discussed superficial things, like our jobs. I'm thinking about scheduling a counseling appointment. He doesn't want to go, but I need to talk to someone to help me process all this anger I've built up." Terri had finally admitted to herself that she'd begun to feel some resentment toward her husband. In order for them to move forward, she needed to get hold of those emotions before they magnified and made things worse.

"I think that's a good idea, Terri," Serenity said. "Hopefully, a counselor can help you figure out the best way to approach communicating with Jon."

She shrugged. "I hope so. But until we have that hard conversation, I can't think about going back home. If I do, I just feel we'll be right back where we started. Yes, last night was amazing—"

"Him leaving at almost four means it was more than amazing," Natasha cut in, fanning herself. "I know how that is."

Terri smiled. "I'll concede that part, but I want it all." She deserved more. *They* deserved more, and she planned to hold out until she got it.

* * *

Wednesday afternoon, Jon drove over to the medical office building adjacent to the hospital. The closer he got, the more his gut churned, his chest tightened, and his breathing accelerated, as if he'd just run an eighty-yard touchdown. By the time he parked, he was two seconds away from calling to cancel the appointment. After wiping the dots of perspiration from his brow and loosening the tie that all of a sudden seemed to choke him, he leaned back against the headrest, closed his eyes, and took several deep breaths in an effort to slow his pounding heart and regain his control. Giving himself a mental pep talk, he got out and made his way to the entrance.

Jon passed a few people who called out greetings, to which he responded. People spoke whether they knew you or not. After living in the town for a few years now, he still hadn't adjusted to it. Or the fact that no one seemed to have a problem getting into everybody else's business. He passed a pharmacy and another medical office and hoped he didn't see anyone he knew, including Antonio's brother, whose optometry practice was also located in the building.

Thankfully, he made it to his destination without encountering a familiar face and breathed a sigh of relief. Three women glanced up at his entrance and stared curiously. The uncomfortable feeling came back, but he forced his feet to keep moving. Jon gave his name to the receptionist and sat in a far corner of the spacious waiting area. He rubbed his hand up and down his thigh, drummed his fingers on his knee, then clenched his fist to stop. Nervous, anxious, and not knowing what to do with his hands, he pulled out his phone and checked his email. He read one from Antonio, letting him know that the materials for the enclosed porch had arrived and that he would stop by later to drop everything off. The work would begin tomorrow. As he pressed the Send button on his reply, the receptionist called him back.

Jon stood, pocketed the phone, and followed the woman down a long hallway. She stopped at a door three-quarters of the way down and gestured him into an office, departing with a smile. A man who looked to be only a few years older than Jon came from behind the desk.

"I'm Ken Walker," he said shaking Jon's hand. "Please, have a seat."

Jon lowered himself into one of the offered armchairs. Taking in his surroundings, Jon realized that, other than the desk, the space had been designed to resemble a living room rather than an office, and guessed Ken had done it that way to make clients feel more comfortable. Yet, it did nothing to put Jon at ease. Even now, he had the urge to cite a work emergency of some sort and bolt out of the room, and it was all he could do to stay seated. Jon clenched his jaw so hard, his teeth ached.

Ken sat across from Jon in the other chair. "I know it wasn't easy to make the decision, so thank you for taking the step to come in. Today, we'll do things a little differently from a regular therapy session. I'll be asking you some questions so I can get a better grasp about what's been going on. I'll also answer any questions you may have. Afterward, I'll share with you my observations to ensure I understand fully. Then we'll discuss my initial thoughts and plan going forward. Okay?"

"That's fine."

"Why don't you tell me what brought you in today?"

You have got to be kidding me. He had spent a good twenty or thirty minutes completing all the questionnaires. Had the man not bothered to look at them? Frustrated, he said, "I wrote all that information on the requested forms that I sent back to your office."

Ken nodded. "You did. However, I'd like to hear it from you directly, just in case there was something else you'd like to share."

This wasn't going the way he'd envisioned. Jon figured the guy would check out the information, offer a few strategies, the end. For a few tense moments, neither man spoke. Jon reminded himself that if he didn't do this, his marriage could be over, despite the fact that neither he nor Terri wanted out. That the pain of his upbringing and anguish of his loss could consume and destroy him. Mama Nora's words, which had been on constant repeat in his mind, rang even louder now: *Don't be afraid to open yourself up and shine the light into those dark places. Let go, sweetheart, so you can be free to love your beautiful wife the way I know you want to do. We're always freed by the truth, no matter how painful the process may be.* "I don't want to lose my wife," he finally whispered.

"Has she given you any indication that's a possibility?"

"She moved out almost two weeks ago." Admitting to a total stranger that his wife had left him was both embarrassing and humbling.

Crossing one leg over the other, Dr. Walker said, "I'm sorry to hear that. How did it make you feel?"

How did it make me feel? Doesn't he know how hard this is? Once again, silence stretched between them. "Angry. Sad. Miserable as hell. Ashamed," he added softly as the emotions stirred in his gut.

"Why do you think she decided to move out?"

Jon seriously wanted to tell the man to read the damn information. As of yet, he hadn't seen one sheet of paper, or even an iPad. *You're here to get your wife back*, his inner voice reminded him for the hundredth time. "Because I haven't opened up to her." Instinctively, he knew what question would come next and his entire body tensed up.

Again the nod. "What's stopping you from opening up to her?"

He scrubbed an agitated hand down his face. *I can't do this.* Leaning back against the chair, he closed his eyes. Unbidden, a long-buried memory surfaced and the words were out of his mouth before he could stop them. "When I was nine, my friends and I were playing football. Darren missed the pass and the ball went into the street." He paused. "He ran after it and didn't see the car. It hit him. Everybody's parents came running out. We were all crying. My father... my father pulled me aside and told me to stop crying. Only girls cried. Men didn't show their feelings because it made them look weak." Jon turned away. "I didn't want to look weak." He'd vowed that day never to cry again or visibly show his emotions. He'd locked everything inside and thrown away the key. He needed that key now, but he had no clue how to find it or what would happen once he unlocked the door.

CHAPTER 14

Terri rushed out of the hospital Wednesday and made the short five-minute walk over to the new memory care center. The calendar had just turned to December and the cold, crisp air reminded her that winter was just around the corner. She'd agreed to meet Dr. Adams on her lunch break for a quick walk-through. As she neared the building, her eyes were riveted to the ingenious design. No one would ever expect it housed a medical facility. It more resembled an upscale condominium. She whipped out her phone and snapped a few pictures.

Dr. Adams glanced up at her approach and straightened from the column he'd been leaning against. "Hey, Terri. What do you think?"

Giving him a bright smile, she said, "I think if the inside looks anything like the exterior, I may be looking for a room here myself."

Chuckling, he unlocked the door, then stepped back and gestured her forward.

The sound of their steps echoed on the polished tile floors

as they entered the lobby area. It was still empty except for a large curved front desk. Soft hues of blue and green gave it a warm, calm feeling. She followed him down a short hallway and veered to the right.

"The patients' rooms will all be on this side of the building."

"How many rooms?" With it being such a small town, Terri didn't think they'd need a large-scale facility.

"Just ten for now. It's my understanding that they left space to add five more, if needed." Dr. Adams stopped at a door and opened it. "They've all been designed like a small studio apartment."

She wandered around the room. The kitchenette had a counter, cabinet space, and a place for a refrigerator. Owing to safety concerns and having a full kitchen staff, they'd forgone a stove. The bathroom was ADA compliant and had grab bars, a walk-in shower with a bench, and a handheld showerhead. "This is really nice," she said after taking a few more pictures and joining him again in the front room.

The two of them retraced their steps and went down a center hallway behind the reception desk. "This will be where the administrative offices are located." Passing four doors, he stopped at the end of the hallway and pointed out the one to the right he would occupy. "This will be your office," he said, gesturing to one directly across from his.

Never having had her own office, she smiled. "I can definitely get used to this." Terri scanned the spacious room and could already visualize what she wanted to do to transform it and made a mental note to call Natasha for her input. After taking a couple more pictures, she crossed the room and stood at the window, which offered a spectacular view of the mountains. "You're going to have to pry me out of here with this kind of scenery."

Laughing as they continued the tour, Dr. Adams said, "I said the same thing, but my wife took exception to the comment."

"I bet she did." She had met his wife at several hospital functions, and the friendly woman had impressed Terri as someone who wasn't afraid to speak her mind. They toured the entertainment room, library, and dining hall, which resembled an upscale restaurant. There was also a dedicated space for a convenience store that they planned to stock with basic necessities and snacks, which would offer residents some measure of independence. Afterward, they went outside, and she marveled at the lush grounds with its walking trails and a small man-made creek. An eight-foot fence surrounded the grounds at the back of the building. The only way in or out was through the front door. Dr. Adams also shared that there would be benches strategically placed along the paths, a few picnic tables, and a gazebo. "This is going to be absolutely amazing." Instinctively, she knew Mama Nora would be ecstatic to finally have her beloved nearby. As they made their way back inside and out front, she asked, "Have they set an opening date yet?"

"When I spoke to the mayor last week, I mentioned to him we'd be ready to open maybe the end of January or first part of February. That means you and I will need to get together soon to start hiring staff. I'd like for you to consider starting full-time here the first of the year."

Terri went still. That was only a month away. She had the

holidays, putting in notice at the hospital... and she had no clue whether her marriage would be anywhere near on track. "Okay. I'll talk to Jessica before I leave work this evening." She had a good rapport with the nurse manager and hoped the conversation would go well. "I'd better get back. Thanks again for the job and the tour, Dr. Adams."

"Thank *you* for accepting, and call me Tyler." He waved a hand. "We don't need to be so formal."

Terri nodded. "Tyler it is. Let me know when you want to meet."

"I'll email you some dates and times, and we'll try to work around your schedule."

"Sounds good. See you later." She threw up a wave and headed back up the street.

The rest of the afternoon sped by, and it wasn't until she'd grabbed her purse and headed toward the hospital exit that Terri remembered she needed to talk to her supervisor. Doubling back, she made her way to the woman's office. Fortunately, she hadn't left, and the short conversation went as easily as Terri had hoped.

"I have to tell you, Terri, we're sad to lose you because you're a phenomenal nurse, but I am happy for you," Jessica said as she stood. "Congratulations again."

"Thanks, Jessica. I appreciate you." Smiling, Terri said her goodbyes and drove home.

After a quick dinner, she sent a text to Serenity to see if she was up for a short visit. Her friend replied almost immediately with "Yes!" She pulled on her coat, grabbed her phone and keys, then cut across the yard. Gabriel answered when she rang the doorbell.

"Hey, Terri. Come on in." Gabriel leaned down and placed a kiss on her cheek.

"Hey, Gabriel." She rubbed her hands together in an attempt to warm them. The evening temperatures had dropped to near fifty degrees. "How're your programs going?"

"Going well. I'm working on a new one now," he said as he led her to the family room where Serenity sat on a chaise lounge, breastfeeding their daughter. To Serenity he asked, "You need anything before I get back to work?"

Serenity smiled up at him. "No. I'm good. Don't be back there working all night."

He held up his hands in mock surrender. "I won't. I promise I'm only going to work for about an hour more before shutting it down for the night."

"Mm-hmm. The only reason I'm not going to fuss is because I know you got a late start after being over Nana's half the day."

"That's why I love you. Oh, Terri, since this one here is getting restless not having her supper club, let Jon know we're doing dinner on Saturday around six. Dana is back for the rest of the year, and my buddy Darius will be here until Christmas, so we'll have a good ol' time. Antonio and I will take care of the food."

Serenity rolled her eyes. "I'm not getting restless. I just want to cook."

"Whatever you say, baby." Gabriel placed a sweet kiss on Serenity's lips before saying his goodbyes to Terri and disappearing around the corner.

Terri envied the ease of their relationship and worried that she and Jon would never get back to that place again.

Pushing away the melancholy thought, she said, "I can't believe how fast she's growing."

"I know. She's almost a month old already." Serenity lovingly stroked Giana's cheek. "So what's been going on? I hate being so out of the loop," she said with a pout.

She chuckled. "You haven't missed anything. Oh, wait. I had a chance to do a walk-through of the memory care center today, and it is *amazing*." She came and knelt next to the lounger and scrolled through the photos she'd taken earlier.

"This is beautiful," Serenity whispered. "Antonio and his friends did a fabulous job. I absolutely adore that the rooms look like apartments. It'll be so much better for their mental health. And the dining hall restaurant has me wanting to call and make a reservation."

"I know what you mean. And this is my office. It faces the mountains and has enough room for me to turn a cartwheel. I'm going to call Tasha to see if she'll help me decorate. Actually, I should recommend her to help do all the patient rooms."

"You have moved up, girlfriend." She finished the feeding, then transferred the baby to her shoulder for burping.

"I'm so excited. Dr. Adams—he told me to call him Tyler—wants me to start there full-time the first of the year. I talked to Jessica, and she's good with it."

"What a way to start the new year. Your work life is on track. What about your marriage?"

Terri went back to the sofa before answering. "I talked to him two days ago, but he still hasn't shared a whole lot. He did text me this morning to wish me a good day."

"It seems like you two are making progress."

"We are, but it's not enough. There's something eating at him. I don't know what it is, but I know in my heart that until we talk about it, things won't ever change." The last couple of times they'd been together, she had noticed an almost tortured look in his eyes. Terri had wanted to ask about it, but didn't out of fear that it would put them back at square one. "I didn't get a chance to tell you, but I went to see a counselor last week."

"Do you think it helped some?"

She shrugged. "Some. I spent several months in therapy after losing Amara, and it helped tremendously. I still miss her every day and often wonder what she'd be like, but I've finally gotten to the point where the grief and moving forward can coexist." *If I could only get Jon to do the same.*

* * *

Friday afternoon, Jon sat in his office tying up a few things before the weekend. A knock sounded on his door. He'd closed it in an attempt to finish his tasks and leave at a decent time. "Come in."

Selena entered the office. "I know it's almost closing time, so I'll be quick."

He gestured her to a seat. "What's up?"

"I just wanted to give you an update on what I found on the winery lawsuit. I did some research, and it seems that not one of the wineries has a record of Mr. Nelson placing an order."

Shaking his head, he said, "So, we're back to the original theory of a shakedown."

"That's the way it sounds to me. I have a call in to his attorney to verify if he actually placed or tried to place an order."

"If he supposedly had difficulties using the website, find out if he called Henley Estates to get some assistance before filing the suit. I know Mr. Henley said they hadn't received a complaint from him, so if Nelson is telling the truth, there will be phone records to corroborate his story."

A smile lit her face. "Already on it. That was the other thing I asked." Selena stood. "I'm going to finish a couple of things and head out, unless you need me to stay late."

"No. Enjoy your weekend."

"You, too."

After her exit, Jon sat a moment thinking about the case. *The things people do for money.* He went back to the document he'd been editing, then put it down again. He hadn't seen or talked to his wife in three days, outside of a couple of texts. He picked up his cell and sent a text asking if he could come by later, then grabbed his pen again. Instead of focusing on the papers in front of him, he rotated his chair and stared out the window and thought about what he would say to her. He wasn't ready to tell everything, but maybe he could start with why he appeared to be emotionally distant. But what would she think? Would she respond the way his father always said she would, or the way Gabriel and Antonio assured him she would? The snap of the pen breaking cut into his reverie.

Jon muttered a curse, tossed the pen into the trash can, and stared at his ink-stained hand. He hadn't even realized he'd been gripping it so tightly. Sighing, he trekked down the hallway to the bathroom to wash his hands. He returned to his office and read Terri's response agreeing to the visit. His concentration shot, Jon decided to call it a day. Ten minutes later, he was on the way home.

Once there, he first noticed the progress on the sunroom and sauntered over to check it out. It had only been a week, but they'd constructed the walls and installed the windows and flooring. The crew had also made two entrances in place of the original large sliding glass door. He was glad he'd taken Antonio's suggestion to widen the area. It had enough space for the twin loungers and small table, as well as a dining set. After they finished, Jon planned to install a sound system throughout the room.

Going back inside, he sent a text to Antonio to see if there was anything he needed for the completion.

Several minutes later, Antonio replied: *Nope. We may be able to finish by the end of the week if the weather holds. Then we can schedule that cooking lesson!*

Rain hadn't been forecasted for the next several days, but this time of year it could change quickly. Chuckling, Jon typed: *It looks good and I'm looking forward to it.*

He headed to his bedroom and placed the phone on the nightstand, then changed into jeans and long-sleeved tee. Afterward, he went back to the kitchen to heat up the leftovers from his last trip to Ms. Ida's. While eating, he read through the document he'd been trying to concentrate on in the office and made notations. When he finished, he cleaned up his dishes, tucked the folder into his briefcase, and left to see his wife.

As the days had passed, he missed her presence more and more, and after parking in the driveway, he sat in the car momentarily with his head against the steering wheel trying to summon up every ounce of courage he possessed. Somehow, this seemed harder than opening up to the therapist. *That's because there's more on the line.* A loud rap on the window startled him. His head came up sharply, and he saw Gabriel standing next to the car. Jon got out and greeted him.

"You okay, man?" Gabriel asked, pulling Jon in for a one-arm hug.

"Yeah. Just thinking about some things."

"How's it going?"

He shrugged. "It's going." He hesitated, then said, "I took your advice and went to talk to someone."

Gabriel clapped him on the shoulder. "I'm glad to hear it." As if he could read Jon's mind, he added, "And whatever you're thinking, don't. Your wife loves you, and I know whatever you tell her isn't going to change the way she sees you."

Nodding around the lump in his throat, he really hoped Gabriel's prediction turned out to be true. "Thanks."

A smile curved his mouth. "That's what friends do. Now get in there and get your woman back. Oh, and we're doing a supper club tomorrow. Antonio and I are handling the food."

"I'll bring the drinks. If you think of something else you need, let me know."

"Will do. Later."

Gabriel cut across the yard to his house while Jon continued up the walkway. The door opened before he could knock. "Hey."

"Hi. I heard voices and saw you talking to Gabriel." Terri stepped back and opened the door wider.

Jon entered and placed a soft kiss on her lips.

"Um, are you hungry?"

"No, but thanks. I already ate. I was hoping we could talk."

She stared at him curiously for a long moment. "Sure. Have a seat." Terri sat on the sofa and tucked her feet under her.

Jon took the chair across from her and rested his arms on his thighs, clasped his hands together, and bowed his head. *I can do this.* He took a deep breath and let it out slowly. Finally, he said, "From the time I was a kid, my father drilled into my head that men should never show their feelings. I cried after my friend got hit by a car when I was a kid, and he literally grabbed me, got in my face, and told me to shut up and stop crying like a girl." He paused to steady his emotions but was afraid to look at his wife. What if Gabriel was wrong? No, Terri had a heart of gold, and she loved him.

Her soft gasp sounded in the otherwise silent room.

"That only weak men—" His jaw tightened.

"Oh, Jon. Baby, there are a lot of words I'd use to describe you, and *weak* is not one of them." She left the sofa, knelt in front of him, and cradled his face between her hands, forcing him to look at her. "He lied to you, Jon. You are the strongest man I know, but none of us can do life alone. You are my heart and my safe place." Terri kissed him. "Let me be that for you. I promise I will always, *always* have your back. I will *never* ridicule you or dismiss your feelings," she said emotionally. "You can let go with me, baby." She placed her hand on his heart. "I love you, Jon."

A lone tear escaped down Jon's cheek before he could stop it, and he quicky swiped it away. He placed his hand over hers and knew she could feel the rapid pace of his heart. He wanted to say something, anything, but his emotions rose up swiftly, overwhelming him and causing him to tremble. He clenched his teeth and his fists, trying to still the tremors, to no avail.

Terri rose, slid onto his lap, and wrapped her arms around him. "It's okay. He was wrong. So wrong. We can work through this."

Relief spread through him. Jon held on to her, grateful that his father had, indeed, been wrong. "I love you," he whispered. He'd scaled this hurdle, and for the next little while, he shared everything about his upbringing. But he didn't envision the next discussion being as easy.

CHAPTER 15

Saturday afternoon, Terri folded the last of her laundry, then went to lie down for a thirty-minute power nap before the supper club dinner. After Jon's bombshell the previous evening, she hadn't slept well. She'd tossed and turned all night, vacillating between sadness for Jon and anger at his father for the antiquated beliefs that almost destroyed her marriage. Sure, she knew men were typically raised to only show their strengths, but the man had gone too far. As a result, her husband had hurts so deep, she feared he might not ever get over them. Terri had wanted to encourage him to talk to a therapist, but she realized it wasn't the right time. It had probably been difficult enough to open up to her, and she hadn't wanted to add more to either of their emotional plates. She'd cried for a good hour after Jon left and seriously toyed with calling her father-in-law and giving him a piece of her mind.

Terri shifted to a more comfortable position on the bed and tried to turn her mind off, but it proved to be difficult. She willed her mind blank. It seemed as if she'd just drifted off when an incessant chime on her cell sounded. Groaning, she reached over, picked up the phone, and turned off the alarm. *So much for getting some rest.* She lay there a few minutes longer, then got up to take a quick shower. She had less than thirty minutes before Jon was scheduled to pick her up. She had been concerned whether he'd still want to go, but he assured her that he hadn't changed his mind and would be there.

When he arrived, Terri pulled him inside the house, came up on tiptoe to kiss him, and hugged him tightly. "Hey, love."

"Hi. Ready?"

"Yep. What's in the bag?"

Jon held it up. "Drinks for dinner. I figure with Gabe and Antonio handling the food, it's the least I could do."

"Or," she said with a smile playing around the corner of her mouth, "you can learn to cook."

"It won't be now, so..." He returned her smile and shrugged.

Terri laughed. "True. I guess we should go." He waited while she locked the door, then they crossed the yard to the Cunningham home.

Serenity answered the door. "Come in, come in." She hugged them and waved them inside. "Natasha and Antonio are already here," she said as they followed her to the kitchen.

Gabriel glanced up from his task of draining potatoes at their entrance. "What's up?"

Before they could answer, Natasha and Antonio came in from the back deck. After rounds of greetings, Jon asked, "Where do you want me to put the drinks?"

Serenity pointed to a tub filled with ice at the end of the counter. "Just put everything in here."

Terri helped Jon add the bottles of wine, sparkling lemonade, and water to the large container. "Where's Giana?" she asked Serenity.

"I just put her down for a nap. Hopefully, she'll stay asleep for a couple of hours." The doorbell rang and she excused herself to answer the door. Minutes later, Serenity returned with Dana trailing.

"Hey, everybody," Dana said. "I see Gabriel and Antonio are trying to make themselves permanent members of the supper club with all this good-smelling food."

They all laughed and Serenity said, "Bite your tongue, girl. They can come *sometimes*. This is a sister-friends only club with a side of hus*baes*," she added, eliciting another fit of laughter.

"Fine," Antonio said, placing his hand on his chest as if he were offended. "We can form our own supper club, and I'll just take these ribs with me."

Terri eased over to the counter where the pan of smoked and grilled meat sat waiting for the sauce cooking on the stove. "Well, let me get mine now, before you run off."

"Aw, don't be like that, baby." Natasha sidled up next to her husband and wrapped her arms around his waist. "We said you can come sometimes, and this is one of those times." She leaned up and kissed him.

"Keep it up, and y'all are going to be on your own for food because I'm going to be doing a different kind of *cooking*." He wiggled his eyebrows.

"I think we need to pour some drinks. It's getting a little warm in here." Dana went to the tub.

"I'll help," Jon said.

As the drinks were poured, the fun and laughter continued, but Terri kept her eye on Jon. Though he interacted as he usually did, she could still see the pain reflected in his eyes. Every part of her wanted to hold him and never let go. She was so focused on her thoughts that she didn't realize he was handing her a glass of wine until he touched her arm.

Jon stared at her with concern. "You okay?"

She waved him off. "Yeah, I'm good. Thanks." She kissed him, then accepted the glass and took a sip. He'd purchased a bottle of her favorite Riesling.

"Hold up. I know you didn't start this party without me."

They all turned to find Darius, Gabriel's friend and business partner, standing in the doorway.

"That's what happens when you disappear when the work starts," Gabriel cracked.

Darius held up his hands in mock surrender. "Hey, first off, I'm a guest. And second, you already know that my cooking repertoire consists of only five things."

"Glad I'm not the only one," Jon said. The two men did a fist bump.

Twenty minutes later, the group sat down to enjoy the meal that consisted of potato salad, green beans, baked beans, honey cornbread, and Antonio's barbecued ribs with a sweet, smoky, sticky sauce that made Terri moan. "You outdid yourself with these ribs, Antonio. They're fall-off-the-bone, slap-yo-mama good."

A chorus of "Amen" and "I know that's right" sounded around the table.

"Thanks, Terri. Does that mean I'll be invited back to the supper club?"

"We already said you could. Just not all the time. How're we going to talk about you guys if you're here?" Serenity asked teasingly.

Jon turned Serenity's way. "Is that what goes on when we're not here?" He divided a look between her and Terri.

Terri wondered if he thought she would share what he'd told her yesterday. Sure, she told her girls some things, but she would never disclose something so intimate, unless he agreed. "Don't worry. It's only the fun stuff." She reached under the table and gave his hand a gentle squeeze of assurance. He repeated the gesture and gave her the smile that had captured her from the first, making her pulse skip. She continued eating and tuned back into the conversation, which went from the NBA standings and the progress on the condo project to the cold and rain predicted to hit the town in the next week or so and the Christmas holiday.

"Ooh, I have an idea for our next joint supper club," Serenity said with excitement. "Since I'm not quite ready to jump back in fully to cooking, what about us cooking with the guys?"

"Like a couples thing?" Natasha asked.

She nodded. "I like that."

"That's all good, but you know I don't do cooking," Dana said. "And if you haven't noticed, this sister is still single."

Darius clapped. "Ditto. But since neither of us cooks and we're single, how about we handle the drinks?"

She pointed her fork his way. "Now *that* I can do. I'm sure we'll come up with some festive holiday libations."

Rubbing his hands together, he grinned. "I did a little mixing in college, so I know we'll make it happen."

"Great," Serenity said. "Now that we've got it settled, what's on the menu? I figure we can do it the weekend before Christmas. That way it won't interfere with any other plans you all might have."

Natasha took a sip of her wine. "Sounds good to me. Good thing my hubby's an ace in the kitchen, because if it was left up to me, you'd be getting something basic."

Terri thought about what she would be doing for Christmas. She and Jon hadn't made any plans for visiting their families or even staying at home. And did she really want to be away from him then? *No.* He was making efforts to fix things, and maybe she could give a little, too. She'd take another few days to think about it before making any decisions. Then she also had to consider them having to prepare whatever dish together. "Does it have to be holiday foods, or can it be something different?"

Gabriel raised his hand. "I vote for different—Italian, Mexican—anything but more of what we'll be eating from Christmas to New Year's. What do you think, Jon?"

"I don't even know why you're asking me. Did we not just establish that me and cooking don't go in the same sentence?"

The guys chuckled, and Gabriel said, "That's why you have your wife."

Jon shifted his gaze to Terri.

She tossed him a wink. "Don't worry. I got you, baby. And I like the idea of Mexican food...maybe a taco bar or something."

"Yes, yes. I agree. Does that mean you're going to make the tacos, Terri? I mean, it *was* your idea," Serenity added when Terri glared at her.

Nodding at Serenity, Terri said, "Sure. We'll handle the tacos."

"Antonio and I will take care of the sides," Natasha chimed in. "Ain't nobody messing with the desserts. That's all you, Serenity."

"Amen, my sister." Terri and Natasha did a high five across the table. An animated discussion about the menu ensued, but Terri noticed that Jon didn't contribute much. She leaned over and whispered, "I can't wait to cook with you."

Jon lifted a brow, then asked slowly, "And exactly where will we be cooking this food?"

"In our home." She could see the relief in his expression.

"I can't wait."

"Neither can I." She was ready to do whatever it took to put her marriage back together and help the man she loved work through his past.

* * *

Thursday afternoon, Jon walked out of his therapist's office after an eye-opening session and headed to the grocery store. He'd believed he only had to deal with the issue of learning to be more open with his feelings. However, today he realized he had layers to unpack, the most startling revelations being that he had a deep-seated fear of failing as a man and husband, and that initially he had subconsciously blamed Terri for losing their baby, thinking that maybe she shouldn't have worked so much or been on her feet all those hours. In reality, neither of them was to blame. It had just been one of those tragic things that happens.

He blew out a long breath. If that hadn't been enough, Ken had asked whether Jon had ever talked to his parents about interfering in his marriage and the reasons he had been shutting down his emotions. Jon admitted that he'd asked his mother to back off, but that was it, preferring to ignore them and believing they would eventually stop. *How has that worked out for you?* Ken's pointed question made Jon acknowledge that it hadn't worked. Of course, the man went straight for the jugular and asked what Jon planned to do about it. He'd definitely have to fly down and have that conversation with them soon, but tonight he planned to focus only on the positive changes in his marriage.

The construction crew was finishing up the sunroom today, and Antonio had decided since he'd already be there, it would be a good time for the cooking lesson. Gabriel was on board, and after discussing Terri's likes and dislikes, the three men had come up with a surf and turf menu. If it turned out well, he would call Terri later and ask her to dinner this weekend. As much as he enjoyed the dating, he really wished he knew when she was coming home.

Jon picked up all the groceries for dinner and made it home minutes before the furniture for the sunroom arrived. It made him more excited than when he passed the bar. After having the delivery drivers load everything into the garage, he went inside and found Antonio and Todd, one of the crew members, putting the finishing touches on the room, and greeted both men.

"It looks good in here, Tony."

Antonio grinned and gave him a sidelong glance. "You doubted? She's going to love it."

"I agree."

"I'm going to head out," Todd said.

Jon reached out to shake his hand. "Thanks for getting this done so quickly."

"My pleasure. Boss, I'll see you tomorrow."

Antonio nodded. After Todd left, he asked Jon, "When does the furniture get here?"

"They just delivered it."

"Cool. I'll help you move it in here. Did you pick up everything for dinner?" Antonio had sent him a detailed list that morning.

"Yep, but I still don't know about this," he said, uncertainty creeping in again. The last time he tried to cook, he'd ended up with steaks that could double as hockey pucks, overdone and dry baked potatoes, and burned sautéed green beans.

Antonio clapped him on the shoulder. "Relax, bro. It'll be fine. Gabe and I are going to turn you into a five-star chef."

Jon laughed. "Again, I'll just settle for it being recognizable and edible," he said as they went to the garage.

It took them less than half an hour to get the furniture positioned to Jon's satisfaction. He surveyed the area and knew instinctively that Terri would spend hours in this space. His gaze lingered on the pair of loungers placed directly in front of the floor-to-ceiling windows facing the lake and mountains. *And I'm going to make sure I spend some of that time with her*, he vowed.

A few minutes later, Gabriel arrived and checked out the new room. "This is nice. Too bad our house doesn't have this view. Otherwise, I'd be asking you to build one for Serenity."

"She'll probably tell you she doesn't need the view, just the room," Antonio said with a chuckle.

"True that." Gabriel rubbed his hands together. "Okay, are we ready to get this party started?"

Jon shook his head. "A party means catered, not do-it-yourself." Gabriel and Antonio roared with laughter as they trailed him to the kitchen. "I left the steaks out like you said."

"Room-temperature steaks cook more evenly than cold ones," Gabriel said as he unearthed two slim bottles from a bag.

"Good to know." Along with the rib eye steaks, they were preparing grilled shrimp, red-skin mashed potatoes, and roasted asparagus. Jon had taken Gabriel's suggestion to purchase the more expensive Wagyu steaks for their tenderness. He'd eaten them a few times and agreed. And since he wanted the dinner to be special, Jon didn't care about the cost. "What are these?" He picked up one of the bottles and saw that it was a type of olive oil.

"Serenity turned me on to these flavored olive oils, and we use this sweet and buttery one on almost everything. We'll brush it on the steaks before cooking and drizzle some on the asparagus."

Antonio frowned. "Flavored olive oils? You've been holding out on me, my brother." He picked up the other bottle, opened it, and sniffed. "I can actually smell the lemon in here. They have any other flavors?"

"Man, they have everything from orange, basil, and garlic to jalapeño. You should order some." He dug out his phone and started typing. "I sent you a text with the company's link."

A chime sounded, and Antonio eagerly clicked on the link and started scrolling. "Oh, I'm definitely ordering some of these."

The two men launched into a discussion of which flavors would pair best with what food, and Jon felt somewhat left out.

Apparently Gabriel noticed, because he said, "Sorry, Jon. We get a little carried away sometimes, and I forgot you're not into cooking like that."

"But he will be when we're done with him," Antonio said.

Jon didn't share his confidence but was all in to pull off the meal successfully. "So, what do I do first."

"Season the meat."

He followed Gabriel's directions, then pulled out his own phone and began typing.

Antonio stared at him. "What are you doing?"

"Writing down notes so I know what to do next time." Both men shook their heads and smiled but didn't comment. "Ready for the next step."

Antonio started looking around the kitchen. "Do you have a speaker?"

Jon pointed it out, and Antonio synced his phone to it. Immediately, "We Don't Talk About Bruno" blared through the kitchen. He and Gabriel laughed and Jon said, "Nice music."

"Hey, it's a catchy groove and Noelle's favorite song. I forgot I still had her playlist up from when we hung out a couple of days ago." He changed it to a different one, and a jazzy R&B tune started.

"Who's this?" Jon asked as he bobbed his head in time with the beat.

"It's called 'Drop' by Plunky. It came up on Spotify one day and I liked it, so I added it to my playlist."

"I'm going to have to add it to mine, too," Gabriel said.

The three men worked while the music played—more like Jon worked, and his friends supervised. As he transferred the steaks from the stovetop grill to a plate to rest, he had a newfound respect for his wife trying to time all the food to be ready near the same time. Between steps, he continued to write detailed notes about cooking times, tenderness of the steak, doneness of the potatoes and asparagus, and cooking the shrimp just until it was opaque.

"Things getting better with Terri?" Antonio asked.

"I think so. We're talking more, and I finally told her why I don't open up. She was pretty supportive."

Gabriel leaned against the bar and folded his arms. "Just like we said. Hopefully, you two will be back under the same roof soon."

"I'll talk to her about it this weekend." Jon recalled her questioning whether he was trying to seduce her to come home, and though it had been soft, he'd heard her sigh of relief. Since then, he'd been hesitant to bring it up, particularly with things going so well between them. But he didn't want to end the year or start the next one this way.

"I can't see her staying away much longer." Antonio watched as Jon cut into a potato, then added, "The trick to not having watery, runny mashed potatoes is to drain them, then put them back into the pot for a few minutes before mashing to allow the rest of the moisture to evaporate. You can pour them into a colander, but I just use the lid."

"Okay." Jon found the top in the cabinet. He picked up the pot, but dropped it, nearly knocking it over as he registered the searing heat on his hand. He muttered a curse while shaking his hand.

"Maybe you should use these," Gabriel drawled, passing him a pair of potholders.

He glared at Gabe as he ran his hand under cool water for a few moments, and grumbled, "I thought these handles weren't supposed to retain heat."

"Obviously, you thought wrong."

Snatching the potholders, he picked up the pot, drained the water, and put it back on the stove.

Antonio pointed to the oven. "You should probably check the asparagus."

Jon seriously considered chucking the entire meal and doing takeout instead. He didn't have the patience for all this. But just as quickly as the thought entered his mind, he dismissed it. He wanted to do something special for his wife, so he stifled the urge and refocused on the task. After removing the now done vegetables, he mashed the potatoes... while using a potholder.

Five minutes later, the three men settled at the table with filled plates and glasses of wine.

"Let's see how you did." Antonio picked up his fork, sliced a piece of the steak, and popped it into his mouth. He chewed slowly, nodded, then sampled the other items on his plate. Raising his glass, he said, "The student gets an A.

Gabe, we should consider turning this into a side gig. I'm sure there are other brothers in town in need of our services."

Gabriel smiled. "You might be right. We need a catchy name." He angled his head as if thinking, then snapped his fingers. "I got it. Cooking for the domestically challenged husband."

"Yeah, I like that," Antonio said, nodding.

"Just eat the damn food without all the commentary," Jon said. The men burst out laughing. However, he agreed that the food was more than just edible. It turned out far better than he'd hoped. *Now, if I can just duplicate it on my own for Terri tomorrow.*

CHAPTER 16

"Hey, Mom," Terri said, cradling the phone on her ear while struggling into a pair of jeans.

"Hello, daughter of mine. Are you okay?"

"I'm fine. Why?"

"You sound a little strange."

She activated the speaker and continued to dress. "Oh, I'm getting dressed for dinner. Jon will be here in about half an hour, and I got off work later than expected because of a multi-car accident."

"Oh, mercy. I hope no one was injured seriously."

"There were a couple who were, but thankfully, no fatalities. Is something going on?" Sitting on the side of the bed, she stuck her feet into her low-heeled boots and fastened the straps.

"No. I wanted to know if you and Jon are coming for Christmas. I'm getting a head count for food purposes."

"We haven't actually talked about the holidays."

"Hmm, what exactly *have* you talked about?"

Terri hesitated briefly. She hadn't shared her conversation with her friends out of respect for Jon, but her mother had always been her confidante, and Terri knew whatever was said would stay between them. "He finally told me why it's hard for him to open up." She relayed the details of the conversation.

"Oh, honey. I'm so sorry to hear that. Somebody should knock some sense into Alan for spewing that nonsense. I'd be afraid to share anything, too," she muttered.

Now dressed, Terri took the phone off speaker and carried it, along with her coat and purse, to the living room. "Believe me, Mom, I had the same thought. All of his archaic crap almost ruined my marriage. Between him and Mama Deb, I don't know who's worse. If we do decide to come to LA, I'm steering clear of them." At this point, she would seriously have to keep herself in check and resist cursing out her in-laws.

"Speaking of home, when are you going home, Terri?"

She'd asked herself the same question several times over the past few days.

"It seems to me that Jon is trying to meet you halfway, and it's time you do the same."

Terri chuckled. "I thought you said you weren't going to interfere."

"I'm not, but it's time for you two to work on your problems under one roof, sweetheart. The fact that he opened up about his upbringing had to be extremely difficult for him. I'd venture that he was probably more afraid of your response."

"What's that supposed to mean?"

"It means he was afraid you'd prove his father right."

Pacing the floor, Terri thought for a moment, then it dawned on her. "Oh, my goodness. He thought I would think less of him as a man," she whispered. "I have to go, Mom." She spun around and headed to the bedroom.

"What?"

"I need to pack. I'm going home."

Laughing, her mother said, "I'm glad to hear it. Give my love to Jon and let me know whether to expect you two. Love you, baby."

"I love you, too. And Mom?"

"Yes?"

"Thank you for being you."

"Hey, that's what moms do. Go pack so you can be ready when Jon gets there. I'm rooting for you two."

Terri sent love to her dad and ended the call. As she lugged out her suitcases, Candace's last words came back to her: *I just want you to consider when what he does will be enough. And, yes, I agree that communication is important, but you can't be waiting for him to say some magic phrase.* No, she didn't need a magic phrase, and yes, they had more to discuss, but her mother was right. It *was* time to have their conversations under one roof. She started tossing in her clothes, not bothering to fold them. She'd deal with it when she got home. Home. She missed sitting on her deck, breathing in the crisp air and staring at the scenery. And she missed cooking in her own kitchen, lounging in her spa-like tub, and being wrapped in her husband's arms throughout the night.

Once she finished packing, Terri went into the bathroom to clean up. Afterward, she did the same with the bedroom and kitchen. There wasn't much food in the refrigerator because she'd planned to shop tomorrow. She glanced down at her watch and smiled. It had taken her less than thirty minutes. "Oh, shoot." She rushed back to the room for her phone and called Serenity.

"Hey, girl. You want to come over for dinner?" Serenity said when she answered.

"Hey. Thanks for the offer, but Jon should be here in a minute. We're going to dinner."

"Ooh, all these date nights. I love it! Hopefully, this means you two will be back together-together soon."

"That's why I'm calling. I'm going home. Tonight."

"*Yes!* I am so happy, sis. What did he say when you told him?"

"I haven't told him yet. He'll find out when he gets here."

"I guess dinner is going to end up like the last one," Serenity said with a giggle. "Are you working this weekend?"

"No."

"I was going to call tomorrow to see how the night went, but I'll just wait until Monday. I think you'll be a little busy." She lowered her voice. "Make-up sex is the absolute best."

Terri burst out laughing. "Get off my phone, girl."

"I'm just sayin'."

The doorbell rang. "Mm-hmm. Now Darius can stay in the house. I cleaned up everything and changed the sheets," she said, ignoring the comment. "Jon's here. I have to go."

"Be ready to tell *all* next week."

Terri opened the door and smiled at her husband dressed similarly in jeans and long-sleeved shirt. "Whatever. Bye." She could still hear Serenity's laughter when she disconnected. "Hey, come on in."

Jon kissed her. "Hi, baby. Ready?"

"Yes. But I'm driving my car."

He lifted a brow. "You don't need your car."

She gestured to the suitcases stacked nearby. "I do because I'm coming home." Before she could blink, he banded his arms around her and lifted her off her feet at the same time his mouth came down on hers. Her arms went around his neck as he deepened the kiss, his tongue tangling sensuously with hers. Had she been standing, she would've melted to the floor. At length, he eased back and rested his forehead against hers.

"This is the best news I've had since the day you moved out. Tonight's dinner will be even more special." Jon lowered her to her feet and reached for the two large suitcases. "Ready?"

Terri recognized that he was asking about more than dinner. Holding his gaze, she said, "Yes. I'm ready. For everything."

He smiled and nodded, then preceded her out the door and placed the bags in her trunk.

She added her toiletry case and the bag of food. "I need to return the key."

"I'll do it." He held out his hand and she placed it in his palm.

As he crossed the yard, she got into the car. Gabriel answered the door and threw up a wave, which she returned. Whatever Jon and Gabriel were talking about made them laugh and do a fist bump. It had been a while since she'd seen her husband so relaxed, and it brought a smile to her face. A moment later, he jogged back to his car. Backing out, she headed in the direction of their place, with him following closely behind her. When they arrived, he hopped out of the car and was at her door before she cut the engine.

"I'll get your bags later."

"That's fine. Where are we going for dinner?" With them casually dressed, she figured it wouldn't be the steakhouse again.

"Right here." Taking her hand, he led her through the garage, cut through the dining room, and steered her directly to their bedroom.

Laughing, she said, "Where are you going? I thought we were having dinner."

"We are," he said, going into the bathroom. "But first I want you to relax while I get everything ready."

She heard the water running and, after kicking off her shoes, peeked inside. The sight that greeted her put a sheen of tears in her eyes. Terri brought her hands to her mouth. "I...I don't know what to say. It's beautiful." Pink and red rose petals floated on top of the rising bubbles in the tub, and he'd lit candles along the ledge. "How did you know I needed this?"

Jon divested her of her top. "I heard about the accident and I know it got pretty crazy in the ER." He continued removing her clothes until she stood naked in front of him. "Are you working tomorrow?"

She shook her head. "Thankfully, I have the entire weekend off. One more week and I'm done at the hospital. I decided to take a couple of weeks off before starting at the memory care center at the beginning of the year."

He kissed her forehead. "Good for you." He tested the

water, then turned it off. "I'll be back for you in about half an hour, okay?"

Though she'd showered a short while ago, she wasn't passing up a chance to soak in her tub. "Yeah." She stepped into the warm water and sank down until she was submerged. Jon placed a rolled-up towel behind her head. A sigh of pleasure slipped out of her, and she inhaled the relaxing lavender scent. The sound of soft music filled the space, and her eyes drifted closed.

Terri didn't realize that she'd dozed off until she heard the door open. "Is it time to eat?" she murmured.

Jon hunkered down next to the tub and brushed a kiss over her lips. "Just about."

She sat up. "I guess I should wash up. This was lovely."

"Then we'll have to put this in the rotation more often." He winked, rose, and walked out.

Staring at his retreating back, her mouth dropped. *What is this man up to?* She figured she'd find out soon enough as she rinsed off.

Five minutes later, Jon came back into the bedroom just as she finished dressing and extended his hand. They shared a smile as he led her back down the hallway. The delectable aroma of whatever he'd ordered hit her nose, and her stomach growled. He stopped before they got to the kitchen and swung her up in his arms. Terri let out a startled squeal. "What are you doing?"

"I have a surprise for you, and I want you to close your eyes until I tell you to open them."

She gave him a curious look. "Jon?"

"Please, baby. It's all good. I promise."

"Okay." Looping her arms around his neck, she snuggled closer and placed a kiss there.

Jon paused. "If you want dinner, don't do that. As much as I want you right now, I'm more than happy to take you back to the bedroom, and I'll be the only one eating."

She clapped a hand over her mouth and giggled. "I'll save it for later then."

"Terri," he said warningly.

"All right." Her smile still in place, she closed her eyes and rested her head against his shoulder as he carried her to the kitchen. A moment later, he stopped walking.

"Keep them closed." He placed her on her feet. "Okay, you can open them."

Her eyes slowly opened and she gasped. "Oh. My. Goodness. This is... When did you...?" In the weeks they'd been apart, he'd had a sunroom built on part of the deck. The stunning wall of windows immediately drew her attention. When she was finally able to get her feet moving, Terri toured the large enclosure with its pair of comfortable loungers, a gas fireplace that warmed the room nicely, and a beautifully set table for two. Jon had used their wedding china and wineglasses, cloth napkins they hadn't used in so long that she'd forgotten about them, and the good silverware. On the plates sat steaks topped with four large shrimp, red-skinned mashed potatoes, and roasted asparagus. He'd filled their glasses with wine she'd purchased on one of her trips to Napa with her supper club sisters. Facing him again, she said, "I don't even have words to describe how much..." Her emotions rose up swiftly, and she choked back a sob. "It's so beautiful. Thank you."

"You're welcome. I know how much you love relaxing on the deck, so I thought I'd make it possible to do it year-round. Come on. Let's eat before the food gets cold." He seated her, then rounded the table to sit across from her.

She spread the napkin over her lap and picked up her fork. "Everything looks so good and pretty, I don't want to eat it." As if on cue, her stomach rumbled again.

Chuckling, Jon said, "I don't think your belly agrees with you. Eat up, beautiful."

She ate a bite of the steak first and nearly swooned in her chair. The rib eye had been prepared to perfection and almost melted in her mouth. She eagerly went for the shrimp, potatoes, and asparagus and found them to be just as tasty. "Mmm. *So* good."

"I'm glad you like it."

"I think I'm going to have to order the steak next time we go to By the Lake."

"I didn't get it from there," he said, then took a sip of his wine.

Terri paused with the glass halfway to her mouth and frowned. She didn't recall Ms. Ida's having this tender of a steak on the menu. "Where did you order it from then?" She brought the glass to her mouth and sipped.

"I cooked."

She choked on the portion going down her throat. Coughing and coughing, she tried to catch her breath.

"You okay?"

Wiping tears from her eyes, she nodded and met her husband's amused gaze. "When did you start cooking?"

Jon shrugged. "When I decided I wanted to cook for you. I'm glad you like it."

"*Like it?* I *love* it." Still amazed, she went back to her food. If he cooked like this, she was never going to go to another restaurant again. As they ate, she asked more about the room.

"Antonio and his guys built it, but I purchased all the furniture."

"You did good. There are two loungers, so I hope that means you plan to join me."

"It does. After you're done, I need you to pack for a couple of days. We're spending the weekend in San Francisco."

Her mouth fell open. "When did you plan this?"

"When you told me you had the weekend off." Jon grasped her hand. "I'm going to be more intentional about us spending time away. I don't want it to be like it's been these past couple of years, and I don't want you to ever doubt how much you mean to me and how much I love you."

She started crying all over again. The fact that he'd cooked, built her an amazing space because he knew how much she enjoyed the view, and booked a last-minute weekend getaway left no doubt in her mind that he loved her. And she loved him. *I don't ever want to be away from him again.*

CHAPTER 17

Jon woke up Saturday morning with his wife cuddled next to him, and he vowed they'd never be apart again. He had planned everything down to the smallest detail to make it a perfect date night, but the surprise of her coming home had topped his surprise a hundred times over, in his opinion. He eased back and studied Terri's relaxed features as she slept. He had begun to wonder if he'd ever see the peaceful expression that used to be a constant fixture in the early days of their relationship or the wide-open smile that never failed to make his heart beat a little faster, or hear the infectious laughter that always had him laughing along with her. Jon pulled her closer and closed his eyes, grateful for this second chance to get it right.

On the drive to the bay last night, he'd asked what made her decide to come home. In response, she'd said that she wanted to meet him halfway, just as he tried to do. She also said her mother told her that it was time for them to work out their problems under one roof again, and Terri had agreed. Jon owed his mother-in-law a big hug the next time he saw her. Unlike his mother, Mama Gina had made it a practice to never butt into their business, and he appreciated it.

"Stop thinking so loud. I'm trying to sleep," Terri murmured.

Jon chuckled. "What? You can't hear what I'm thinking."

"No, but I know you're thinking about something because I can feel it. And you've been restless for the past fifteen minutes."

He dropped a kiss on her forehead. "Sorry, baby. I didn't mean to wake you. And I'm not restless. Quite the opposite. Having you in my arms again relaxes me."

She lifted her head and a smile curved her lips. "Me, too."

"I'm glad to hear it."

"Now that I'm awake, what's on the agenda today?"

"I want to do whatever you want, whether that's chilling here at the hotel all day or doing some sightseeing. Is there anything you'd like to do?"

Terri shifted until her head was laying on his chest and her arm across his midsection. "I want to walk around Pier 39 for sure and check out some of the shops. I know it's kind of chilly out, but maybe we can take a sunset cruise to the Golden Gate Bridge, too."

"Sounds like a plan." He glanced over his shoulder at the nightstand clock. "It's a few minutes before ten now. What time to do you want to leave?"

Her head popped up. *"Ten?"*

"Yep." With both of their careers requiring them to get up early, neither of them tended to stay in bed past eight or eight thirty, even on weekends. So he was just as surprised that they'd slept so late. Then again, he shouldn't have been shocked since he doubted he'd gotten more than four or five hours of sleep a night while they were apart.

"I can't believe I slept this late."

Jon idly ran his hand up and down her spine. "Relax, sweetheart. You're supposed to sleep in. That's what this weekend is all about. For both of us."

Terri let out a soft sigh. "You're right. It's been so long since we've done this, I've forgotten what it's like."

So had he, but he was determined to do better about incorporating some downtime in their schedules at least once a month, even if it was only a day trip.

They lay quietly for a while longer, then she asked, "Instead of going out for breakfast, can we order room service?"

"Yeah, we can. Breakfast in bed sounds good to me." After poring over the menu, they made their choices and Jon called it in. He pulled her back into his arms. "I could stay here with you like this forever."

"Mmm, me, too. Do we have to go back?"

"Eventually. But for now, we aren't going to think about anything but us." Content, they stayed in bed until the food arrived, then fed each other the waffles, scrambled eggs, and bacon.

They made it to the pier by midafternoon and strolled hand-in-hand through the area, stopping at the various shops. Despite the cool temperatures, it was fairly crowded.

"Ooh, a tea store. Let's go inside." Terri pulled him into the store.

From the window display, he assumed it would be a place

to purchase teapots and other accessories, as well as cups of tea. However, the store also had a large variety of loose teas, from black and green to herbal and chai. Jon stood off to the side as Terri wandered around, pausing here and there to read labels or smell samples. She went back to the front, grabbed a small basket, and added several of the clear packages.

"You might need one of these." He held up a mesh tea ball infuser.

"Thanks." Terri plucked it out of his hand and dropped it in the basket. She started to walk away but turned back and added three more.

"Why so many?"

She shrugged. "Just in case my supper club sisters want to join me for tea." She brushed her body against his and gave him a sensual smile. "Or if my sexy husband wants to join me in my new sunroom while we watch the sunset."

"Then we're going to need a few other things." Jon found matching tea mugs for the ladies and a larger one for him. They took their haul to the counter, and he overrode her protests and paid for everything.

Terri leaned up and kissed him, and then hooked her arm in his as they left the store. "Aww, thank you. You're the best sugar daddy a girl could have."

He laughed and shook his head. "Does being a sugar daddy come with benefits?"

"Yep," she said, wiggling her eyebrows. "And I'll show you a few tonight."

His body reacted with lightning speed. "I vote for now." He pulled her flush against him so she could feel just what her words did to him. Leaning down, he whispered, "As you can feel, I'm more than up for the challenge." Their eyes locked for a charged moment.

Terri backed out of his arms. "Stop tempting me. You promised we'd do the sunset cruise. Now come on."

He lifted a brow. "Who's teasing whom? I'm not the one out here making these bold promises."

"And I can back them up. *Later.*" She strutted off, putting a little extra sway in her hips and winking at him over her shoulder.

Smiling at her playfulness, he caught up with her and slung an arm around her shoulders. "Since we still have a good forty-five minutes before we need to board, let's drop this bag off in the car first."

"Okay, but I want to get there early so we can have our pick of the best seats."

Jon nodded. In the summer months, he wouldn't hesitate to choose to sit outside. But with the temperatures hovering in the low fifties, he knew it would be even cooler over the water, so inside seating would be his preference.

As they exited the pier, Terri stopped. "Wait. We have to get a picture with the Christmas tree behind us." They found a spot just as another couple finished.

She whipped out her phone and moved it back and forth. "I can't get a good angle. Here, you're taller."

He took the phone, snapped a few shots, then handed it back. "These okay?"

"Perfect," she said while scanning the photos.

After putting the bags in the trunk, they continued up the street to the dock. Only a few people stood in line, and they were able to secure window seats and a good view of the approaching bridge. She coaxed him outside for more photos before returning to the warmer interior. Afterward, they enjoyed dinner at Bubba Gump Shrimp Co. and then returned to the hotel.

Terri rubbed her hands together. "I'm so cold."

Jon came up behind her and wrapped his arms around her. "I'll keep you warm." Lowering his head, he traced a path with his tongue along her neck. "I think I'm ready to experience a few of those benefits," he murmured, turning her at the same time as he slanted his mouth over hers, losing himself in the sweetness of her kiss. Without breaking the seal of their mouths, he slowly stripped away her blouse. His hands mapped a path over the curve of her hips, her slim waist, and up to her breasts. Her soft moan fueled his desire. He reached behind her and unsnapped her bra, dragging the straps down and off, and letting the lacy scrap of material drop to the floor. "So beautiful."

"Jon?"

"Hmm." He dipped his head and took one taut nipple in his mouth. She called out his name as he suckled, stroked, and teased, first one, then the other. He dropped to his knees and transferred his kisses to her stomach. He pulled her jeans and panties off and was instantly engulfed in her womanly scent, arousing him even more.

"I thought I was the one who's supposed to be showing you."

Jon rose to his feet and spread his arms. "I'm all yours."

He closed his eyes and shuddered when her hands slid beneath his shirt and touched his bare skin. She pulled his shirt up and off, tossing it aside.

"I love touching you, kissing you, tasting you."

Her warm tongue skated across his chest and stomach and sent a jolt straight to his groin. She unbuttoned his jeans, slid the zipper down, and pushed them and his underwear down his legs. Jon kicked them off.

Terri walked him backward to the bed and gently pushed him down. She lifted one long, toned leg, straddled his body, and lowered herself inch by inch onto his erection, swirling her hips in a figure eight.

Jon groaned. "Terri—"

She cut him off with a kiss. "I just want you to feel how much I love you."

She braced her hands on his chest and slowly moved up and down. His hands made a path up her smooth skin and settled on her breasts. The play of passion on her face matched what he felt. He massaged the full mounds, then leaned up to capture a pebbled nipple between his teeth and tugged gently, drawing a sharp cry from her.

Throwing her head back, she let out a sharp cry of pleasure. Holding his gaze, she slowly slid up and down his engorged length, repeating the process again and again.

His breathing increased, his muscles quivered, and a low growl erupted from his throat. She continued to torture him with deliberate movements until he thought he would explode. Unable to take it any longer, Jon grabbed her hips and guided her to move faster. Her hands dug into his shoulders, and each time she came down, he thrust up to meet and match her strokes, going deeper and deeper. The moment a gigantic explosion hit him, Terri screamed out his name. Their bodies bucked and shuddered for what seemed like hours before she collapsed on him. When he could finally catch his breath, he said, "I think I like being a sugar daddy."

"Good, because I've got more *benefits* to show you."

Just like that, he was aroused again. In one fluid motion, he flipped her on her back and surged back inside her. Unlike the first round, this one was hard and fast, and Jon knew if he made love to her every night for the next hundred years, it would never be enough. She was the only woman who'd ever have his heart, his everything.

* * *

Jon wished they had more time, but Sunday came, and he had to prepare for another week of cases and Terri would be finishing up her job as an ER nurse. He loaded their bags into the car and turned to find her leaning against the door. Her somber expression mirrored his. Gathering her in his arms, he said, "I know. I'm not ready to leave, either. But I promise we'll make time for another getaway after the holidays."

"It just seemed to go so fast. I wish the work week would do the same," Terri grumbled.

"I hear you." He chuckled and closed the door behind her after she dropped down on the seat, then rounded the fender and got in on the driver's side. They were content to listen to the music playing softly through the speakers. Halfway into the drive, he asked, "Do you want to stop and pick up a Christmas tree before we get home?"

Her eyes lit up. "Ooh, yes."

"I saw the way you were looking at the tree on Pier 39."

There was a tree farm a few miles outside of town, and he knew how much she loved Christmas and decorating the house.

"Yeah, well. What can I say? Speaking of Christmas, my mom called and wanted to know if we were coming down. We can just stay here if you don't want to go," she rushed to add.

"No. We can go." They had spent Christmas with his parents a couple of years ago and, after that fiasco, stayed home last year. "It's been a while since we've seen your family, so I'm good." He slanted her an amused glance. "Besides, your mom's yellow cake with chocolate frosting is calling my name."

Terri frowned his way. "I'm still mad about her making that cake for you in place of *my* favorite lemon cake."

Jon laughed. "Aw, baby, don't hate just because Mama Gina loves me." When her mother found out it was Jon's favorite cake, she had baked it instead of her standard lemon one the first year he'd joined them for the holidays. Terri had been outdone, especially when Mama Gina had said sweetly, "Oh, honey, you can make your own lemon cake. I had to make my son his favorite this time." She'd made the cake each time they visited, and Terri never let him live it down.

She rolled her eyes. "Whatever. All I know is I'd better see a lemon cake this year, or I'm going to start flipping tables."

Still chuckling, he grasped her hand and placed a kiss on its back.

She snatched it away. "Don't try to kiss up. You just better tell my mama it's my turn to be the favorite child."

Jon switched the playlist to one with some of her favorite holiday songs. Almost immediately, she started humming. Smiling inwardly, he refocused on the road. Twenty minutes later, he drove into the tree lot. "Looks like they still have some good ones."

Terri was out of the car before he could get to her side. "Hurry up. There are a lot of people here, and I don't want them getting my tree." She grabbed his hand and dragged him toward the mass of trees.

The thick scent of pine mingled with the brisk breeze. The sun had been shining the entire weekend, but now the sky had become increasingly cloudy and it was forecasted to rain by midweek. He observed her serious expression as she inspected each tree for fullness, size, and shape. It took a good thirty minutes for her to finally find one to her liking. They paid for it, the attendant helped secure it to the roof of his car, and he drove the rest of the way home. The happiness on her face was something he wanted to see for the rest of his life.

CHAPTER 18

Monday morning after the staff meeting, Jon sat behind his desk feeling more relaxed than he'd been in a long while. He attributed it to the positive changes in his marriage and, as much as he didn't want to admit it, going to therapy. Ken, with his direct and sometimes blunt approach, had helped Jon to dig deep inside and resurrect all the things he'd buried and given him steps to move forward. Now that they were going to LA for Christmas, he planned to make a short visit to his parents' house—alone—to have the conversation he probably should have had years ago. He glanced up from the file he was reading when the intercom buzzed on his desk. He hit the button.

"What's up, Gail?"

"The mayor is on line one for you."

The mayor? "Thanks." He picked up the line. "Good morning, Mayor Brewer. How can I help you?"

"I've got a problem, and I need you to stop by my office at your earliest convenience. I have a one o'clock opening. Will that work?"

Apparently, Jon's earliest convenience translated to the mayor's availability. "I'll be there."

"Thanks. See you then." The line went dead.

He leaned back in his chair, curious about the issue that had the man needing an attorney. Jon hadn't heard anything floating around town, so he figured whatever it was, the mayor was keeping it quiet. He was also curious about why, because he recalled there being an attorney on staff there. Rising to his feet, he went across the hall to his partner's office and tapped his knuckles on the partially closed door. "Got a minute, Brian?"

"Come on in."

He leaned against the doorframe and crossed his arms. "Got an interesting call from the mayor. Apparently, something's going on and he wants to meet with me this afternoon."

Brian leaned back in his chair and ran a hand through his blond hair. "Whoa. Must be serious. I haven't heard anything going on in town."

"Me either, but I'll fill you in when I get back. I'll probably stop at Ms. Ida's and pick up something for lunch while I'm out."

"About time you start remembering you have a lunch hour," he said with a chuckle.

"Kettle, pot," Jon said with a smile as he straightened from the wall. "I'll let you know what I find out." Back in his office a few seconds later, he thought about Brian's comment. He knew he worked a lot, but the fact that his partner noticed it enough to mention it told Jon he needed to make some changes. He knew he wouldn't always be able to take a formal lunch, but he had to be more conscious of making time for those breaks he insisted the employees take.

Jon worked steadily until it was time to leave. He slipped into his suit coat and made his way out front, stopping to check in with his assistant. "I should be back in a couple of hours. I'll call if I'm going to be later."

"Got it," Gail said. "I hope nothing serious is going on in town."

He simply nodded and left.

The mayor's administrative assistant, Mrs. Rogers, greeted him with a wide smile as soon as Jon walked in. "Well, hello, Mr. Rhodes. I don't think I've seen you in the office before." She lowered her voice conspiratorially. "Must be something big to bring in a lawyer."

"Good afternoon. Is Mayor Brewer ready to see me?" According to the town rumor mill, the sixty-something woman had been a fixture in the mayor's office for many years and had a penchant for being a little too concerned about other people's affairs.

"Have a seat and let me buzz him."

He sat in one of the quartet of chairs in the spacious area and flipped through a magazine on a side table. A minute later, he heard the mayor's voice, and he stood.

"Mr. Rhodes, I'm glad you could make it," Mayor Brewer said, rushing over and extending his hand.

Jon shook the proffered hand. "You mentioned a problem?"

"Yes, come on back to my office." Once there, he gestured Jon to a chair as he rounded the massive desk and reclaimed his seat. As soon as Jon sat, the mayor passed him a stack of papers.

He leafed through them. "A lawsuit from Whitman Land Developers? I thought you had an attorney here on staff to handle things pertaining to the town."

"We do, but Earvin is on an extended medical leave right now, so I need you to handle this."

Jon nodded, relieved. He had no desire to get caught up in some government bureaucracy. "I thought Davenport Family Construction was handling the condo project. This says Whitman is suing the town for backing out on the deal."

"We never made a deal with them. I approached them initially because Charles Davenport elected not to take on the project. I spelled out what we wanted, and they seemed amenable to the small number of units we requested. They also agreed to use Davenport employees first, then supplement, as needed. However, when I received the contract, it was for a six-hundred-unit, multi-building complex when we asked for no more than thirty or forty."

He made notes on his iPad as the mayor spoke. "And their reasoning?"

"They mentioned it being a great opportunity for us to expand the town and bring in more residents to increase the tax base," Mayor Brewer said with disgust. "I told them we liked the size of our town just fine."

Jon flipped a page and read, then frowned. The contract not only outlined the larger number of housing units, but also had a clause stating that they would choose the construction employees. "So, I assume you signed the contract," he said, still making some notes.

"Not hardly."

His head came up sharply. "Excuse me?"

"My thoughts exactly. I'm not sure how they think this is legal, since I never signed anything. When I told this to their representative, he said I didn't have to sign anything, that it was a good faith agreement. I didn't agree to anything other than what I asked for." He punctuated each word with a jab of his index finger on the desk.

Jon knew what a good faith agreement entailed, and this raised several red flags. "I need every single piece of correspondence you have—emails, notes, letters—everything."

The mayor passed him a file folder. "Already done. I had my assistant gather them in anticipation of our meeting." He hesitated, a hint of vulnerability in his expression. "You will be able to get this dismissed?"

"From what I've read, it doesn't appear that they have a case, but I don't want to make any promises until I review everything."

"I really appreciate you taking this on."

"I'm not sure how much I'll be able to get done before the holidays." He'd found that staff availability decreased significantly during this time of year, and most things carried over into the new year.

"Understood. Thanks again."

"I'll be in touch." Jon stood and shook the mayor's hand, then made his exit. He toyed with walking the couple of blocks to Ms. Ida's, but nixed the idea because it would mean walking back to where he parked his car. Timewise, it would be more efficient for him to drive. Fortunately, with the lunch crowds gone, he found a spot a door down from the restaurant.

He nodded greetings to the people he passed and held the door open for a couple of older women entering the establishment at the same time.

"Such a polite young man," one of the women said, smiling up at him.

Ms. Bernice was on duty as hostess and had to hold an entire conversation with the women before seating them. She came back and asked, "For here or to go?"

His automatic reply of "to go" was poised on the tip of his tongue, but Jon changed his mind when Brian's taunt came back to him. "Here."

She grabbed a menu and led him to a booth in the nearly empty place. "Someone will be with you in a minute."

"Thanks." The moment he opened the menu, he heard someone call his name. Jon glimpsed over his shoulder and saw Mrs. Hayes and her best friend, Gabriel's grandmother Ms. Della, approaching. He came to his feet and greeted both women. "Mrs. Hayes, Ms. Della, would you like to join me? My treat." It was a dangerous offer, he knew, recalling all the incidents and matchmaking with his friends. His only saving grace was that he didn't have to worry about the matchmaking part.

"No, thank you, Jonathan," Mrs. Hayes said. "And you can call me Mama Nora like everybody else. We're on our way out. I just wanted to know how you're doing, but I see things are better with you now."

Jon contemplated asking what she meant, but again...

dangerous. The conversation they'd had on Thanksgiving still baffled him.

As if reading his mind, she said, "I can see it in your face. You're more relaxed, and there's a peace that wasn't there a few weeks ago."

"That's because things are better between him and Terri. I'm so glad you two are back under one roof," Ms. Della said.

He didn't know how to respond.

"Uncle Jon!"

He spun around in time to see Noelle barreling toward him. *Saved!* She launched herself at him and wrapped her arms around his legs. Jon picked her up and placed a kiss on her cheek. "Hey, Noelle. School is out already?" Her bright smile and pure affection always grabbed his heart.

"Yes, and I'm going to get a treat because I was a good helper in school today."

"That's great. What kind of treat are you getting?" He loved her bubbly personality.

"Ice cream," Noelle said, raising her arms with excitement.

"I'm proud of you, and that's a great treat." Jon noticed the smiles on Mama Nora's and Ms. Della's faces, and warning bells went off in his head. Noelle's mother stood off to the side with an amused gaze. "How's it going, April?"

"Good. Noelle saw you come inside and insisted we come say hello."

He smiled and tickled the little girl, whose giggles touched him in an unexpected way. "I'm glad you did." The hole in his heart magnified. What he wouldn't give to hear this sweet sound every day.

* * *

Half an hour later, Terri hurried into Ms. Ida's and ran into what felt like a brick wall. "I'm sor—*Jon?* What are you doing here?"

Jon gave her a teasing smile. "It's a restaurant, so..."

She playfully punched him in the arm. "You know what I mean."

He gave her a quick kiss, then whispered, "The mayor called and wants me to handle a case. We'll talk about it at home."

Several people had stopped to view their exchange. Laughing softly, she said, "You're probably right. Seems like we're the main attraction at the moment."

"Then we should probably give them something to talk about."

Before she could ask what he meant, Jon slid an arm around her waist, dipped her, and kissed her until she could barely stand. Applause broke out, and she buried her head in his chest, her cheeks warm with embarrassment. "I am so going to get you for that."

"If it's part of that benefit package, I can't wait."

Terri tried to hide her smile but failed. "Don't you need to go back to your office?"

"I have a few things to finish, but I should be home no later than six or six thirty."

"I'll be waiting."

"Will you be naked?"

Clapping a hand over his mouth and taking a hasty look

around to make sure no one had heard, she pushed him toward the exit. "You need to go. Always starting trouble," she muttered.

Jon's smile widened, and he tossed her a wink. "See you later."

She watched his sexy stroll until he got to his car, then went inside. To say she enjoyed their banter was an understatement. *Maybe I should be waiting...and naked.* Giggling at the naughty thought, she searched the restaurant and saw Serenity waving her over. Terri had taken off a couple of hours to take care of some paperwork for her new job and, since she had some extra time, texted her friends to see if they were available to meet for a late lunch. When she got to the table, she hugged her three friends. "Sorry I'm late. Tyler and I started talking about the center, and I lost track of time."

"Looks like you were actually just in time, if you ask me," Natasha said, fanning herself.

Serenity scooted over to make room for Terri in the booth. "I know, right? I was hoping to grill you about the weekend, but I think we can all agree that it went well. *Really* well."

Once again, Terri felt her cheeks warm.

"Oh, girl, don't be shy," Dana said. "I'm glad to see you two smiling so much."

"So am I. And the weekend was *amazing.*"

"Weekend?" Serenity asked. "I thought you said you were going to dinner."

"We had dinner at home. In my new sunroom that he had built while I was gone." The women's mouths fell open. Grinning, she added, "And he cooked."

They all screamed like teenagers, and started talking at the same time. "He *cooked?*" "Wait. A sunroom?" "I thought he couldn't cook."

Terri dug her phone out of her purse, opened the photos of the sunroom, and passed it around. "I was so surprised. He knows how much I love sitting on the deck facing the mountains and wanted me to be able to do it year-round. We'll have to have one of our supper clubs there soon." She fell back against the seat and placed her hand on her chest. "It is so beautiful. For dinner he made grilled rib eye steaks, shrimp, mashed red-skinned potatoes, and roasted asparagus. And let me tell you, that food was the best I've ever eaten. It had me swooning in my chair."

Dana laughed. "I would've been swooning, too. This is gorgeous, and I can't wait to really see it." She handed the phone back to Terri. "I bet *after* dinner was even better."

"Yes, girl, *yes*! Oh, wait." She waved a hand. "I forgot that when we got to the house, he ran me a bubble bath with rose petals in the water, candles, and music. It was absolutely wonderful." Terri still couldn't get over the evening. It had been a night that surpassed any fantasy she'd ever had. "When I told him I had the weekend off, he booked us a room in San Francisco for the weekend."

Serenity whipped her head around. "Just like that?"

Nodding, Terri said, "Yep. Just. Like. That."

"That's what I'm talking about," Natasha said, snapping her fingers.

She shared the details of the trip and told them how much fun it had been just hanging out with no schedules and no work. "It was the best time I've had in a very long time.

We've also been talking." She briefly mentioned Jon opening up but kept the particulars to herself.

"Oh, Terri, I'm so happy for you guys. I don't think I've ever seen Jon smiling so hard."

Terri bumped Serenity's shoulder. "Girl, I'm happy, too, and you're right. He has been smiling *a lot*." She did a little shimmy in her seat.

The laughter and catching up continued as they ate their shared seafood platter. Natasha asked, "How does it feel being out of the house, Serenity?"

"Girl, I almost skipped down the block. I love my little one, but I needed some sister-girl time. Gabriel was more than happy to send me on my way, most likely so he can hold Giana nonstop for the next hour." She shook her head. "He is spoiling her too much."

"That's what girl dads do," Terri said. It made her wonder if Jon would have been the same way. She instinctively knew the answer was yes. He was more excited than she when they found out about the pregnancy. And he'd been beside himself when the sonogram showed they were having a little girl. For a brief moment, the sadness rose, but she forced it back down. Changing the subject, she said, "Dana, what's been going on with you? Are you going to be playing with the orchestra next year?"

"They asked, but I haven't decided yet." She dipped a piece of fish in tartar sauce and said nonchalantly, "I met a guy."

"Who?" Terri, Natasha, and Serenity chorused. "And where did you meet him?" Terri asked.

When Dana didn't answer immediately, Natasha said,

"Girl, don't make me snatch that shrimp out of your hand. Quit stalling and spill the beans."

Dana chuckled. "I met him during my last concert series. We were leaving after the performance, and he was parked next to my rental. He was having some car trouble, and I helped him out. Long formal dress, heels, and all."

"I bet he didn't know what to say," Serenity said.

"He didn't. Just kept staring at me. Then he said, 'You play like an angel, fix cars like an angel, look like an angel, so you must be one. And I'm fortunate to be the one entertaining an angel.'"

"*Whaaaat?* Oh, my goodness. I probably would've fainted."

"Terri, girl, I almost did. He was holding my hand the whole time, and then he kissed it. I couldn't say one word. He asked me to dinner as a thank-you. I said yes, and the goodnight kiss at the end made me say yes, again, when he asked if he could visit me."

Natasha grasped Dana's arm. "What's his name, and when is he coming?"

Dana didn't say anything for a long moment. "His name is DeAngelo Murray, and...he got in last night and said he's staying for a week."

Serenity clapped. "Perfect timing. Invite him to the supper club dinner on Saturday."

"What about the couples drink thing I'm doing with Darius?"

She waved her off. "You aren't dating Darius." Dana opened her mouth to protest, and Serenity added, "How would it look if you told him you were going to dinner with friends without him when he came *all* this way to visit you?"

She rolled her eyes. "I can't stand you sometimes."

"But you're going to invite him," Natasha said confidently. "Otherwise, I will march right over to the Firefly Lake Inn and do it myself. And you *know* I'd go door-to-door to find him, if necessary."

They all laughed. Terri loved her girls. This dinner was going to be the best one yet. Dana had finally found a guy who didn't mind her working on cars. She and Jon were closer than ever. Yep. She couldn't wait.

CHAPTER 19

Friday evening, Terri and Jon carried in the rest of her going-away gifts. A part of her would miss the fast-paced emergency room, and she'd definitely miss her colleagues, but Terri couldn't be more excited to start this next chapter. "It's nasty out there," Jon said, placing two gift bags on the dining room table.

"I know." She rubbed her hands together to warm them. A storm had blown in two days ago with heavy rains and wind gusts of up to forty miles per hour. He came and wrapped his arms around her, and she rested her head on his shoulder. "Thank you for being there this afternoon. It meant a lot to me." She hugged him tightly. The best part of the party had been when Jon showed up, surprising her. She couldn't hold back the tears that had streamed down her face. Even now, just thinking about it made her emotional all over again.

"I'm glad I was able to make it. I'm so proud and happy for you, baby." He placed a lingering kiss on her lips. "Ready to get this tree decorated?"

"Yep. Can you bring in the boxes of ornaments?" They were finally getting a chance to decorate the tree. Both had busy work weeks, but unlike in the past, they still managed to eat dinner together twice. They'd even braved the weather to take her back to By the Lake to celebrate her new job.

"Okay. Are we still prepping the food for tomorrow?"

"Yeah. But I want to get the cake in the oven first."

A smile lit his face. "7Up cake?"

She nodded slowly and leaned up to kiss him. "Mm-hmm."

Jon took over the kiss, deepening it until they were both gasping for breath. "I don't know which is sweeter, the cake or your kiss." He slanted his mouth over hers again, teasing, tasting. "Your kiss. Definitely your kiss."

Terri slumped against him, her heart racing, her body pulsing. He released her and went out to the garage. She stood there with her eyes closed for several seconds, gulping in air to regain some semblance of calm. When she finally opened her eyes, it took a moment to remember why she was standing in the kitchen. *The cake.* As she pulled out the ingredients, a big part of her wanted to skip cooking and go straight to the bedroom. But they had all night, she reasoned, and she focused on measuring flour into a bowl. While creaming the sugar and butter a few minutes later, Jon came up behind her and trailed kisses along the side of her neck, sending shockwaves of pleasure straight to her core.

"I can start prepping the food for tomorrow, if you want. You'll have to walk me through it, though."

"Um...you can season the short ribs to start." She rattled off the spices she wanted him to use.

Jon washed and dried his hands, then quickly covered the meat with the seasoning mix. "You want me to put them in a Ziploc bag?"

"That'll work. I'll put them into the slow cooker in the morning." She gave him directions on starting the chicken to boil for the second type of tacos. Terri found she had an easier time shredding the chicken when using that cooking method. They worked in tandem, and she finally understood what Serenity and Natasha meant. There seemed to be a special kind of intimacy that came with preparing food together. And she liked it.

"It's really coming down out there," Jon said, looking out the kitchen window.

"I know. It's the wind that I don't like." She could hear the gusts getting stronger, sometimes shaking the house. "I'm glad we're not out in that weather."

"Same." He came back and leaned against the counter. They conversed quietly while she made the batter.

She stuck the cake in the oven and set the timer, then they went to start decorating the tree. There were four boxes of ornaments lined up. "I didn't realize we had that many decorations."

Jon gave her a sidelong glance. "That's because I'm the one who always puts everything away. You're the one who keeps buying more every year."

Unable to refute his statement, she smiled and said, "So what's first?"

He burst out laughing. "Yeah, that's what I thought."

They sorted through the first box, which held the blue and white tree ornaments. "I don't know which color to use this year. Which do you like best—the blue and white, or the gold?"

"I like the blue and white." He stood. "I forgot to turn the music on." He made it halfway across the room before the lights flickered, then went out.

"Oh, no! My cake is in the oven." She hopped up and, feeling her way, rushed as quickly as she could into the kitchen. Because they had a gas stove, the chicken was fine and still boiling. Her cake was another story. Maybe if she didn't open the door, it would be okay. *Please don't let these lights stay off long.*

"Is it okay?" Jon had a flashlight and several candles.

"Depends on how long the power stays out." They lit the candles and placed two in the kitchen, two on the fireplace mantel in the living room, and two in their bedroom. Jon went back through the house and turned off all the lights except one, to prevent a power surge.

He returned to the bedroom, where Terri stood looking out at the pitch-black night. "See anything?"

Terri turned to face him. "It looks like the entire town is out." She shrugged. "Well, so much for decorating the tree."

"I can think of a few other ways to occupy our time, and I *promise* we'll generate plenty of power," he said with a wicked grin, unbuttoning his shirt as he came toward her.

"I bet you can." She stood transfixed as her husband stripped for her, baring every inch of his hard, toned body. "I think you missed your calling as an exotic dancer."

Jon shook his head slowly. "Baby, you're the *only* woman who'll get a peek at this exclusive show." He angled his head. "I think you have entirely too many clothes on, Mrs. Rhodes."

Playing along, she gave him a sultry smile. "And what do you plan to do about it, Mr. Rhodes?"

"I'll be glad to show you."

He unbuttoned her sweater, one button at a time, kissing each newly bared inch of her skin. Her breath stacked up in her throat, and her legs started to tremble. "Jon." He carried her the short distance to their bed and continued to torture her with his hands and his mouth as he undressed her. She moaned. Suddenly, the light came on. Terri jerked upright. "The cake."

He groaned and rolled over onto his back. "Great."

She scooted off the bed, pulled her pants and sweater back on, and hurried to the kitchen. Carefully cracking open the oven door, she checked the cake. It hadn't fallen, so she reset the oven and hoped for the best.

* * *

"I guess we can decorate the tree," Jon said, coming into the kitchen. He'd put on a pair of sweats and a T-shirt.

He could see her biting her lip to stifle a grin at his disgruntled expression. Attempting to soothe him, she said, "Tree now, *us* later." Terri took his hand and led him into the living room.

He turned on the music, and pretty soon they were laughing and hanging ornaments, stopping every so often to sing a chorus or do a dance step. It was the best time of his life. "Let It Snow" by Boyz II Men came on, and Jon pulled her into his arms. He sang as they started a slow sway. She rested her head on his chest, and he held her closer, relishing the moment. The song ended and Luther Vandross's "Mistletoe Jam" came through the speakers. Jon swung her out, and they changed their rhythm to the up-tempo beat. Terri raised her hands in the air, shaking her hips and pressing her body sensually against his. When the chorus of the song invited everybody to kiss somebody, Jon produced a little package with mistletoe and did exactly what the song said.

As the song ended, they shared a smile and continued decorating. Jon opened another box that had various special ornaments she'd collected over the years. He unwrapped each one and handed them to her to place, all while teasing her about needing a bigger tree because they were close to running out of room. He opened a small box and his heart stopped and started again. His hands shook as he stared at the photo. He'd completely forgotten about the ornament that came with the memory photos of their daughter. Ones he'd purposely never viewed. They were a family of three for less than a day.

Terri glanced down. "Jon."

"I'm going to check the chicken." He was out of the room before she could say another word. After finding the chicken ready, he turned off the flame and paced. They'd been having such a great time, and now all he wanted to do was leave. Jon stayed in the kitchen another minute before bracing himself and returning to the living room. His steps slowed as he watched Terri kneel and picked up the sepia photo surrounded by bronze. She lightly ran her finger over the surface, then placed it against her heart. He must have made a sound because she turned his way. Their gazes held.

"Please don't shut me out."

He closed his eyes. "Terri, I can't do this right—" If he looked at the picture, he'd remember the pain, the one long beep on the machine that had been keeping his sweet baby girl alive, the one that said she was gone forever. He'd completely lose it.

"Please," she whispered.

Trying to summon all the courage he'd worked on in his therapy sessions, he haltingly started in her direction. She held it out to him, but he didn't take it. He couldn't.

"I miss her," Terri said on a broken sob.

Her tears were his undoing. Jon dropped to his knees beside her and gathered her in his embrace. He wanted to say something, anything that would ease her pain. Ease *their* pain, but he couldn't. If he opened his mouth, he feared the only thing that would come out was a tortured cry, just like hers.

"Why, Jon? Why our baby?"

"I...I..." He clenched his jaw. "I don't know," he choked out. With those words, everything he'd held inside over the past four years rushed to the surface. His body trembled as he fought to keep the emotions locked away. He sucked in several deep breaths in an effort to maintain control, but it didn't help. None of it helped. Despite his best efforts, the pain and anguish refused to be denied this time, and the tears he tried to hold back broke free. At first in a trickle, then a flood. "My baby. My sweet baby girl," he cried. He wept for the laughter and sound of her saying "Dada" for the first time that he would never hear. For all the hours he prayed for her to live. For not being able to comfort his wife like he should have. He wept for it all. At length their tears slowed, then stopped. Jon cradled Terri in his lap as they clung to each other, neither of them speaking. They stayed that way until the oven timer went off. Terri tenderly wiped away his tears and kissed him softly before rising to go check the cake.

Jon picked up the ornament, staring at the two of them kissing their daughter for the first and last time and wishing he could kiss Amara just once more. He slowly came to his feet, rubbed his thumb over her beautiful face, pressed his lips to it, then carefully placed it in the center of the tree, just as she was in his heart. And always would be.

CHAPTER 20

Terri eased out of the bed Saturday morning, slipped into her robe, went to the bathroom to brush her teeth and wash her face, then made her way to the kitchen. She stifled a yawn as she removed the Ziploc bag of short ribs from the refrigerator. After the emotional night she and Jon had, all she wanted to do was crawl back into bed and stay wrapped in her husband's arms. Her wish for him to open up about his feelings had turned into a double-edged sword. While she'd been happy they could finally grieve together, she hadn't been prepared for the impact seeing him completely break down would have on her. As she browned the meat, tears filled her eyes. After Terri had taken the cake out of the oven, she'd returned to find Jon standing in front of the tree staring at the ornament of them with their daughter. He'd placed it in the center of the tree and said that Amara would always be in the center of his heart. They'd finished the tree without speaking, then sat on the sofa and held each other for a long while.

She placed the now seared meat into the slow cooker, along

with onions and a little more of her seasoning blend, and poured beef broth over it.

"What are you doing up so early, babe? It's barely eight."

Terri whirled around and brought her hand to her chest. "You scared me."

Wearing only a pair of basketball shorts, Jon straightened from the doorway, walked to where she stood, and pulled her into his embrace. "Sorry about that." He nuzzled her neck.

She melted into his arms, his minty breath feathering over her jaw and down to her neck and shoulder. "I'm getting the short ribs into the slow cooker so they'll be ready for later." Even though dinner wasn't until six thirty, the meat needed to cook for eight hours, and she didn't want to rush. The chicken and shrimp would take far less time.

"Need some help?"

"Nope. All done," she said, placing the lid on and starting the timer.

"Good. Then you can come back to bed."

Terri let out a little squeal when Jon swept her into his arms and strode toward their bedroom. "I need to clean up first."

"I'll do it later. We need to just relax for a while." Jon deposited her on the bed and removed her robe and his shorts, then climbed in and wrapped his arms around her. "Now, isn't this better?" he murmured.

"Mm-hmm." She snuggled closer, wiggling her backside against his front. His hand stilled her. "What?" she asked innocently, feeling his rapidly growing erection.

"If you keep that up, there won't be any *relaxation* going on."

"I'm just trying to get comfortable." She shifted again and sucked in a sharp breath when his hand slipped between her thighs and he slid two fingers inside her.

"So am I."

Removing his hand, he lifted her leg over his and entered her with one hard thrust. Unlike last night, when he'd loved her slowly and tenderly, this time was hard and fast. It only took them both a few minutes to explode in ecstasy. Terri screamed out his name at the same time his low growl sounded in her ear. Her breaths came in short gasps, and her body continued to tremble with aftershocks.

"Now, we can relax."

The only thing she could manage was a soft moan. *I could get used to this*, she thought before drifting off.

When Terri woke up, two hours had passed and she was alone in bed. Sitting up, she listened for sounds of Jon moving around but only heard the faint strains of music coming from the front of the house. She flipped the covers back and headed for the bathroom to shower. After dressing, she made her way to the kitchen to check on the meat, but changed direction when she spotted Jon seated on one of the loungers in the sunroom. He'd left the sliding glass door open, and she could clearly hear the jazzy instrumental music playing from the hidden speakers he'd installed in the space.

He seemed deep in thought, and she wondered if he was replaying everything that had happened last night, as she'd done earlier. "Want some company?" she asked, touching his shoulder.

Jon's head whipped around. "Hey, baby. I didn't hear you."

He pulled her down on his lap and shifted her until she was sitting between his outstretched legs. "Did you sleep well?"

"I did. What about you?"

"Okay, I guess. Couldn't shut my mind off, so I got up and came out here."

Rubbing his hands, which were wrapped around her, she asked, "Anything you want to share?" He didn't answer for the longest time, and she hoped it didn't mean he was going to revert back to shutting her out again.

"I was thinking about the case the mayor wants me to look into," he said finally. "And I was thinking about last night."

"Oh, yeah. You never got around to telling me about the case."

"Apparently, the development company that was originally supposed to do the condo project is attempting to sue the town for breach of a contract that was never signed. They're saying the town reneged on a good faith deal."

"Oh, please. You can't just decide to bring your own people in and try to build something completely different from what was requested, then sue when the town goes with someone else." She recalled the town hall meeting they'd had at the beginning of the year when the mayor shared that he'd stopped negotiations with the company because they'd wanted to bring in their own workers and build a much larger residential area. "Do you think they have a legitimate claim?"

"Not sure yet. I have a call with them scheduled next week."

"Well, if anyone can handle this, it's you."

Jon kissed her temple. "Thanks for the vote of confidence."

"And about last night?" she asked, going back to the other thing he'd mentioned thinking about.

"Nothing specific." He fell silent for a few seconds. "Do you ever wonder what Amara would've been like now? Who she'd look like, her personality?"

A sad smile touched her lips. "All the time. Especially when I see Noelle, or any of the other little girls in town. I think about what her laugh would sound like and how it would feel to hear her say *mama* for the first time."

His arms tightened around her. "I think about all of those things, too."

Terri had often thought about trying again, but with her and Jon struggling in their own relationship, she hadn't wanted to add more stress by bringing it up. She was also afraid that history would repeat itself. Terri didn't know if she could handle a second loss. They sat in companionable silence for a few minutes, just staring out at the dreary day. Though last night's storm had passed, the temperatures remained in the midfifties, and dark clouds continued to hover over the town. "I should probably check the meat in the slow cooker."

"I checked it right before you came out, and it looked fine. There was still a little over two and a half hours left on the timer. It smells really good."

"Thanks for checking on it. Once it's ready, we can start prepping everything for the taco bar. I'm looking forward to tonight."

"So am I. I didn't realize how much I was missing out on by not being there."

Terri was somewhat surprised to hear him admit it, but glad. "Well, you know I love it when you come, and I miss you when you aren't there. I noticed that you're hanging out with Gabriel and Antonio more often, too." It made her happy to see him finally taking time to develop friendships with them. In her mind, women weren't the only ones who needed good, dependable friends.

"Does that bother you?"

She leaned back to look up at him. "Absolutely not. It's just that—" She cut herself off, not wanting to say anything that might mess up the closeness they'd reclaimed.

"What?"

"Nothing," she said, turning back toward the window.

Jon shifted her to sit crossways on his lap, tilted her chin and kissed her softly. "Talk to me, baby. What were you going to say?"

The sweet kiss melted her resistance. And him calling her *baby* never got old. "I was only going to say I didn't remember you having these kinds of friendships in LA."

"You're right. I didn't. Most of the guys I grew up with moved away after college, and when I started working, everything became a competition. Kind of hard finding someone to trust with my secrets."

"I hear you. You remember what happened with Sabrina?"

"Yeah. I still can't believe she went behind your back like that."

"Me, either." She and Sabrina Davis had been friends since high school, went through college and nursing school together, and ended up working at the same hospital. Everything went well until a promotion came up and Sabrina made up lies about Terri not pulling her weight on the floor and missing key things with patient care. It backfired, however. Not only did Sabrina not get the job, but she also lost her best friend. She'd tried apologizing, but in Terri's mind, there was no way to repair the damage done to their friendship. She felt a rumble behind her. "Is that your stomach?"

Chuckling, Jon said, "I guess it's telling me I need to eat."

"You haven't had breakfast?" she asked, incredulously. "It's after noon."

"I wanted to wait for you."

"Aw, that's so sweet." She patted his cheek. "Since you were so nice to wait, I'm going to fix something special." They rarely ate a big breakfast, both usually grabbing something simple in the mornings like toast, muffins, boiled eggs, or some fruit. She stood. Today, she would make pancakes, scrambled eggs, bacon, and if there was still juice in the fridge, mimosas.

"I'll help."

"Nope. I got it. You just relax, and we can eat out here when I'm done." Smiling, she went to the kitchen and got busy, humming all the while.

* * *

As Jon sat across from Terri devouring the breakfast she'd made, contentment washed over him. After last night's emotional upheaval, he hadn't known what to expect. However, his wife had been her same beautiful self. He realized that what his therapist had said was right—hard conversations were sometimes necessary and a natural part of every healthy relationship. And that's what he wanted...a *healthy* marriage. A touch on his hand drew him out of his thoughts.

"You okay?"

"Huh? Oh, yeah. I'm good."

"Where did you go? I called your name three times," Terri said, viewing him with concern.

Jon frowned. He hadn't heard her once. "I was just thinking about last night. I'm glad we talked, or rather *I* finally talked." It dawned on him that he hadn't told her about him seeking out a therapist. With everything going on, it had honestly slipped his mind. A brief moment of panic gripped him, but he forced it down. She'd already proven that she had his back. "I also meant to tell you that I finally started seeing a therapist."

Terri grasped his hand. "I know that had to be hard for you, but it took a lot of strength and courage, and I'm *so* proud of you. I went to talk to someone, too, and she's helped me a lot. Do you feel like it's helped you in some way?"

"It's helped a lot. You were right, and I'm sorry I didn't take it and you more seriously. I didn't realize how much crap I've been carrying around, stuff I'd buried so deep, I'd forgotten. And I'm finally learning it's okay to talk about my feelings. Especially with you. I talked a bit with Gabe and Antonio, too." When she'd initially suggested it, Jon had shut her down cold, and he wasn't surprised that she'd sought out a therapist.

"Oh, honey, that's great. There's nothing like having a few good friends you can talk to or be a sounding board, if needed. It's one of the things I love most about Serenity, Dana, and Natasha."

Jon nodded. He was finding that out. "Maybe...we...we could go together." It would serve him right if she did the same thing to him now. But that wasn't her. His wife had a heart of gold, and he considered himself blessed to still have her by his side.

She placed her fork on the plate and leaned forward. "You just tell me the time and place, and I'll be there."

"I have an appointment on Tuesday at two." Then they'd be flying out to LA later that evening for the Christmas weekend, and he'd be making a trip to talk to his parents. Jon definitely wasn't looking forward to the conversation.

"*We* have an appointment."

They shared a smile and resumed eating. "By the way, these are the best pancakes I've eaten in a long time." Most likely because he hadn't taken time to be home when she cooked. It wouldn't happen again.

Terri eyed him. "Mm-hmm. Are you trying to butter me up for some reason?"

Laughing, he shook his head. "Not at all. You know I love your cooking. What time do you want to get to supper club?" Jon asked, changing the subject.

"Maybe around five thirty. That'll give me time to heat the meat and fry the corn tortillas. We can just warm the flour ones and they'll be good to go."

"Sounds good."

"Oh, I forgot to tell you Dana met a guy while she was traveling, and he's here visiting. He'll be there, too, so you guys make him feel welcome."

"Really? If he's cool, it'll be no problem." Theirs was a tight-knit group, and while he was happy that she'd found someone, he hoped the guy treated her with respect. Otherwise, he'd be on a quick trip back to wherever he came from.

She shook her head and finished her juice. "I forgot about that big-brother protective thing you have."

Jon shrugged. "Just sayin'. I'm sure Gabe and Antonio would back me up."

"No doubt. Well, at least give the man a chance before y'all run him out of town."

"That's up to him." He stood and collected their empty plates. Terri picked up their glasses and followed him to the kitchen. While he rinsed the plates and loaded them into the dishwasher, she checked the short ribs.

Terri got a fork from the drawer, dug out a small piece, and blew on it. She held it out to him. "Tell me what you think."

He accepted the portion and groaned with the first taste. The perfectly seasoned tender meat nearly melted on his tongue. "Oh, this is good, baby. I vote for just taking the chicken and shrimp, and leaving this here for us."

She sampled it and nodded. "It is good, but it's too late to come up with another meat, so you'll just have to share. I'll make you more anytime you want." She came up on tiptoe and kissed him.

As soon as her lips touched his, he took over the kiss, deepening it. Her hands roamed over his chest and belly. She reached into his sweats and wrapped her hand around his rapidly growing erection. Jon gasped sharply and jerked back. "Don't do that."

"Why?" she asked with a sultry smile.

"You want to make it to dinner tonight, right? If you keep

that up, we'll be sending out regrets and having our own private celebration."

"That sounds tempting."

"Just say the word." He pulled out his phone.

Laughing, she said, "We can't cancel. But we can still celebrate later." She tossed him a bold wink and strutted over to the sink to wash her hands, then to the refrigerator with a little extra switch in her hips.

Later can't come fast enough.

CHAPTER 21

"We're here!" Terri said when Serenity opened the door to her and Jon Saturday evening.

"Oh, my goodness," Serenity said, hugging her and stepping aside so they could enter. "Whatever is in that slow cooker smells *so* good. Hey, Jon."

"Hey, Serenity." Jon placed a kiss on her cheek and followed them to the kitchen. "I need to bring the rest of the food in." He placed the large tote on the counter.

Gabriel entered holding Giana. "What's up, y'all?" He kissed Terri's cheek and gave Jon a fist bump.

"Hey, Gabriel. Let me wash my hands so I can say hello to my goddaughter." Terri went to the sink.

Serenity took the baby. "Babe, can you help Jon bring in the rest of the food?"

"Sure." He lifted the lid of the pot. "Oh, man, this smells good. Let me just have a little taste real quick. Does it taste as good as it looks, Jon?"

"Yeah, it does. But I barely got a taste."

Terri laughed as she dried her hands, then playfully

swatted him on the arm. "Oh, please. You know that's a lie. Just get the rest of the food."

Grinning, Jon dropped a kiss on her lips and trailed Gabriel out.

She stared after him until he was out of sight. This more relaxed and playful side of him never failed to put a smile on her face and in her heart.

"Well, now," Serenity said, handing her the baby. "Looks like things are back to normal with you two."

She smiled down at Giana as she stared up at Terri. "Actually, it's better than before. We finally talked and he opened up to me. It's not my place to give the details, but let's just say I wasn't the only one broken by the loss of our little one."

Serenity brought her hand to her chest. "I don't need all the details—that's between you two—I'm just happy to hear that you guys are back on track. And I don't ever think I've seen Jon look so happy or relaxed."

"It has been a long time, but I'm happy, too." Terri kissed Giana's small hand, and the little girl wrapped her chubby hand around Terri's finger. Her emotions swelled with the memory of Amara's brief grasp before her body went limp. Pushing the painful thoughts aside, she focused on the little girl in her arms.

"Did you leave anything for everybody else to bring, Terri?" Gabriel said as he and Jon returned. "I thought you were doing a taco bar."

"I am." She handed the baby back to her mother. "I decided to do three different meats—beef, chicken, and shrimp. The other containers are the condiments. We came a little early so I can warm up everything and fry the tortillas."

Gabriel rubbed his hands together. "I can't wait to dig in. So, Jon, what did you make? Or did you actually make anything?" he asked teasingly.

"Ha-ha. I did the chicken and the shrimp."

Terri wrapped her arm around Jon's waist. "Oh, don't be shy. Tell Gabriel everything." When he didn't say anything, she continued. "He helped shred the cheeses, chicken, and cabbage, and even mixed the ingredients for the cilantro lime sauce for the shrimp tacos." Gabriel's and Serenity's eyes widened and their mouths fell open. "Yep, my man is cooking now!"

"Aw, I'm so proud," Gabriel said with mock emotion. "Wait 'til I tell Antonio we've gotten our first A-plus student."

Jon just shook his head, but he was smiling. "Man, don't you have something to do, like answer the door?" he added as the bell sounded.

They all burst out laughing, and Gabriel left to let in whoever was at the door.

Terri and Serenity shared a smile.

"What do you need me to help you with, sweetheart?" Jon asked.

"Nothing right now, really. The slow cooker is already plugged in and on warm, and we just need to stick the other pans in the oven. You can relax for a minute."

Serenity walked over and placed Giana in his arms. "Perfect. You can bond with your goddaughter while I put the finishing touches on dessert."

Terri thought she saw a flash of fear in his eyes, but it was gone so fast, she might have imagined it.

"I guess it's just you and me, baby girl," Jon said, placing a gentle kiss on Giana's forehead. He sat at the kitchen table and cradled the baby against his chest. "So how are you liking this crazy world so far, Giana?"

The sight of Jon smiling and talking softly to the baby set off a longing so strong in Terri, she had to look away. So many times, she'd wanted to broach the subject of them trying again, but with their marriage floundering, she'd kept it to herself. Now that they were on solid ground again, she hadn't mentioned it for fear that it would plunge them back in that dark place. Laughter drew her out of her troubled musings. She glanced over and saw Serenity staring at her curiously.

As if interpreting Terri's thoughts, Serenity whispered, "Everything will work out."

Gabriel returned with Natasha, Antonio, and Dana with her new love interest. He said, "I found the rest of the food. Now, we can really party."

Rounds of greetings ensued, and Dana made introductions. "Everybody, this is DeAngelo Murray. DeAngelo, meet the supper club crew." She pointed to each person as she called out their names.

"Nice to meet you all. I've heard a lot about these meet-ups, and it sounds like y'all have a good time."

"*They* have a good time," Gabriel said. "We only get an invite every now and then." Everyone laughed.

Serenity slid her arm around Gabriel's waist. "Keep talking, *darling*, and those every-now-and-again invites will become you-ain't-invited-*ever*."

"Man, shut up. You're about to get us kicked out," Jon said, still rocking the baby.

Gabriel chuckled and held up his hands in mock surrender. "Aw, baby, you know I was just playing."

"Mm-hmm," Dana said. "Let's get this party going. Where's Darius? We put together a nice festive drink menu." She pointed to the large bag DeAngelo held.

Terri rubbed her hands together. "Ooh, I can't wait." She opened her mouth to say something else just as Darius entered the kitchen.

"What's up, good people? Sorry about the delay, but when Mom calls, I have to answer. I can't be messing up and not getting all the great holiday food she'll be cooking when I get home," Darius added with a little laugh. "Dana, did you tell them what we're having?"

"Not yet, but you can go ahead. Oh, and this is DeAngelo. DeAngelo, this is Darius. He's Gabriel's friend and business partner visiting from Atlanta."

The two men greeted each other, then Darius said, "All right, for your drinking pleasure we have a cranberry cocktail containing triple sec and champagne—substituted with 7Up for those unable to indulge—and spiked eggnog with your choice of whiskey or coffee liqueur. For you Scrooges, we have a Grinch cocktail—Midori, rum, and 7Up. Again, we have a mocktail alternative with lime sherbet. Last, but certainly not least, we've got a little homemade Irish cream, courtesy of Dana. Oh, and she made the coffee liqueur, too."

Every head turned toward Dana. Terri said, "Girl, you've been holding out on us."

"I know I've only been back less than a year, but I've come to at *least* four or five of these supper club dinners, and I haven't heard one word about my favorite Irish cream drink," Antonio said. He rubbed his hands together. "The first glass of Irish cream is mine. Of course, a little later I'll need to sample the coffee liqueur, too."

"I gotta tell y'all. They both taste amazing," DeAngelo said.

Gabriel lifted his hand. "Hold up. Man, you can't be just coming in here sampling all the good stuff before we do. And Dana, how're you giving him all the good stuff first? And like Antonio said, we ain't heard one word about this. I've been to more supper clubs than him."

Dana held up a hand. "Yeah, yeah, I know. I completely forgot about the fact that my mom had the recipes. So, are we going to stand around all night, or are we gonna get our eat and drink on?"

A loud roar went up from the men, who chorused, "Let's eat!"

Someone turned on the music, and Dana and Darius stepped in as bartenders, with DeAngelo assisting. Jon handed a dozing Giana to Serenity and came over to where Terri stood frying the tortillas.

"Let me help you," he said, dipping his head to nuzzle her neck.

Tiny bolts of electricity flowed through her as his tongue circled the sensitive spot below her ear. "This isn't helping," Terri murmured.

"Speak for yourself." But he stepped back, washed his hands, and handled the tortillas in one pan while she did the other. "I think I like cooking with you."

She glanced up at him. "I know I like it, and I hope we can do it more often."

He smiled. "I assure you we will."

Her heart leaped. She thought their first Christmas together had been the best, but this one was shaping up to be even better. They finished the cooking, then assembled everything on the bar on trivets Serenity had provided. "Okay, everybody, food's ready."

"Oh, my goodness. This smells *sooo* good," Natasha said, grabbing a plate. "I think I'm having one of each kind of taco. What's this white sauce, Terri?"

"It's a cilantro cream sauce, and it's great with the shrimp, but you can put it on everything. I mixed a little in with the shredded cabbage for extra flavor." Along with the tacos, they'd done side dishes of Mexican rice, black beans, and fried corn, and included a host of condiments from guacamole and a few varieties of salsa to sour cream, cheese, and tomatoes.

After everyone had filled their plates, they gathered around the dining room table. Serenity laid Giana in a bassinet that had been placed in a corner. Gabriel and Serenity stood side by side, and Gabriel held his glass aloft and said, "To the first of many holiday couples supper club celebrations." They all lifted their glasses in a toast and sipped. "DeAngelo, we welcome you and hope to see you again."

His eyes fixed on Dana, DeAngelo said, "Oh, you'll definitely be seeing me again."

Terri, Serenity, and Natasha exchanged knowing looks as Dana blushed. Terri was happy for her friend and hoped DeAngelo turned out to be the one for her.

"Before we dig in, I have something to share," Natasha said. "Antonio and I are expecting our first child."

"Which is why my baby is now part of the mocktail crew." Antonio leaned over and placed a sweet kiss on Natasha's lips.

They all clapped, cheered, and raised another toast. Terri was so happy for them, but at the same time she wondered if it would ever be her turn. As if sensing her turmoil, Jon reached under the table and gave her hand a reassuring squeeze. She didn't have time to dwell on it as lively conversation ensued. The topics went from sports and weather to holiday plans and gift wish lists. Over the meal, they found out that DeAngelo's family owned a chain of boutique hotels and that he was the oldest of three boys and the only one who worked in the business.

"Do you all eat like this at every get-together?" DeAngelo asked.

Dana nodded. "Serenity usually does all the cooking, but we're giving her a break since she recently had the baby. But we've done a good job filling in until she's ready to take over. Of course, I'll still only be doing the drinks. Me and cooking aren't best friends."

He lifted her hand and placed a kiss on the back. "Don't worry about it, baby. I can do a little sumthin' sumthin' in the kitchen."

"Well now," Terri said, fanning herself. Dana shot her a look, but Terri just smiled.

"You'll fit right in with this bunch." Jon toasted DeAngelo

with his drink. "We may have to do our own dinners. But let me go on record and say that I'm still working my way up to cooking well, thanks to Gabe and Tony."

Terri turned his way. "What are you talking about? You helped with this meal, and let's not forget about the *amazing* dinner you prepared for me. I'd say you've more than worked your way up to cooking *well*."

"Nothing like having your wife giving you props," Antonio said.

Jon touched his glass to Antonio's. "Nothing like it in this world." He leaned over and kissed Terri. "Nothing," he whispered against her lips.

Her heart started pounding, and she bit back a moan. She couldn't recall the last time he'd been so openly affectionate. She was still reeling when dinner ended. The guys volunteered to do dishes while they waited for their food to settle before eating dessert. The women gathered in the family room.

"Terri, I have never, in the years that you've been here, seen Jon be so open and loving with you," Dana said. "Y'all must've made up *real* good."

"I was thinking the same thing," Natasha chimed in. "I had to fan myself a couple of times."

Terri waved them off but was smiling. "I don't know what you're talking about. And what about the way DeAngelo was looking at you, Dana? I think we're going to have a new resident in Firefly Lake soon."

Serenity adjusted Giana as she breastfed her. "Exactly. That man is totally into you, Dana."

"I'll concede that point. DeAngelo is one of the nicest guys I've met in a long time. He makes me feel... I don't know. I really like him. He hates drama, and so do I, which makes the relationship easy."

Terri placed a hand on Dana's arm. "We've all been there, and we get it, sis. The only thing that matters is he makes you happy."

"He does, but in some ways, I feel like things are moving way too fast."

"How old is he?" Natasha asked.

"Thirty-six, and he's never been married or had children."

"Old enough to know what and who he wants," Terri said. "Jon and I met and married within three months. Although things went south for a while, I wouldn't do anything different." The conversation with her cousin rose in her mind. She'd mentioned wondering whether she'd taken enough time to get to know him before jumping into marriage. However, she realized that no matter what, she loved Jon and would still have said yes to his proposal, regardless of the time frame. "Only you two will know when and if the time is right to take things to the next level."

"Okay, okay. Enough about me. Tasha, how're you just gonna drop that little bombshell at the dinner table, and how long have you known?"

Natasha grinned. "I'm three months along and we've known a few weeks. We wanted to keep it to ourselves for a while before the Firefly Lake rumor mill got started." The women laughed and agreed. "You all are the first ones we've told. We plan to tell our families next week at Christmas, since everyone will be here." She must have noticed Terri's expression, because she added, "Terri, I just know you and Jon will be next. Have you guys talked about trying again?"

She shook her head. "We've only recently talked about the loss. I think we're both afraid to bring it up and worried history will repeat itself. I don't think either of us would be able to handle if it happened again."

"Did the doctor say there were any residual problems?" Serenity asked.

"No. He said there shouldn't be any issues, but with all the stress lately, my cycle has been erratic at best." Over the past year and a half, she'd missed several periods and gotten her hopes up, only to realize it was the strain and anxiety taking its toll on her body.

"Then maybe it's something you two can discuss after the holidays. Jon looked right at home holding Giana."

Terri held Serenity's hopeful gaze. "Maybe." She agreed. Jon would make a wonderful father, and she wanted nothing more than to see his eyes light up as he held their own child.

CHAPTER 22

"Are you almost ready, Terri?" Jon asked Tuesday afternoon as he added a flash drive to his laptop bag. They had decided to drive to Oakland for their flight right after the therapy session.

"Yep. I just need to grab my light jacket. I'm kind of looking forward to a little sunshine and warmth." Terri came out of the closet, added the jacket, and zipped the suitcase.

"Same, but we won't be there long enough to really enjoy those nice seventies temperatures. It would've been nice to stay a couple more days and relax on the beach."

She sighed and laid her head on his chest. "I totally agree."

Jon wrapped a hand around her waist and kissed the top of her head. "As soon as it warms up, you, me, and the beach, whether it's LA or Tahoe." He tried to recall the last time they'd taken a vacation, a real vacation, and realized that they hadn't since the first year they moved to Firefly Lake. Somehow, they both had become so lost in work—him, especially—that those things they typically enjoyed had gotten pushed so far to the side, they were now nonexistent.

Never again would he allow anything to come between them. *Even me.*

Terri smiled up at him. "Sounds like a plan, but it won't be now, so we should probably get going. Don't want to be late for our appointment," she added with a little laugh. Backing out of his arms, she picked up her tote.

Jon slung the laptop bag over his shoulder, then picked up their suitcases and started toward the garage. He wouldn't admit it out loud, but he had some apprehensions about the session. It was one thing to reveal his vulnerabilities to his wife and his therapist separately, and although it didn't make any sense, airing his dirty laundry—*their* dirty laundry—together in one room almost made him want to cancel. Almost. He placed the luggage in the trunk of the car. Going around to the passenger side, he held the door open for Terri and closed it behind her.

As he got in on the driver's side and started the engine, she reached for his hand. "I can sense you worrying about what's going to happen today. Just remember we've got this. Together."

He released a deep breath and brought her hand to his lips. "Have I told you how much I love you?"

She angled her head thoughtfully. "Hmm, you might have mentioned it once or twice, but I wouldn't mind hearing it again."

Her serene smile and playful banter relaxed him. "I love you."

"I love you, too. Now, let's do this!" Terri cranked up the music and danced in her seat.

Yeah, I love her. Grinning, he got them underway. By the time he reached Ken's office, Jon felt a little more at ease.

"Good to see you, Jon," Ken said, ushering them into his office and closing the door. "And it's nice to meet you, Terri. Please, have a seat." He gestured to the two armchairs placed side by side.

"Nice to meet you, as well," Terri said, sitting.

Jon lowered himself next to her.

The therapist sat across from them and picked up his iPad. "Thanks for filling out the information, Terri. How about you tell me what you hope to gain from these sessions."

"I just want us to be able to communicate openly and get back to the closeness we used to have." She glanced over at Jon. "I think we're on the right track now. We've been talking more, and it's helping tremendously."

"Do you agree, Jon?"

"Yes. I finally told Terri about my upbringing."

"How did that make you feel, Terri?"

"Honestly, I wanted to book a flight to LA and cuss my in-laws out. But that probably wouldn't go over too well," she added with a shrug.

Jon chuckled and shook his head. He noticed Ken trying to keep a straight face.

"As I said, we seem to be making good progress getting back to where we were, so I'll keep my peace."

Ken cleared his throat. "You mentioned making good progress. Jon, do you think you two are progressing?"

"Yes." He shared some of the things they'd starting doing and how he was making a concerted effort to have more quality time together again. "We've been eating together most evenings and on the weekend, we took a trip to the Bay, and I've opened up some to share my past with her."

Ken nodded. "Terri?"

She smiled over at Jon and reached for his hand. "It's been amazing being able to spend time talking and just being together. He's even learning how to cook, and being in the kitchen together is becoming one of my most favorite things. It's all I've ever wanted for us."

Jon kissed her hand. "I want that for us, too."

"It sounds like you two are on the right track now," Ken said.

Still staring at his wife, he said, "We absolutely are, and I couldn't be happier."

By the time the session ended, Jon wished he'd done this as soon as their relationship began to crumble. It would've saved them years of heartache and pain. He and Terri had agreed to continue with a few more sessions, and he was actually looking forward to them.

"That wasn't so bad," Terri said as he drove out of the parking lot.

"I was just thinking the same thing." He slanted her a quick glance. "And that I wished I'd done it sooner."

"Better late than never, as the saying goes. Maybe we needed to go through this to strengthen our marriage. If we can get through this, I feel like we'll be able to handle anything life throws our way."

"I agree." Jon checked the traffic on the car's GPS. "Looks like there's not too much traffic, so we should get there around four fifteen."

"Good. That means we'll have plenty of time to eat before the six forty flight." She pulled out her phone. A minute later she said, "The flight is still on time, so that's good." It rang in her hand. "Hey, Mom. Yes, we're on the way to the airport now. I just checked and the flight is on time. We should get in around eight."

"Hey, Mama Gina," he said.

"She said hi. And that your cake is waiting for you," she grumbled.

A wide smile spread across his lips.

"Did you make the lemon cake, too?"

The way she was frowning told him no, and he chuckled inwardly.

"How are you just gonna not make my favorite cake? I haven't had it since the first time Jon came home with me. That's just wrong, Mom. I'm your *only* daughter. Doesn't that count for something?"

Jon's eyes left the road briefly and caught her glaring at him. "Why are you mad at me? I'm not the one making the cake."

"Mm-hmm. We'll stop by tonight before going to the hotel." Terri ended the call, then shifted in her seat. "I can't believe her."

"Aw, don't be mad, baby. I'll share my cake with you."

"I don't want your tired little cake."

He laughed and reached over to smooth her frown, and she slapped his hand away, which made him laugh even harder. For the first time in years, he was looking forward to enjoying the holiday.

* * *

Two days later, Terri helped her mother, aunt, and Candace bring out the desserts. After enjoying a huge Christmas dinner earlier, everyone agreed that they needed to let the food settle before tackling the wide array of sweets. When she and Jon had stopped by that first night when they arrived, her mother had, indeed, baked Jon's favorite yellow cake with chocolate frosting—a full-sized one and an individual one that he'd eaten after they'd gotten checked in at the hotel. The heated memories of what they'd done with the frosting tempted her to see if her mom had made extra so she could bring back an entire bowl tonight.

"Girl, those must be some thoughts," Candace whispered as she set a peach cobbler on the table. "You're just standing there with the cake and smiling."

She glanced down and realized she still held the cake in her hands and quickly set it next to the other desserts.

Her cousin chuckled. "I'm just glad to see you and Jon smiling. Things must be better."

"They are, and I couldn't be happier." Terri went still for a moment. Jon had said those identical words during their therapy session, and it meant everything to her that he felt the same.

"Is that everything?" her mother asked, coming in with two pies.

"Aunt Gina, if we have anything else, it won't fit on the table," Candace said with a little laugh. "There are only ten people here, and there is enough to feed three times more. You and Mom went a little overboard, I think."

Terri gave her mom a quick hug. "You and Aunt Naomi outdid yourselves." The two sisters had always been deemed queens of the kitchen, and her mother was very particular about who she allowed near her stove. Terri's paternal aunt and her two daughters had joined the festivities, but none of them could cook well, so they had been relegated to bringing the paper goods, water, and drinks.

"And because *someone* was whining about a lemon cake, I got up early to make one."

"That's why you're the best mom *ever*!"

"Mm-hmm, I know." The three women burst out laughing. "Terri, let the guys know dessert is ready. Candace, I left the plates in the kitchen. Can you get them, please?"

"If it means I get first dibs, absolutely."

"You'd better not cut my cake first," Terri said, heading for the family room at the back of the house, where the rest of the family had assembled to watch a football game. "Dessert is ready to be served, y'all." She caught Jon's gaze, sauntered to where he was sitting, and whispered, "You'd better get your cake before my two cousins over there beat you to it."

Jon jumped to his feet, grabbed her hand, and nearly dragged her back to the dining room. "You know I don't play about my cake."

Laughing and handing him a plate, she said, "I guess not." She went around to the other side and cut a large slice of the lemon cake and a small portion of peach cobbler.

"Mama Gina, this cake is amazing," Jon said, toasting her with his fork.

"Thank you, baby. I'll make sure you have enough to take home."

Terri rolled her eyes, and he winked at her. "Don't make no sense how spoiled you are," she muttered.

He dropped a kiss on her lips. "Don't hate. And I don't know how you can call me spoiled when you're stuffing your mouth with that lemon cake I'm sure wasn't on the original menu."

She shoved a forkful of the cake in her mouth and gave him an innocent look. "Hmm."

"Thank you, Jon," Candace said, shaking her head. "Just rotten to the core."

Terri skewered her cousin with a look. "I know you're not talking, Miss Begging for Peach Cobbler."

"I don't know what you're talking about."

"I bet you don't." They burst out laughing. The rest of the family got their desserts and drifted back to the family room.

"I don't have to take this. I'm going to eat my dessert in peace." Candace shoved another spoonful of cobbler in her mouth, then pivoted on her heel and strutted off.

Jon chuckled. "You two are like siblings."

Terri said, "We are. So, are you enjoying yourself?"

"I am. It's the best Christmas I've had in a while. I think it's because we're in a good place now. And because neither of us had to deal with my parents and their shenanigans," he added with a wry grin.

Terri smiled. "Amen, and I agree. This has been a really good day." She came up on tiptoe and pressed a kiss to his lips. Being able to relax without having to listen to his mother's "suggestions" to improve their marriage was definitely a bonus. "Speaking of your parents, do you still plan to talk to them?"

"Yep. I'll head over tomorrow. She called earlier, but I

didn't tell her we're in town. I'm going to pop over just like they did us."

She burst out laughing. "You know your mom hates people showing up unannounced."

"But she has no problem doing it to other people, so..." He shrugged. "Enough talk about that. I'm trying to enjoy my cake." He ate another bite and groaned. "You think if I asked, your mom would send me one of these once a month?"

"Probably," she muttered with a roll of her eyes. Terri narrowed her eyes and pointed her fork his way. "You'd better not even think about it, unless you're campaigning for my lemon cake, too."

"Have I told you how much I absolutely adore you?" He eased her closer and trailed kisses along her jaw and neck.

"Don't try to sweet-talk me."

"Is it working?"

Of course it was, but she wouldn't tell him. Each kiss had her ready to go back to the hotel. "I plead the Fifth."

The low rumbling of his laughter vibrated against her ear. "I'll just take that as a yes."

She stepped away from him. "Go eat your dessert."

A wicked grin tilted the corner of his mouth. "That's what I was trying to do."

"Behave."

"I promise you I'll be on my *very best* behavior." Jon dipped his head and kissed her again.

"Hey, hey. Y'all need to get away from the dessert table before you melt everything."

Terri jumped and spun around. Candace stood there with her hands on her hips and a wide grin on her face.

Jon chuckled. "I'll be in the family room."

She watched until he was out of sight, her body still in sensual turmoil.

Candace cleared her throat.

"What?" Terri asked.

"I just think y'all cute." She hooked her arm in Terri's and led her to Terri's old bedroom. "I can't believe Aunt Gina hasn't changed one thing since you moved."

"Me, either." All Terri's books still sat on the bookshelves, and her framed high school diploma hung on the wall, along with every award she'd ever received. The only thing that had been changed was the bedding. They sat on the bed and relaxed against the headboard, then smiled at each other. "This brings back so many memories."

"So many. We dreamed in here, shared secrets, talked about all the cute boys we liked." They broke out in a fit of laughter.

"Those were some good times." She ate another bite of her cake.

"It looks like you and Jon are all straightened out," Candace said around a mouthful of sweet potato pie.

She smiled. "We are, and it feels even better than before in some ways." Because they'd always been each other's confidante, Terri shared a little of what Jon had told her about his parents and his reasoning for shutting down.

"That is so freakin' unbelievable!" She pointed her fork Terri's way. "See, this is why men have such a hard time with their emotions. Don't make no sense," Candace muttered.

"I agree. He's been going to therapy, and I went with him to the last session."

"That's great, Terri. Has he talked to his parents about it?"

"He's going over tomorrow before we leave. And no, I will *not* be going with him." That would be a sure way to ruin her holiday.

"Well, I hope it goes well."

"So do I." Terri didn't know what she'd do if it turned out any other way.

CHAPTER 23

"Are you sure you don't want me to come with you to your parents' house?"

Jon gathered Terri in his embrace. "I'm sure. I appreciate you offering, especially because I know they're not exactly at the top of your favorites list at the moment." Truth be told, they weren't at the top of his, either, and he had to wonder if he'd end up off their lists after the conversation.

Terri placed a loving hand on his cheek. "No, they aren't, but for you, I'd do it anyway because I love you."

"I love you too, sweetheart." He would forever be grateful that he'd been given a second chance to get it right with his wife, and he planned to make sure she never regretted coming back home. Jon covered her lips with his, intending it to be a light kiss, but Terri took over, holding him in place and deepening the kiss as if she knew he needed the strength.

"That should hold you until you get back. But if you get there and you need my support, promise you'll call. I can have Candace or my mom drop me off."

"I'll be fine. I should be back in a couple of hours, but I'll text if it's going to be longer." They would be having an early dinner with her family before their flight out later that evening.

"Okay." Terri gave him a strong hug. "No matter what, know that I love you and I am *so* very proud of you. Remember, I'll always have your back. *Always.*"

Jon released a deep sigh. "I just wish I'd done it a long time ago. Maybe things wouldn't have gotten so bad between us." He would always regret not taking her up on her many offers to go to counseling.

"You're doing it now, and that's what counts."

He nodded. She walked with him to the front door. "I'll be back in a little while. Are you and Candace still going shopping?"

"Just a short trip. She wants my opinion on a couple of outfits she already picked out. We're trying to get all our time in before going home." She gave his hand a gentle squeeze. "I hope everything goes well."

"Me, too. See you in a bit." Jon loped down the walkway and slid behind the wheel of the rental. Terri stood lounging in her parents' doorway, a worried expression lining her face. He wanted to reassure her, but even he wasn't certain of how things would turn out. Backing out, he threw up a wave and made the twenty-minute drive to his parents' home.

He sat there for a moment, trying to decide how to start the conversation, but for a man who made his living talking, he didn't have a clue. "Might as well get it over with," he muttered and got out.

After ringing the doorbell, he shook his head at all the decorations. His mother tended to go overboard, as she did with everything else.

"Jon! Oh, my goodness. I didn't expect you," his mother said the moment she opened the door.

"Hey, Mom." Jon hugged her and kissed her cheek. She peered around him. "Terri's not here." He followed her to the family room, where his father sat watching a college football game.

"So you just flew in for a visit?"

"No. We got in a few nights ago. Hey, Dad." He leaned down to hug him.

A hand on her hip, his mother said, "You spent Christmas with Terri's family and didn't even bother to let us know you were here?"

Jon sat on the sofa. "Mom, you know good and well why we didn't come over here for dinner yesterday. And that's why I need to talk to you. To you both." He waited until she took a seat in her favorite recliner before continuing. She looked upset but didn't seem to know why, when he'd asked her over and over to stop badgering his wife.

"Everybody was disappointed that you two weren't here. And Barbara asked whether you and Terri were expecting another baby yet. I couldn't tell her anything—"

"Really, Mom?" He ran a weary hand over his face. "That's exactly why we didn't come. Every time we step foot in this house, the first thing you do is start telling us what we need to do in our marriage. You have to stop. Yes, we've been having problems, and a big part of that is you constantly trying to tell my wife what she should be doing to keep me happy. The phone calls, the texts, the links to articles... all of it has to stop *now*." While he'd known about the calls and texts, he'd had no idea his mother was sending Terri articles about keeping the spice in marriage and lists of things to do when there's trouble in the relationship. The one that had him ready to take an immediate flight had to do with moving on after loss of a child. She'd sent that one a couple of weeks ago, and it had sent his wife into a crying spell that broke his heart.

"I told you to stop interfering, Deb. You're always trying to tell somebody what to do with their lives. Don't make no sense," his father said, shaking his head.

"I'm not that bad," she mumbled. "And what's wrong with wanting your son to have a happy marriage?"

"There's nothing wrong with it, but you can't keep badgering them. They need to work it out themselves."

"Mom, you *are* that bad. And do not ever send my wife another article about losing a baby."

"I don't know why you're so upset, Jon. It's been years, and neither of you is getting any younger. I want grandbabies, and—"

"Stop, Mom. Just *stop!*" Jon jumped up and started pacing. He dragged an agitated hand down his face. "Did you not hear anything I said? You're making everything worse, not better. And if it continues, then be prepared not to see us. No visits, no phone calls, nothing." He didn't want to go there, but sometimes with his mother, he found that drastic measures were needed to get her attention.

Her eyes widened in surprise. "You wouldn't."

"For Terri's well-being, and the well-being of our marriage, I'd do it in a heartbeat." He saw her gearing up to dig her heels in and cut her off before she could start. "You don't want to test me on this, Mom. We've already missed two holidays, and I don't think you want to make it permanent." She folded her arms, and her lip trembled as tears filled her eyes. Sighing, he hunkered down next to her. "I love you, Mom, but I'm not your little boy anymore. I'm a grown man with a wife, and you have to let me live my own life, *my* way." He kissed her temple and returned to his seat. For a few moments, no one said anything. The next part of the conversation would be harder. He bowed his head and struggled to force the words out. "There's more. Dad, I almost ruined my marriage because I wouldn't open up to Terri. I bought into all the years of you drilling into my head that sharing my feelings would somehow make me less of man, and in doing so, I lost myself and nearly lost my wife. She left me, and that scared me more than anything you've ever said." Jon lifted his head and stared directly at his father. "You were wrong. It's not a weakness to tell someone you love that you're hurting. There's no shame in crying over a loss. And there's not one thing wrong with needing to talk things through with a professional."

"I can't believe you went and—"

Jon raised a hand to stop his father's familiar rant. "Yes, I went to talk with a therapist, and I've also started talking to Terri about what I'm feeling inside. You know what? She doesn't look at me differently, and our marriage is back on track. I understand that Grandpa said those same things to you, and that society tells us as men we have to always be strong, but we don't. And we can't. We're human and have emotions, too, and it really *is* okay to talk about them. It doesn't change who you are, but it does help to work things through. Maybe you should try it," he added softly.

His father turned away, seemingly staring at some spot on the wall, and didn't respond.

He hoped he'd given them both something to think about that would positively affect their relationship. They sat in strained silence for a minute. Jon checked his watch, then stood. "I have to get going. We're flying home this evening." His parents slowly came to their feet, both with expressions of apprehension.

"So you're cutting us out of your life now?" his mother asked.

"No, not now, but you're going to have to change your ways. And you should pass the message to your sisters. Terri is my number one priority, and I will not let any of you disrespect her anymore. We've tried to be nice about it, but I'm done. I love her more than my own life, and I'm grateful that she's given me a second chance. I'm not going to mess it up. If that means spending less time with you all to keep the peace, then so be it. It's up to you what happens next."

She burst out in tears. "I'm sorry. I don't want to lose you, Jon. You two seemed miserable, and I just want you to be happy."

Jon wrapped his arms around her. "I know, and I am happy, Mom. Terri and I are finding our own way, and we're good." They were better than good, in his opinion because *he* was better. "You're not going to lose me."

Swiping at her eyes, she stepped out of his embrace. "I'll call Terri and apologize, and I promise to do better."

"She'd like that." He turned to his father. "I'll see you later, Dad." They shared a rough hug, and he whispered, "If you ever want to talk about anything, call me." Maybe having a conversation about his past hurts would do them both good. Though his father tried to hide behind his stoic persona, Alan Rhodes harbored some deep wounds, and Jon could see right through it. His parents had been married for almost forty years, and Jon knew things hadn't always been good between them, mostly due to some of the same reasons as he and Terri dealt with. He only hoped the man would do something to help himself and his marriage. If nothing else, they'd be too busy to interfere with his and Terri's lives.

After saying his final goodbyes, Jon started down the walkway to his car feeling as if a weight had been lifted from his chest. He found it ironic that he communicated for a living but had never applied those skills to his personal life until now. It had been freeing in a way, and he never wanted to go back.

* * *

"Are you sure you can't stay in bed a little longer?" Terri asked as she lay sprawled atop Jon. Since returning from LA four days ago, he'd hit the ground running but had made it home no later than six thirty or seven.

Jon groaned. "Baby, you know I'd like nothing more, but I've got a full day."

"I know, and I'll probably be the same way in a couple of weeks." Though she'd spent a few hours there the past couple of days, the memory care center wouldn't open officially until the end of January, which gave her a good three weeks to get in all her relaxation time.

"What's your day look like?"

"We're having an impromptu supper club lunch here since Dana and Tasha have some time. I'm anxious to show off my new sunroom. Did I tell you how much I appreciate you having it built?"

"You may have mentioned it, but feel free to refresh my memory," he murmured while trailing kisses along her jaw.

"Mmm, starting something is a sure way to make you late for work." She moved onto the bed.

"And since I have a couple of meetings with clients this morning, and the hearing with the mayor and the construction company this afternoon, being late probably isn't the best idea. Gotta love small towns. No way would the case have made it to the docket this soon in LA." Jon sat up and swung his legs over the side of the bed.

She agreed. Things moved much faster here. "Probably not. But we can pick up where we left off tonight."

"Now, *that* is an offer I can't refuse," he said over his shoulder. He leaned back to kiss her once more, then went to shower and get dressed.

Terri rolled onto her back and smiled, thinking about how well things were going with them. She'd been worried they'd have a setback after he talked with his parents, but he had assured her that wasn't the case.

Several minutes later, Jon emerged from the bathroom dressed impeccably in a gray tailored suit with a white shirt and coordinating printed tie. He stood staring at her for a lengthy moment.

"What's wrong?"

"I'm trying to figure out a way to kiss you without touching you, because if I do, I'll be sending the mayor my regrets. You are beyond tempting, baby."

Chuckling, she pulled the sheet back up to cover her nakedness. "How's that?"

"Disappointing." He bent and kissed her softly while keeping his body from making contact with hers. "How was that?"

"Disappointing," she said, tossing his words back to him. "Can't even get a little rub or touch." Terri sat up and the sheet slipped.

He shook his head but was smiling. "Stop tempting me."

"Who me?" she asked innocently, pointing at herself.

Instead of responding, he said, "I should be home no later than six. If something pops up, I'll text you." Jon pivoted on his heel and strode out of the room.

She fell back on the bed and burst out laughing.

"It's not funny," he yelled from the hallway, which made her laugh harder.

Once she finally calmed, she lay there a while longer before heading for the shower. After dressing and having breakfast, she searched the cabinets and refrigerator for items needed for lunch. They'd decided on a salad bar to offset some of the holiday calories. Terri figured she'd sauté shrimp and grill chicken breasts for proteins and make a crab dip with toasted baguette slices for an appetizer. She made a list of what she had to pick up from the store, grabbed her purse and keys, then started to the garage.

As soon as she settled in the car, her phone rang. She froze when she saw her mother-in-law's name on the display. Terri briefly toyed with letting it go to voicemail, but went ahead and answered. *She'd better not start with me today.* "Hey, Mama Deb."

"Hi, Terri. I hope I didn't catch you at a bad time."

"Actually, I'm just leaving to run a few errands."

"I won't take up too much of your time." There was a pause, then she said, "I wanted to apologize for meddling."

Terri stared at the phone for a second. *Did she say what I think she did?* The words caught her off guard, and she didn't know what to say.

"I don't want to lose my son or you," Mama Deb continued, her voice cracking. "So I'm going to do better. I won't send you any more articles or stuff like that."

"I would really appreciate that, and thank you for the apology."

"Well, that's all I was calling for. You go on and do your errands. I'll talk to you later."

Before she could respond, Mama Deb ended the call. *Well, alrighty then.* Still shocked, she backed out and drove to the store.

Three hours later, her friends arrived. After several rounds of hugs and greetings, Terri led them back to her new room. "What do you think of this space? Isn't it gorgeous?"

"The pictures did not do this justice," Serenity said, walking over to the wall of windows facing the mountains. "I would probably never leave."

"Right?" Dana said. "Antonio did a fabulous job. If I had space, I would seriously consider asking him to build me something similar."

Natasha smiled. "I told y'all my baby is the best."

"That he is," Terri agreed. "But *my* baby made sure I had

everything I needed in here to enjoy myself all year round." She'd turned on the fireplace to ward off the chill and had music playing through the concealed speakers. When he found out she wanted to host her friends, Jon had gone out to purchase a rolling cart for serving food. "Let me go get everything and bring it back. Y'all get comfortable." She went to the kitchen, loaded up the cart, then made her way to the sunroom. "Okay, sisters, let's eat!"

"Honey, this is just what I need," Serenity said, patting her stomach. "The way I ate over the past couple of weeks, you'd think I was still eating for two. And I haven't lost all my maternity weight." She filled a plate with her choices from the salad bar.

Dana opened her tote and pulled out a large thermos. "But you still look good. I don't think Gabriel has a problem, the way he was staring at you at supper club."

"Yeah, you're right, especially now that he can get some of my good stuff since I've been cleared by the doctors." She wiggled her eyebrows, and the women fell out laughing. "But I'm not the only one with a man staring at her like she's his favorite dessert. DeAngelo has it bad for you, girl."

"I thought he was going to sneak you off to the back room for a minute, especially after that comment about being able to do a little sumthin' sumthin' in the kitchen," Terri said. "Has he gone home yet?"

"He left on Sunday. They have a few New Year's parties scheduled at the hotels, and he needed to get back to handle the planning. But he said he'll be visiting again soon, perhaps even New Year's Eve, if he can hand off the event coordination to someone else." She poured the fragrant hot apple cider into the mugs placed at each place setting, then fixed her plate.

Natasha claimed a chair. "Speaking of New Year's, are we going to do anything? I don't think it has to be big, but maybe dessert and a toast. We can do it at our house. I'm sure Tonio won't mind," she said using the nickname she'd given her husband when they were high school sweethearts. The two had been separated for seventeen years before reconnecting.

"Sounds good to me," Terri said, taking a seat. "I'm enjoying being a woman of leisure and want to have all the fun before starting full-time at the center."

"Speaking of that, I heard there's going to be a ribbon-cutting ceremony the second week of January. When are they allowing the residents to move in? Mama Nora is so excited about finally having Papa Fred close by."

"From what I understand, it'll be two weeks after the ceremony. And speaking of that, I'd planned to ask you about helping me decorate my office."

"Oh, girl, yes. You know I've got you. I don't have to go back to LA for a few weeks, so I've got some time. We'll coordinate schedules before I leave."

"Thanks, Tasha." While eating, the women talked about everything from the storm that blew in with wind gusts that had caused damage to a few houses when trees fell on them to plans for the upcoming year.

"How've you been feeling, Tasha?" Dana asked.

"Not too bad. Thankfully, I didn't really experience morning sickness, but my energy has been in the pits. Hopefully, that'll change soon. Things have been a little slower with the holidays, which is good. As soon as the new year hits, I'll be back at it."

Terri had been the same way, and wondered if she'd be just as lucky the next time. *If there is a next time.* "Speaking of work, did you decide when you're going back, Serenity?"

"Probably not for another two or three months. I had always planned to take three months if and when I had babies, but I'm enjoying this time with Giana and want some extra time with her. I've already told the office I'd be off for four months." She sipped her cider. "Now, how did the holidays go in LA, and did you visit your in-laws? Spill *all* the tea."

Terri chuckled. "Christmas was great because I *didn't* see my in-laws, but Jon went over to talk to them. He said it was tense for a while, but things ended on a positive note. Whatever he said must have worked, because my mother-in-law called me earlier and apologized for interfering in our marriage and said she was going to stop sending me all the relationship crap." The three women all stared. "I know. I had the same expression."

"Hold up," Dana said. "What do you mean sending you stuff? I know you mentioned her always trying to give you suggestions during your visits and whenever she calls."

She nodded. "Suggestions, texts, links to articles...you name it. I was this close to cussing her out." She put her thumb and forefinger together.

"I am so glad I don't have to deal with that," Natasha said, shaking her head in disgust.

"And now, neither do I. Jon told her if she didn't back off, we would not be visiting or attending any family functions."

Terri had never meant for him to issue the ultimatum, because they were his parents, and she didn't want to come between them. However, he'd assured her that the choice had been as much for his own peace as for Terri's. She hoped going forward the relationship would be better.

"If the threat of Jon cutting them off was what it took to make them stop, then..." Serenity shrugged. "With how long it's been going on, I'm surprised it took this long for him to put his foot down. Then again, it's always difficult when they're your parents. I hope it hasn't affected you and Jon now that you two are doing so well."

"He's asked her to back off over the years in a nice way, but that never worked. But we're still good." She thought about that morning. "We're really good."

CHAPTER 24

Jon slid into the chair across from Selena after introducing himself to Mr. Nelson's attorney, Mr. Carson. She'd asked him to sit in on the meeting with the man suing a host of wineries. One look at the lawyer's smug expression told Jon all he needed to know about the man. Only Carson would find that this time, his little scheme would be anything but easy.

"I know we all have busy schedules, so shall we get started, gentlemen?" Selena asked. She opened a folder. "I see that you're requesting a twenty-five-thousand-dollar settlement from our client Henley Estates Winery. Can you—"

"It's their responsibility to allow patrons to be able to fully access their website, and they should've done something about it," Mr. Carson said, cutting her off. "With all the laws regarding disability on the books, this should be a no-brainer, and my client paid for his inconvenience."

"How many times did Mr. Nelson try to access the site?"

"Several times, of course."

"And did he ever contact the winery about placing an order or having difficulty using the website?"

"Where is this going, Ms. Bailey? We've already forwarded all this information."

She leaned forward and clasped her hands together. "Actually, Mr. Carson, the only thing we have is a copy of the lawsuit. Neither you or your client has provided us with any other documentation, like the number of times Mr. Nelson tried to use the site or how many times he called the winery to complain and make them aware of the problem. Or whether he ever purchased wine from them."

Jon bit back a smile. He'd known hiring Selena had been a smart idea. Now he was even more grateful. Not once had she raised her voice, although Mr. Carson's continued to increase as he became more agitated.

When the man didn't reply, Selena slid some papers across the table. "These are Mr. Nelson's telephone records beginning three months before the lawsuit was filed. Can you please point out which of those calls were made to Henley? Here's the phone number and a highlighter to help you." She placed both items in front of him, sat back, and shared a look with Jon.

Jon knew he wouldn't find the number, because the man had never called.

"I also have information from Mr. Nelson's computer detailing his internet searches during the same time." She handed him another stack of papers.

Mr. Carson's light brown face blanched. "You have no right to—"

"Let's cut the bull, Mr. Carson," Jon said. He'd had enough. "We both know that your client never called the winery or made an attempt to purchase anything off the website. In fact, the only mention of Henley Estates was in the search engine. So, no, we won't be settling, and we'll see you in court."

Shock and anger lined the man's features.

Selena stood, and Jon followed suit. She said, "We'll let you know when we have a court date." She pressed a button on the phone sitting on the table. "Gail, can you please show Mr. Carson out?"

Within a few seconds, the administrative assistant appeared in the doorway with a smile on her face. "Mr. Carson, if you'll follow me, please."

He threw a hostile glare their way and brushed past the assistant.

Once the door was closed again, Jon said, "Nice job. I think he underestimated you."

She shrugged. "He did, and I don't think he's going to want to continue down this road. My hope is that he'll convince his client to drop this one, as well as the others."

"I agree. Once the other wineries find out, they'll probably adopt our stance." He checked his watch. "Keep me posted. I need to head out."

"Oh, yeah, the other frivolous lawsuit." Selena rolled her eyes and chuckled. "Not that you'll need it, but good luck, boss."

"Thanks. I hope you're right." Jon hoped the judge agreed that the lawsuit was indeed ridiculous. He had to hand it to the mayor. The man had followed up every phone conversation with an email to confirm, leaving a nice paper trail. He went back to his desk to retrieve the folder containing the documents and stuck it, along with his laptop, into his bag. Normally, Jon would return to the office after the court hearing, although it would most likely be near closing time. However, today, he planned to go home to his wife. His partner could handle anything that came up.

On the way out, he stopped to talk to his assistant for a moment, then drove over to the courthouse. With the mayor's office being housed in the same building, he headed that way first, since they still had a good half hour before facing the judge. As soon as he stepped off the elevator on the third floor and turned the corner leading down the hallway to the town's administrative offices, he saw the mayor.

"Oh, good. You're here," Mayor Brewer said, extending his hand.

Jon shook his hand. "How are you, Mayor Brewer?"

"Ready to get this farce over with. They figured since we're a small town, we must be stupid. The only one not operating in good faith is Whitman Land Developers." He shook his head and wore an expression of disgust.

"Hopefully, the judge will see it the same way. Do you have any questions before we head over?"

"No. I know I said it before, but I appreciate you stepping in to handle this."

"I'm glad to do it." This town had become his home, his wife's peace, and, lately, his own. Jon had no problem doing whatever it took to keep this small slice of paradise exactly that. The two men headed back to the elevator and took it to the ground level.

"I was hoping not to see Whitman and his crew until we

got inside," the mayor muttered. "I'm not in the mood for his lawyer's foolishness today." The land developers and their attorney stood in front of the courtroom doors.

He'd spoken with Avery Dobson twice and agreed with the mayor's assessment. Jon found the man to be a blowhard with an inflated ego.

"Ah, Mayor Brewer, Mr. Rhodes. I'm looking forward to adding another win to my extensive list," Avery said with a smug smile.

Jon barely stifled a snort. Dobson was a piece of work. "With all due respect, Mr. Dobson, that'll be up to the judge. If you'll excuse us, my client and I will see you gentlemen inside." He shifted his gaze to the mayor and held the door open. "After you, Mayor."

Once inside, they took their seats at the front of the room, which was almost filled to capacity. With it being close to three, he hadn't expected a large turnout. Then again, he'd found out early on that the residents of Firefly Lake were a tight-knit community and turned out for anything that affected the town. He leaned over to ask the mayor a question but went still when, in his peripheral vision, he spotted Terri. She gave him a bright smile, blew him a kiss, and mouthed, "You've got this." Jon returned her smile, his heart full. Her support meant everything to him. Before he could say anything, the bailiff entered and called the court to order.

Judge Collins sat and said, "Be seated." He sifted through the stack of papers in front of him. "Okay, it's already after three and we don't want to be here all day, so let's get started. So, Whitman Land Developers, you're suing Firefly Lake for breach of a good faith agreement?"

Mr. Dobson jumped to his feet. He took a moment to look around the court, his chest puffed out. "Yes, Your Honor." He paced for a few seconds. "They backed out of a very lucrative deal that has impacted my client's construction company and caused financial harm to his employees. We feel restitution should—"

"I've read the documents, Mr. Dobson," the judge said, cutting him off. "One more thing. Your reputation precedes you. I know you have a flair for the dramatic, but I won't put up with those shenanigans in my courtroom. Do I make myself clear?"

The attorney looked as if he wanted to challenge the judge but thought better about it. "Yes, Your Honor."

"Good."

"As I was saying, we feel that restitution should be made in light of the fact that Mayor Brewer did not follow through on his promises. I have an email communication from the mayor stating that he couldn't wait to work with my client." He held up a piece of paper.

The judge nodded to the bailiff. The young man retrieved the sheet of paper from the attorney and handed it to the judge, who briefly scanned it. He shifted his gaze to Jon. "Mr. Rhodes."

Jon came to his feet. "Your Honor, Mayor Brewer never made any promises on a deal for more than six hundred units. The agreement was for no more than forty, which the entire email chain that Mr. Dobson is referring to shows." He handed the stack to the bailiff, and as Judge Collins read through them, Jon detailed how the land development company initially agreed to the request for the small number of units as well as using Firefly Lake's local construction company employees first, and then hiring as needed to supplement. "Those are the emails leading up to the one that Mr. Dobson entered. However, when the contract arrived, it was for a six-hundred-unit property, and it stipulated that they would have full control over hiring and bring in their own people. The mayor declined the offer, as it was not the original agreement. Their claim lacks any arguable legal basis, and we're asking for this case to be dismissed and that they be responsible for all fees incurred."

"Objection!" Mr. Dobson shouted.

"Overruled. Mr. Dobson, are you saying that your client didn't change the terms of the original agreement?"

"My client was looking out for the town. The larger condominium complex would bring in more residents and, in turn, more revenue."

The judge held up his hand. "Mr. Dobson, I've heard enough." He held up the stack of papers. "Do you deny that your client agreed to build forty units and use local construction workers?"

"Your Honor, we—"

"Yes or no."

"Well," he hedged. "No, but—"

"So the town didn't actually back out of the deal. You don't have a case, Mr. Dobson. This case is dismissed, and your client is ordered to pay all legal fees." He banged his gavel. "Court is adjourned."

The crowd erupted in cheers, and the mayor pumped Jon's hand so hard, Jon thought it might fall off.

"Excellent work, Jon."

"Thanks. I wish all my cases were this easy." He packed up and headed for the exit. It took a while because many of the townspeople stopped him to offer congratulations. When he finally made it to the hallway, his wife was there, leaning against the wall.

Terri rushed over, hugged him, and brushed a kiss across his lips. "You were so wonderful, baby. I bet they won't try to get over on this small town again."

He chuckled. "I hope not."

"Good job, my brother," Antonio said, joining them.

"Thanks."

He leaned down and kissed Terri's cheek. "Hey, Terri."

"How's it going, Antonio?"

"Busy, as usual. I'm headed back to the office, so I'll catch you two later. Oh, if the weather holds, we're shooting around on the basketball court Sunday."

"Count me in."

Antonio nodded and disappeared in the crowd.

Jon turned back to Terri. He grasped her hand, and they exited the building. "I didn't expect to see you."

"I wanted to surprise you. I haven't had a chance to see you in action since we left LA, and I figured with me having time off, it was a good time to come." They stopped at her car, which was parked in the lot. "I think we should celebrate your win. I'm taking you out to dinner, then later, we can have our own private celebration." She winked.

"I like those plans, especially the private ones for later."

"I anticipated you winning and made reservations at By the Lake for six thirty."

He grinned and pulled her closer. "That gives us a good

two hours to get this party started. I'll meet you at home in fifteen minutes."

Terri frowned. "Don't you have to go back to the office?"

"Nope. I'm all yours tonight."

She got into the car and started the engine. "Then let's make it ten minutes."

Laughing, he said, "You're on." They might not make those reservations, after all. *Life is good.*

CHAPTER 25

Terri fastened the buckle on her boot, then stood. "Jon, are you almost ready?" They were headed to hang out with the supper club for New Year's Eve.

"Give me five minutes," he said from the bathroom.

She crossed the room and leaned in the doorway, watching as he pulled on a sweater. The past month had been the best in their marriage since moving to Firefly Lake, and she couldn't be more pleased with the amazing changes in their relationship. She hoped it would be even better in the new year.

Jon paused and stared at her. "You okay?"

"Yep. Just thinking about us and how far we've come in the last few weeks."

"We've made a lot of progress. *I've* made a lot of progress, and I agree that we're better than we were before." He came to where she stood and brushed a kiss over her lips. "And my hope and prayer is that we grow even closer in the upcoming year."

Terri looped her arms around his neck. "It's mine, too." He had made a lot of positive steps, and she would be forever grateful that he'd continued to open up to her. She felt that they'd finally reached a place where they could weather any storm life threw their way.

"We'd better get going. We don't want to be late."

"Mm-hmm. More like you don't want to be late for anything Serenity, Gabe, and Antonio are cooking." The three had decided to share the cooking duties.

Jon laughed. "Hey, you can't blame me." He helped her with her coat, then put on his own. "Is DeAngelo going to be there? The man has it bad for Dana."

"He does, and I love seeing it." Dana had all but given up on finding someone who didn't mind that she got her hands dirty for a living, but DeAngelo seemed to be just the man her friend needed. And if all the impromptu flights he'd taken in the past month were any indication, she suspected it wouldn't be long before their small town gained another resident. "Dana said he planned to be here and stay for a few days." He led her out to the car and helped her in before sliding into the driver's seat and getting them underway.

"He's racking up a lot of frequent flier miles. Gabe, Antonio, and I were thinking he should just go ahead and relocate."

She smiled. "I was just thinking the same. Maybe he could open a boutique hotel here or nearby."

"This hasn't hit the rumor mill yet, but I think the owners of the inn are thinking about retiring. Apparently, the last time DeAngelo was here, he got into a conversation with Mr. Copeland, and the topic of DeAngelo's job came up. The discussion took off from there. He doesn't want to say anything until the details are hammered out."

Terri whipped her head in his direction. "Are you serious? That would be so cool. I'll keep it to myself until Dana says something." She sent up a silent prayer that things would work out for her friend. When they arrived at Antonio and Tasha's place, Jon parked behind Gabriel's car and rushed to the door as the heavens opened up.

"Oh, my goodness. Come on in, you two," Natasha said, waving them inside. "I can't believe how that sky went from a few clouds to a downpour in seconds."

"Girl, me either," Terri said, removing her nearly soaked coat. Thank goodness it had a hood, or she'd probably look like a drowned rat.

Natasha took the coats to the mudroom, so they wouldn't drip all over the floors. "Dana and DeAngelo should be here any minute, then we can start dinner," she said as they made their way to the kitchen. "In the meantime, there are some appetizers, courtesy of Serenity and Gabriel, as well as wine and hot cider."

Serenity hopped off the stool where she'd been sitting. "Hey, y'all. I'm so ready for a grown folks night without interruption. Thank goodness for great-grandmas!"

They all laughed, and several rounds of greetings ensued. Rubbing her arms to warm up, Terri said, "I think I'm going to have the cider for now, so I can warm up, and save the good stuff for later." She and Jon washed their hands in the half bath off the kitchen, then filled their plates with the spinach dip, bruschetta, cheese, meat, crackers, and chicken and cheese empanadas.

Jon waved a hand over the spread lining the bar. "With all this, I don't know if I'm going to have room for dinner."

Antonio clapped Jon on the shoulder. "You don't want to miss out on this meal, my brother, because it's gonna be better than good. We decided on a little elegance for tonight."

"Oh, I can make room for that."

Gabriel and Jon did a fist bump, and Gabriel said, "Same, man."

A few minutes later, Dana and DeAngelo arrived. After another round of greetings, Antonio and Natasha cleared the appetizers and replaced them with broiled lobster with drawn butter, filet mignon topped with shrimp, roasted potatoes, and sautéed green beans.

Terri shook her head. "Okay, am I the only one here who's thinking that we should just hire Antonio instead of going to By the Lake?"

A chorus of laughter and agreement sounded as everyone filled their plates and took them to the formal dining room that had been set as if the friends were dining in a five-star restaurant. Natasha and Antonio had pulled out the fine china, crystal glasses, and linen napkins, and two small bouquets of red roses surrounded by greenery were placed in the center at each end of the table.

"Tasha, you outdid yourself," Terri said as Jon seated her.

"Thanks. I thought this would be the perfect way to end the year. It may have started out rocky, but it turned out to be a good one."

Terri knew her friend was thinking about all the fireworks between her and Antonio before they got back together. But she wholeheartedly agreed. For her, the year had ended far better than she could have imagined—her marriage was back on track, and she would be starting a new and less stressful job soon. She shared a look with Jon, and he kissed her temple. Yeah, things were really good. Over the fabulous meal, the friends laughed and talked about everything from their jobs and families to the new memory care center and the off-and-on rainy weather.

As they were finishing, Dana said, "I have something for each couple." She and her date left the dining room, then came back with gift bags. "Since y'all enjoyed the Irish cream and coffee liqueur so much, I made some for everybody."

Before she got the words out, a loud roar went up from the men. Gabriel reached for the first bag. "I'm definitely going to be starting the new year off right."

"Amen, brother. Amen!" Jon said, claiming a bag.

Grinning, Antonio said, "This will be the perfect nightcap."

Natasha folded her arms. "You know I love you, Dana, but right now I can't stand you."

Dana laughed and shrugged. "I'll make you and Serenity some next year."

"In the meantime, I'll enjoy this for both of you," Terri said, plucking the bag out of Jon's hands.

"Same, girl," Dana said.

"So much for sisterhood," Serenity grumbled. Everyone burst out laughing.

Minutes later, the group left the table and went to the family room to finish their drinks and conversation. After the food settled, Serenity laid out desserts, which included her grandmother's prized pound cake, peach cobbler with homemade vanilla ice cream, and her boozy berries.

"I'm just going to take this entire plate of berries, and you all can have the rest of the desserts," Dana said. "I know these are your favorite, Tasha, but you'll have to wait to get some."

Natasha frowned. "I'm going to need an entire dozen after this baby is born."

Everyone laughed.

"If anybody wants those strawberries, you'd better get them before Dana," Terri said and she reached for one.

DeAngelo added some of everything to his plate, starting with the dipped strawberries. He bit into one and groaned. "What's in these? They're amazing."

Serenity smiled. "The one on your plate was infused with whiskey." She pointed to second serving dish. "These have been infused with champagne."

"I wouldn't mind paying you for a weekly order of these. My hotel guests would love them."

"As much as I'd love to, no way would I be able to fit it into my busy schedule."

"And I can't have you interfering with our supper club stash," Dana said, snagging another berry from the plate.

He held his hands up in surrender. "Since I'm a newcomer to these gatherings, I don't want to get myself uninvited, so I'll just take these and keep my mouth shut." He added two more to his plate and, with one finger lifted, tiptoed over to the other side of the room.

Everyone erupted in laughter. They took the desserts back into the family room and sat around eating and talking. Terri moved closer to Dana. "I really like DeAngelo. He fits right in with this group, and it sounds like he plans to be around for a long time."

Dana glanced over at him briefly. "We'll see. I really like him, too. He's the first man who accepts me as I am and has no problems with me being a mechanic."

"The fact that he's been here twice in the last two weeks tells me he's pretty serious. Oh, and don't think I haven't noticed that he can't keep his eyes off you, and you can't stop looking at him, either. You two have fallen fast and *hard*." She playfully bumped Dana's shoulder. "Are you blushing?" she teased.

"Oh, hush." Dana rolled her eyes and tried to hide her smile.

"What are y'all talking about?" Serenity asked as she and Natasha joined them.

"About all the heat Dana and DeAngelo are generating," Terri said.

Natasha fanned herself. "Honey, you noticed it, too? I can just turn the thermostat down while you two are here."

Serenity chuckled. "Girl, we are so happy for you. I think he's a keeper."

Dana shrugged. "He's been great so far. We've only been dating a couple of months, so we'll see." She paused. "Do you think it's crazy that I've fallen for him so fast? I mean, it's been so long since I've actually dated someone, I feel a little out of my element."

"And? Sometimes, it doesn't take long to know if someone is the right one," Serenity said, pointing her spoon Dana's way.

Terri nodded. "Amen to that. You know about my whirlwind love story." She shifted her gaze to Jon, watching as he laughed with the guys. "And I wouldn't change one thing."

Even with everything they'd been through, she would do it all again.

"He's kind and generous to a fault, and he makes me feel as if I'm the most important person in his life."

Natasha gave Dana's shoulders a gentle squeeze. "Sis, that's the way a *real* man should make you feel. This is a good thing."

"Okay, everybody. Gather around." Antonio's voice rang out in the room.

"Do you know what he's going to do?" Serenity asked Natasha.

"Yep." She grinned and made her way to Antonio's side.

"We have about ten minutes before the new year. Tasha and I thought it would be a great time for us as couples to spend a couple of minutes sharing with each other your hopes and dreams for the upcoming year. So, my brothas, claim your woman and let her know what you're looking forward to with her in the new year. Ladies, you do the same. Then, when the clock counts down, we'll lift our glasses in affirmation of those dreams." The men nodded and did just that.

Jon came and slid his arm around Terri's waist. They moved to a quiet corner, as did the other couples, and for a moment, he just stared at her.

"What's wrong?" Terri asked.

"Nothing. I'm just counting my blessings. These past couple of years have been hell on our marriage, and I know a big part of that is on me."

She placed a finger on his lips, then came up on tiptoe and

kissed him. "All water under the bridge." She'd already forgiven him, but she wanted him to feel it tonight.

"I love you, Terri. This year I want us to continue to talk openly, spend more time together, and grow even closer."

"I want those same things, Jon. I want us to be intentional about our time, even if it means making a schedule, because I know there will be times when our jobs will require more hours."

"I *will* be more intentional when it comes to us. I want date nights every week, whether we go out or cuddle up at home, and at least once a month, a date weekend."

Tears filled her eyes as her emotions surged. Those were the things that had kept them close at the beginning of their relationship and everything she had hoped to reclaim. "I'm looking forward to it all."

Jon gently wiped away the tear that escaped down her cheek. "So am I, baby." He bent and placed a soft kiss on her lips.

"Okay, people, we've got about two minutes before the ball drops," Natasha said as she passed around champagne flutes.

Antonio followed with bottles of champagne and sparkling apple cider and filled everyone's glasses. He turned on the TV just as the countdown started. Everyone joined in and counted down from ten. "Happy New Year!" they all shouted.

"Happy New Year, sweetheart," Jon said.

Terri cupped his face. "Happy New Year, my love." The kiss that followed was one of healing and promise.

After the rounds of hugs and good wishes, DeAngelo said, "This is the best New Year's celebration I've had in years. I want to thank you all for including me in your supper club. I can't think of a better way to end the year." He handed his glass to Gabriel, then grasped Dana's hand. "But I do know the best way to start it." He dropped to one knee.

"Have mercy," Dana whispered.

"Dana, from the moment I laid eyes on you, I felt something different. I sat mesmerized as you played the piano—the passion hit me here." He pointed to his heart. "And when you fixed my car in your beautiful gown, then smiled at me, I *knew* you were my one. The one I'd been waiting for. When I look into your eyes, I see a reflection of the two of us and the life I hope we'll share. I want to spend the rest of my life loving you, cherishing you. Will you marry me?"

"DeAngelo," she said as tears ran unchecked down her face. "Yes. Yes, I'll marry you." He slid the ring on her finger, and a loud cheer went up.

Terri, who was standing closest to Dana, hugged her. "I'm so happy for you, girl. Like I told you, sometimes it doesn't take long."

After all the congratulations and another toast to the newly engaged couple, everyone said their goodbyes. Thankfully, the rain had stopped.

"Oh, my goodness. I'm so happy for Dana," Terri said as she and Jon entered their home. She went into the family room and dropped down onto the sofa.

"So am I. DeAngelo is good people. I guess that means he'll definitely be relocating."

"For real," she said with a laugh. "Now, that was a great way to start the year."

"I agree, but I can think of a better way for us to bring it in." He whipped his sweater over his head, tossed it aside, and kicked off his shoes.

Terri's breathing increased as she watched her husband strip. She loved every inch of his sexy body.

Jon crossed the room, stood in front of her, and extended his hand. He gently pulled her to her feet and slowly, erotically undressed her. "Let me show you another one of my dreams for this year."

"Show me." *This is going to be our best year yet.*

CHAPTER 26

Sunday afternoon, Jon parked in front of Gabriel's guesthouse, headed up the walkway, and rang the bell. He couldn't help but recall the last time he visited this place, a time when he didn't know if his marriage would survive. The painful memories rose, and he bowed his head. He'd come so close to losing the only woman who'd ever had his heart, and he planned to make damn sure it never happened again.

"Hey, man. You okay?"

His head came up and met Gabriel's concerned expression.

"Yeah, I'm good. Just thinking about the last time I was here."

Gabriel nodded in understanding. "Come on in. DeAngelo's here, and Antonio is on his way."

Jon followed him inside. With the weather still threatening rain, their usual meetup at the high school to play basketball or one of the parks to run had turned into an indoor affair. "Smells good in here."

"Next time, you can cook."

"Nah, man. I've got my one meal and I'm good," he said with a laugh.

Gabriel smiled and clapped him on the shoulder. "I told you, Antonio and I are going to have you preparing meals like a gourmet chef."

"So you say." However, his aversion to cooking had lessened tremendously due to being in the kitchen with his wife. And he finally understood what Gabe and Antonio meant about the intimacy they experience with their wives. "Hey, DeAngelo."

"What's up, Jon?" DeAngelo stood and pulled Jon into a one-arm hug.

"I guess you're really going to be a member of the couples supper club."

"These gatherings are the icing on the cake, but nothing tops having Dana in my life." He shook his head. "I fell for her so fast, I *still* don't know what happened."

Jon and Gabriel laughed and nodded. Jon said, "Man, I've been there." The doorbell rang. Gabriel went to answer and came back with Antonio.

"Let the first men's supper club party begin!" Antonio said, unloading a box that held several covered containers onto a six-foot table set up on the other side of the living room. A loud roar went up.

"DeAngelo was just telling us how fast he fell for Dana," Gabriel said. "I think we all had the same experience. Of course, I fought like hell *not* to fall for my sexy neighbor."

DeAngelo swung his head in Gabriel's direction. "What? Why would you fight falling for a woman like Serenity? She's beautiful and smart, and she can cook better than just about everybody I know, including my mama."

He waved a hand. "I was only supposed to stay here for a few months, then convince my grandmother to move back to Atlanta with me. She shut me down cold," he added with a chuckle. "It didn't help that Serenity and I didn't start off on the right foot." Gabriel shook his head as if remembering. "She overheard me talking to one of my buddies, and I'd told him that so far I hadn't seen anything *serene* about her. The next thing I knew, a container hit me upside my head, and Serenity was standing there, mad as hell."

DeAngelo burst out laughing. "Sweet Serenity? I can't believe it," he said, trying to catch his breath.

"Believe it. Her aim was dead on. She should've been a starting pitcher with some pro ball team. I opened that container and found the best brownies I've ever eaten. I apologized and was prepared to beg if I had to to get more."

"Yeah, Tasha mentioned you always eating all the brownies," Antonio said. "I'm the only one who grew up here, and Tasha was my high school sweetheart. She broke it off our first year of college, and I was mad at her for more than a decade. I moved back home at the beginning of last year and thought I was over her."

"With how fast y'all got back together and down the aisle, obviously, you were lying to yourself," Jon said.

"Ain't nobody asked you, Jon."

Jon let out a short bark of laughter. He thoroughly enjoyed his friendship with these guys, and DeAngelo fit right in. They spent the afternoon eating barbecue pulled pork sandwiches with sides of baked beans, potato salad, corn on the cob, and rolls. Dana had made more of her liqueurs, and they enjoyed them, as well.

"So, DeAngelo, are you ready for small-town living?" Jon asked later as the men sat around talking.

"It'll take some time to get used to it, but I think I can handle it. Didn't you move from LA, too? That had to be a huge change, especially after being an attorney in a large firm."

"Oh, it was definitely a change, but I still work for the same firm. That promotion to partner made the transition much easier." While he'd shared some of it with Antonio and Gabriel, he didn't know DeAngelo well enough yet to spill his personal business and decided not to share the other reason he and Terri decided to relocate.

"And so will adding another boutique hotel to the Murray brand," DeAngelo said, lifting his glass in a mock toast.

Gabriel set a plate of brownies on the coffee table between them. "Are you planning to make any changes? I think right now there's only what... seven or eight rooms?"

"Eight. I was thinking about adding a few more, so I need to get on your schedule, Antonio, to see what we can do. I like the charm of the town, and I think trying to make something larger would be counterproductive."

Antonio reached for a brownie. "Finally, somebody who understands. We just went through an issue with a real estate development company wanting to build a six-hundred-unit, multi-building condo project when we asked for no more than forty." He shook his head. "But Jon handled that without breaking a sweat."

Jon chuckled. "Glad I could help."

"Just give me a call when you're ready to talk," Antonio said, continuing his conversation with DeAngelo. "Any idea when you'll be moving here permanently, and did you and Dana set a date yet?"

"My goal is to be here by the end of March, and we haven't had a chance to talk about it too much with making all the calls to our families. I know I don't want to wait an entire year, though."

"None of us had a long engagement," Gabriel said. "Mine was the longest, and it was only five months."

"Two months for me and Tasha."

They all looked at Jon. He said, "I met, proposed to, and married Terri in three months."

"That's what I'm talkin' about!" DeAngelo said. "Although, the way our mothers were going on and on about all the things that needed to happen from announcements and engagement parties—yeah, that's *plural*—to bridal showers and formal dinners, they'll need two years of planning. I'm two seconds from asking Dana if she just wants to elope and have a reception later."

"My only advice is to do what you two want to do," Jon said. "My mother was probably worse with the list of everything she wanted us to do. In the end, I told her it was our wedding and she needed to get with *our* program." She hadn't been happy and didn't speak to him for a good week, thinking the guilt trip would make him change his mind. It didn't, and she eventually realized neither he nor Terri was going to budge on their positions.

DeAngelo reached over and tapped his fist against Jon's.

"Thanks for the advice. Six months is going to be my limit, and that's pushing it."

They discussed their weddings for a few minutes longer, then Jon asked the question that had been on his mind. "Antonio, I wanted to ask how you and Natasha came up with the idea to do the New Year's goals thing."

"We all have careers that require a lot of our time, families, babies being born, and I figured it would be a good way to be more intentional in our relationships. Sort of recommitting to the most important person in our lives."

He nodded. *Recommitment. Maybe that's what I need to do with Terri. Something like a recommitment ceremony.* The more he mulled it over in his mind, the more Jon warmed up to the idea.

"Uh-oh," Gabriel said with a smile. "Jon, I can see that lawyer brain at work. What are you thinking?"

Chuckling, he said, "I was just thinking that with everything Terri and I have been through in the last couple of years, I might want to do something like a recommitment ceremony." He held up a hand. "Nothing big. Just a little something with the supper club couples." The last thing he wanted was to get into another clash with his mother. So far, she'd kept to her word about not interfering in their relationship, but he didn't plan to give her any ammunition. No, this would be something private.

"Valentine's Day is right around the corner and would give us plenty of time to plan something," Gabriel said, his head angled thoughtfully. "Do you want this to be a surprise or not?"

"I'd like to surprise her. You think your wives would be willing to help?"

Antonio laughed. "Man, you know they'll be all in. Terri's not going to know what hit her."

He pulled out his phone and brought up the calendar. "Valentine's Day is on a Friday this year. We could do something Saturday evening."

"Dana and I aren't married yet, but just let me know the time and place, and I'll be here. We do a lot of weddings and commitment ceremonies at our hotels, so if you need anything, I've got you," DeAngelo said.

Jon regarded the men he now considered more than friends. They'd developed a brotherly bond he wouldn't trade for anything. "I appreciate y'all." And he couldn't wait to see his wife's surprised face.

* * *

"Girl, you've been holding out on us," Terri said to Dana. While the guys were next door, the women had gathered at Serenity and Gabe's primary home for an impromptu supper club to congratulate Dana on her engagement.

"I don't know what you mean. Didn't you see my face? I had no idea he was going to propose. He only said last week that he was falling in love with me. My head is still spinning."

"But are you happy?" Serenity asked as she rocked Giana.

"Yes. But—"

"No buts," Natasha chimed in. "You and I have been friends for as long as we could talk, and you complained about guys having a problem with you doing one thing or another. Now, DeAngelo is here and loves everything about you. Let him love you like you deserve to be loved."

Dana laughed. "I am. I accepted his proposal, didn't I?"

"So when's the big day? Whenever it is, it better not be around the time this baby is due in July."

"We haven't gotten around to discussing it, and don't worry. We called our families, and my phone has been blowing up with calls and texts from every aunt, uncle, cousin, first cousin, second cousin once removed...*everybody*. I've been here for twenty minutes and have gotten eight text messages since then. I don't even want to get started on my mother. I knew she'd be happy, but my head was hurting by the time I got done talking to her."

"Oh, come on. She couldn't have been that bad," Terri said, trying not to laugh at the frustrated look on Dana's face.

Dana skewered Terri with a look. "She'd have to climb several notches to be *not that bad*. She was talking about finding venues from Napa to San Francisco, and every place in between, all these crazy engagement parties I need to have, searching for wedding gowns. One of my aunts called and was going on and on about making sure I have addresses of family across the country and telling me I should have my wedding someplace other than Firefly Lake because there isn't enough room for everybody. I haven't talked to most of those folks in years. They only show up to weddings and funerals, eat up everything, then leave. *Ugh!*" She shook her head. "Maybe we should just elope," Dana muttered.

Terri shrugged. "Or do something small. Whatever you decide, let it be what you and DeAngelo want. No one else."

"Exactly," Serenity said, laying the baby in the bassinet. "Girl, don't let those people try to bully you into doing something you don't want to do. What do *you* want for your wedding?"

She sat back and sighed. "I really want something small and intimate. Maybe a sunset wedding on the lake." She waved a hand. "Y'all know I'm not one for a lot of hoopla."

Terri brought her hands to her chest. "That sounds absolutely beautiful, Dana. If that's what you want, we'll do whatever it takes to help you make it happen."

"You're probably looking at some time in mid to late June then," Natasha said. "The weather won't be as cool in the evening. But with the way this weather has been lately, you might be okay to have it in May."

They all agreed. Last year, May had been unseasonably warm and had several days of ninety-degree temperatures.

"I'm all for May, if it's warm enough. I'll talk to DeAngelo about it tonight. He'll only be here for a couple more days before heading back to LA."

"But he'll be back real soon, I'm betting," Serenity said with a huge grin. "And with a moving truck behind him."

Terri and Natasha screamed with excitement, then hurried and covered their mouths. Both had forgotten about the baby sleeping. However, Giana didn't even flinch and kept right on sleeping. Terri said, "I wish I could sleep that soundly."

Chuckling, Serenity said, "Girl, same. When she's out, she's *out*. Anyway, Dana, you let us know what you want us to do."

"And if you two decide to elope, we'll be there for that, too," Natasha said.

"That's why I love y'all. I know neither of us wants a long engagement, so that elopement is looking better and better. Of course, my mother would probably have a heart attack if we did. Anyway, enough about me. Terri, it looks like I'm not the only one who was heating up the house New Year's Eve. You and Jon were over there stealing kisses and whispering all night. Jon looked like he couldn't wait to get you home and have a private celebration."

Terri grinned, recalling every sensual moment. "And what a private celebration it was." She fell back against the sofa and fanned herself. The women laughed. "I know I wasn't the only one, though."

Natasha raised a hand. "Guilty."

"Hey, I've got to make up for lost time. I was on lockdown for over two months," Serenity said.

They all looked at Dana, who confessed with a sly smile, "What? We had to celebrate our engagement." The women broke out in a fit of laughter.

"Well, isn't there a saying that whatever you were doing at midnight—in our case, shortly after—you'll be doing all year long?" Serenity asked.

"If so, it's gonna be a *good* year and a whole lot of nights of passion," Natasha said, wiggling her eyebrows.

Terri waved her hand in the air. "Amen, sister. *Amen!*" She hoped this would be her and Jon's best year yet.

CHAPTER 27

Terri stood off to the side talking with Jon, Natasha, and Antonio as streams of people rushed inside the new Harmony Cove Assisted Living Center after the ribbon-cutting ceremony. Serenity and Gabriel had gone inside for a quick tour, then left to take the baby home. "The mayor was pretty excited, wasn't he?"

"Announcing that the entire cost had been covered through donations would make me dance, too," Natasha said with a laugh. "He had a hard time keeping the names of the donors anonymous. And just like when they broke ground for the condo project, I thought he was going to crown Antonio king of the town. *Again.*"

Antonio gave his wife a sidelong glance. "I don't think so."

"She has a point," Terri said. "I seem to recall him going on and on about being proud of one of the town's own taking on the project. Sort of like last time with the condo project." What was supposed to be a short affair had turned into one that lasted much longer because the mayor couldn't stop singing Antonio's praises.

"Again, it wasn't all that."

Jon laughed. "I don't know, bro. It did seem like he was ready to hoist you on his shoulders and chant your name in the streets."

"Kind of like he was ready to do with you after you sent those real estate developers packing," Antonio shot back.

They all laughed and Terri threaded her arm through Jon's. "Okay, let's just say you two are amazing at what you do and deserve to be celebrated."

"I agree," Natasha said, sliding her arm around Antonio's waist. "It looks like the crowd is starting to thin out. I can't wait to see your office, Terri."

"I can't wait for you to see it, either. I'm counting on you to use your design expertise to make my office the most coveted one in the building."

She rubbed her hands together. "Girl, you know I got you. I can't wait to get started. What?" she added when both Antonio and Jon shook their heads.

"Baby, you *know* you get a little out of control when it comes to interior design," Antonio said with a chuckle.

Jon raised his hands in mock surrender. "I'm staying out of this. The only thing I plan to do is check out my baby's office, then head back to mine."

"In that case, let's go," Terri said. They made their way through the few stragglers who remained in the lobby area and headed to the back, where the offices were located. She stopped at hers, opened the door, and gestured with a flourish. "This is *all* mine."

"Girlfriend, now this is an office!" Natasha made a slow circle in the empty space. "Ooh, I'm already getting some ideas."

"I knew you would. I want it to be professional but with a homey feeling." The only things currently in the room were a temporary table and two chairs. Her new desk was scheduled to arrive at the end of the week.

She nodded. "That would fit perfectly with the center's aesthetic."

Jon walked over to the window. "This is a great space, and the view ain't bad, either."

Antonio joined Jon. "I'd take a beautiful view of the grounds and distant mountains any day. Well, I need to do a little walk-through for Ced and Zo to make sure nothing was missed."

"I'll walk out with you," Jon said. He bent and placed a lingering kiss on Terri's lips. "I should be home no later than six thirty. If something comes up, I'll call."

Still in the circle of his arms, Terri stared up at him. While Jon had always been affectionate, he didn't often show it in public. Lately, however, he'd been more demonstrative wherever they happened to be, and she loved it. "Okay." He gave her one more sweet kiss, then he and Antonio left.

"Girl," Natasha started, fanning herself, "I don't think I've ever seen you two this way. You're going to burn down your office before we even get it decorated with all that heat."

She laughed. "I can't even lie and say I don't like it. I *love* it! Things are really good with us now, and I pray it stays that way." When they'd first reconciled, Terri had been reluctant to let her guard down for fear that all their progress would crumble with the least little thing. However, over the past few weeks, she'd relaxed with Jon's assurance that they would never go back to that dark place in their marriage. "Anyway, enough about that. Let me tell you what I'm thinking for the office." For the next several minutes she shared her likes and dislikes, favorite color schemes, and type of furniture.

"I think keeping to the calm blues and greens is a good idea. You have space for a loveseat, and maybe a small table with two or three chairs."

"I didn't think about the table. That's a great idea. It would work well when meeting with families." She paused as Natasha continued typing notes on her tablet. "Oh, I'd also like to have a bookshelf. Nothing too large and wide, but with at least four shelves." Along with her books, she planned to add some greenery and maybe a photo or two. She took a step, and a wave of dizziness hit her. Terri brought her hand up to her face.

"You okay?" Natasha asked, concern lining her features.

She waved her off. "Yeah, just felt a little dizzy. It's probably because all I've had today was some yogurt and a boiled egg this morning, and I've been running around ever since. I'll be fine after I eat something." She and Tyler had been going nonstop for the past couple of weeks overseeing staffing and supplies, and Terri had missed more than a few meals.

"Are you sure?"

"Yeah, girl. I'm good."

"Okay," Natasha said, although she didn't sound convinced. "When are the clients scheduled to move in? I want to get as much of the big stuff in here before they arrive."

"The beginning of next week. I think there are only five, so far."

"Mama Nora is so excited to have Papa Fred nearby."

Terri smiled. "I know. She stopped by the other day with Antonio to look around. I saw her eyeing one of the benches in the garden, and I suspect it'll be one of their favorite spots."

"That's the same thing Tonio said."

"Knock, knock." Antonio stuck his head in the partially opened door. "You about ready, Tasha?"

"Almost. We were just talking about Mama Nora and Papa Fred."

He nodded. "I'm glad he's still here to take advantage of this place."

Terri knew how much his grandparents' separation had affected Antonio. The very fact that the town now had a place like this was a testament of his love for them. "We can talk later, Tasha. I'm going to do a few more things, then call it a day." She turned, and another wave of dizziness hit her hard, making her grip the edge of the desk to steady herself.

"Terri!" Natasha and Antonio rushed to her side. "Maybe you should sit down for a minute," Natasha said.

"Yeah, maybe." She made an attempt to take the few steps to her chair, but the lightheaded feeling magnified and wouldn't let her move. Terri felt herself falling as everything went black.

* * *

"How was the grand opening of the center, aside from Mayor Brewer being long-winded again?" Gail asked when Jon got back to the office.

Laughing, Jon said, "It's a really nice place. The Hunters did a great job."

"I'll have to go check it out one day later this week. You'd think if he wanted to do the opening during the week, he'd keep the comments short." She rolled her eyes. "He talked so long, I couldn't even stay for the tour."

He dug his phone out of his pocket, opened it to the photo gallery, and handed it to her. "I took a few pictures."

"Oh, my goodness. This is gorgeous. When it was mentioned that the place would resemble a neighborhood instead of a medical facility, I figured they meant having a little garden and a couple of walking paths. But this looks like an apartment complex." She paused and enlarged one of the photos. "Wait. What is this? Did By the Lake add a new dining area?"

Jon frowned and leaned over to see the photo she referenced. Then he smiled. "No. That's the dining area for the residents. From what I understand, they wanted it to have a restaurant feel."

"Mission accomplished," she said with awe. "Antonio did an amazing job with the design, and those brothers knew what they were doing. And this little store is fabulous. My aunt has started to show some symptoms of dementia. I wonder if they'll be full to capacity when it opens next week." Gail handed the phone back. "My cousins would love to have her in a place like this."

"From what I understand, only about half of the beds are filled at the moment."

"I'll definitely be calling my cousins tonight, then. They're closer to Napa, but I'm sure making the drive won't be a problem, especially once they see the photos and get some information."

"I'll send some of these to you. Terri mentioned that the website would be up by the time it opens, but I'll ask if she has a brochure or something." Jon selected a few that he thought would give the best overview and sent them.

Gail brought her hands to her chest. "Oh, Jon, that would be great. Thanks." She handed him a small stack of messages. "I'll let you get back to it so you can leave on time today."

"I will be gone on time. I just have to meet with Brian about a few things and finish up some paperwork." He took a moment to leaf through the messages and didn't see anything pressing as he headed for his office. Everything else could wait until tomorrow. If Jon was being honest, he'd admit that even though he'd reduced his work hours some, his productivity had soared.

Fifteen minutes later, Brian knocked and came in. "I heard there was a good turnout for the opening," he said, dropping a folder and notepad on the small conference table.

Jon joined him. "It was. I guess people had no problems closing up shop for a short time." He opened his mouth to say something and the intercom buzzed. He went back to his desk. "Yes, Gail."

"Antonio Hayes is here to see you, and he says it's important."

Jon frowned. "Tell him I'll be right out." He turned back to Brian. "I'll be back in a minute."

Brian nodded.

He stepped out and closed the door. One look at Antonio's

face stopped Jon in his tracks. The hairs on the back of his neck stood up. "What's going on?"

"It's Terri. She passed out and they took her to emergency."

Jon's heart beat in alarm as stark fear gripped him. "What happened? I've got to go. Gail, I need—"

"You go, and I'll tell Brian."

He nearly sprinted to the parking lot with Antonio on his heels.

"I'm driving," Antonio said, pointing to his truck.

Instead of arguing, he just hopped in on the passenger side. Driving in his current state probably wouldn't be a good idea anyway. His hands shook, his heart still raced, and every imaginable scenario ran through his head, none of them good. "I don't understand. She was fine when I left her an hour ago," he said as Antonio sped through the streets.

"She said she was dizzy. Tasha mentioned Terri saying that she hadn't eaten anything since this morning."

"But that doesn't make sense, either. Working in ER, she always complained about missing lunch or not eating until later in her shift. She did that for *years* in LA, which is far busier than here, and never had a problem. I can't lose her, Antonio." They'd lost their little girl, and that had crushed him. If he lost Terri, he wouldn't survive.

"She seemed to be coming around when the ambulance arrived, and Tasha is with her. Just keep a good thought. She doesn't have any health problems, right?"

"No."

"Then she'll be fine."

Jon leaned his head back and closed his eyes. *She has to be fine. I can't deal with anything else.* He sat up when Antonio pulled into the hospital lot. The car had barely stopped before he was out and striding purposely through the emergency room doors and toward the receptionist desk.

"Jon."

He whipped his head around and saw Natasha hurrying toward him. She hugged him.

"I'm so glad you're here. She was awake when they got here, but she's still somewhat out of it. I came out when Tonio texted me to let me know you were here. We'll be waiting here for whatever you need."

"Thanks, Natasha." Their small circle had become more than merely friends. They were family, and he appreciated them more than he'd ever be able to express. Antonio came through the doors, and she went to greet him while Jon went to the desk.

"Mr. Rhodes, come on and I'll take you to Terri," a nurse who happened to be standing nearby said.

"Thanks," he said, grateful that she'd recognized him and he didn't have to go through the hassle of getting information. They went through double doors and past a few curtained-off beds before the woman stopped at one. She pulled back the drape, and the sight of his wife lying so still nearly dropped him to his knees. He finally got his feet to move and slowly approached her. Bending, Jon placed a soft kiss on her lips. Her eyes fluttered open and relief spread through his chest. "Hey, baby."

"Jon," she whispered, tears filling her eyes. "I don't know what's wrong. I'm scared."

Pushing down his own fear, he stroked a finger down her cheek and, keeping his voice as steady as he could, said, "I'm sure everything is going to be okay. Have they given you any reason why this might've happened?"

Terri shook her head. "They've just been running all these tests. I need to know what's wrong."

So did he, and he sent up another silent prayer that it wasn't anything serious. He took the chair next to her and held her hand, encouraging her to relax and assuring her that everything would be okay. He didn't know who he was trying to convince more—her or himself. Her eyes drifted closed, and a few moments later, her breathing became deep and even. Jon leaned back and kept stroking the back of her hand with his thumb. He didn't know how long they sat this way before the curtain lifted and Dr. Adams appeared. Jon leaped to his feet. "Dr. Adams." The movement caused Terri's eyes to open.

"Jon. Terri."

Jon moved closer to Terri, grasping her hand and bracing himself for whatever the doctor would say.

A faint smile lifted the corner of the doctor's mouth. "First, you're going to be fine, Terri. Second, congratulations. You're going to be parents."

Terri sat up abruptly, her eyes going wide. "What did you say?"

"I assume that's rhetorical," he said with a chuckle.

"We're having a baby," she whispered, falling back against the pillows.

Jon couldn't utter one word. All the emotional turmoil and fear from the last time were like a vise around his heart and lungs so tight, he could barely breathe.

Dr. Adams continued. "Sometimes, the surge in your hormones can cause the lightheadedness, dizziness, or passing out. I know about your history, but there's no reason to assume the same thing will happen again. All the tests came back fine, so you can go home. Take tomorrow off, and I'll see you on Wednesday if you're feeling better. And follow up with your ob-gyn. The nurse will be here shortly to get you discharged."

"Thanks, Tyler. I will," Terri said.

Dr. Adams turned to Jon and extended his hand. "Good to see you again, Jon."

"Thanks, Doc." He forced the words out. As soon as the doctor walked out, Terri stared up at him with tears in her eyes.

"I'm scared, Jon. What if we lose this one, too?"

It took everything inside him not to bolt. He felt the old baggage trying to surface. The fear in Terri's eyes told him she knew what he was thinking and was begging him not to go back to that place again. *You've come a long way, so don't blow it*, his inner voice reminded him. Finally, he perched on the edge of the bed and rested his forehead against hers. Pushing his own uneasiness aside, he said, "I'm afraid, too. I want to tell you not to worry, but I don't know how to do that. I am glad that you're okay. You scared the hell out of me, baby," he whispered, his voice cracking. "I don't know what I'd do if something happened to you."

Terri reached up and palmed his face. "I don't know what I'd do without you. Are you...are you...happy about the baby?" she asked almost tentatively. "We never talked about trying again."

It had been the one conversation both of them had steered clear of, and he knew it stemmed from their anxieties about the same thing happening again. "I know we haven't, and I know why. But yeah, I'm happy. Very happy." Jon laid a hand on her still-flat belly, then bent and placed a kiss there. He wanted this baby, their baby. He had to hold on to the belief that nothing would go wrong this time. Yet, on the off chance that something did happen, he knew this time they'd get through it. Together.

CHAPTER 28

"You feel okay, sweetheart?"

Terri angled her head and smiled at Jon. "I'm good." It had been three weeks since they found out about the pregnancy, and both of them continued to have bouts of anxiety, but they were coping. Together. They'd celebrated with their friends, and she, Serenity, and Natasha were excited that their babies would grow up together. The women had laughingly told Dana she needed to speed up her wedding plans so she could join the club.

He lowered himself in the lounger next to her and reached for her hand. "That was my mother calling. Again."

She chuckled. Mama Deb had called them twice a week to see if everything was going well. "At least she hasn't tried to offer any advice, so that's a positive." Her own mother had been doing a weekly check-in, as well, and they'd had a long talk about not borrowing any trouble. Terri had seen her ob-gyn, and so far, the baby was developing fine.

"She didn't offer advice, but she did ask whether we were doing anything special for Valentine's weekend. When I mentioned we were hanging out with the supper club, the first words out of her mouth were 'That's not romantic,' then she quickly said it wasn't her business." He shook his head.

"That's a big step for her, right?"

"Yeah. Are you good with us doing the group thing?"

"Of course. I love that we're going to have a quadruple date. I still can't believe that we were able to get reservations at By the Lake."

"It helps that we made them right after New Year's while everybody was still thinking about the holidays and worrying about how they were going to get rid of all that turkey and ham."

She let out a little giggle. "Your mother was wrong. I think what you guys did is very romantic." She glanced down at her watch. "I'd better get ready. Natasha will be here in a little bit." The ladies had decided to get manicures and pedicures for the evening, then get dressed at Natasha's place. Jon would pick her up, and the group would carpool over to the restaurant. She'd purchased a special dress for the occasion, and she wanted it to be a surprise for Jon. The weather had decided to cooperate, and the temperatures were forecasted to reach the low seventies for the weekend. She rose from the lounger and bent and kissed Jon. "What are you going to do today?"

"Not much. Maybe the guys should've thought about something to do."

Terri shrugged. "It's not too late to call and find out. Dinner isn't until six, and it's only two thirty now."

"Hmm. I'll see. Speaking of dinner, you're still not going to show me what you're wearing?"

"Nope," she said with a smile. "I do promise it'll be worth the wait."

Jon lifted a brow. "I hope it isn't something that'll get dinner canceled and the dress ripped off your body."

She sashayed out of the room. "We shall see."

"Tease!" he yelled after her.

"But I can back it up," Terri called back, laughing. *I love that man!*

Her smile still in place, she gathered her toiletries, makeup, and other accessories, then added them to a duffel that already held her shoes. Going to the closet, she took down the garment bag in the far corner where she'd hidden the dress and laid it across the bed. The eggplant-colored, long-sleeved, one-shoulder dress hugged every one of her curves and emphasized her now fuller breasts. It stopped at her calf, but had a slit that ended mid-thigh, which was guaranteed to grab her husband's attention and hold it tight. She had her own Valentine's plans for them after they returned home.

Terri headed to the bathroom for a quick shower, so she wouldn't have to worry about it when they got back. As she stuck her feet in her flip-flops after dressing a few minutes later, Terri realized this would probably be the last time she'd be able to wear something fitted for the next several months. Her hand went to her stomach, and she closed her eyes briefly. *Please let everything go well this time.*

She heard the doorbell and carried everything out front. Natasha and Jon were laughing when she rounded the corner. "Hey, Tasha."

"Hey, girl. Ready for a little pampering?"

"More than ready." She came up on tiptoe and kissed Jon. "I'll see you later."

"You ladies have fun."

"We will," Terri and Natasha chorused.

Dana and Serenity were waiting in the car. They greeted each other with hugs, and after placing her bags in the trunk, Terri slid into the back seat next to Serenity. As they drove off, she said, "This was such a good idea. It's been so long since I've gone to get a pedicure."

"Same. I've been doing them myself. But we deserve a little pampering every now and again," Natasha said.

Terri clapped her hands. "Amen, sistah!"

Dana wiggled her hands in the air. "Y'all know why I don't get manicures often."

Serenity chuckled. "I bet you'll be getting them now so you can run your hands all over DeAngelo's body." They screamed with laughter.

"Girl, I haven't had a man in so long, I might need some help remembering how to do it."

Terri reached up and playfully shoved Dana's shoulder. "DeAngelo will be more than happy to give you some... *instructions*. Trust me." Her statement brought on another round of laughter. The women were still laughing when they arrived at the day spa.

As the four of them settled into their luxury chairs with the warm water swirling around their feet, Serenity said, "Okay, who's with me on making this part of our supper club fun?" Three pairs of hands shot up. "I say we add this at least every other month. I know with everyone's busy schedules that timeframe might work better."

"Sounds like a plan to me," Terri said. "This year, I'm really going to start making my me time a priority."

Natasha placed a hand on Terri's arm. "We're both going to need it with these babies coming."

"Speaking of babies," Dana said, "how have you been feeling, Terri? You scared us to death."

"Tell me about it. At least you didn't see it. If Antonio hadn't been there, I probably would've completely lost it."

"Tasha, I can't tell you how grateful I am for you and Antonio. You both kept me calm. To answer your question, Dana, I'm feeling good. I still get a little tired, but having a job that doesn't require such a fast pace and no overtime has helped tremendously. Jon has been amazing. The doctor said I'm progressing well, but Jon and I still have a little fear about something going wrong. We're talking about it, though, and it's been the best thing ever." Jon had made a concerted effort to be home on time, started to do a little more cooking with her, and ensured that she built in some time to rest after she got home from work. The conversation tapered off as the manicurists came over to do their nails. Having her feet, legs, hands, and arms massaged at the same time felt so good, Terri vowed to schedule her next two or three appointments before she left.

By the time they made it home, it was almost five. Natasha parked in the driveway and Terri, Serenity, and Dana unloaded their bags from the trunk.

"We have a good half hour to get dressed before the rest of the guys get here," Natasha said unlocking the front door and leading them inside. "If you want to freshen up, feel free to use the two bathrooms."

"You two can go ahead," Terri said. "I showered right before I left."

"Then I'll show you where you can change."

She followed Natasha to the downstairs bedroom that faced the side of the house. Terri's nearest neighbor's house was only about twenty feet away, affording them a modicum of privacy, but the closest house here stood more than double that distance away. She couldn't complain because the homes in LA were built almost on top of each other.

Terri changed into her dress, applied her makeup, and bumped the ends of her shoulder-length hair with the curling iron. She took a seat on the bed to fasten the strap on her heeled sandals. Going back to the mirror, she turned one way, then the other, and smiled. *Yep. Jon isn't going to know what hit him.*

After placing her other clothes in her bag, she went out to the living room to wait. Natasha and Antonio were coming down the stairs when she entered.

Antonio let out a long whistle. "Jon is going to be in trouble tonight. You look beautiful, Terri." He kissed her cheek.

"I agree," Natasha said. "I can't wait to see his reaction."

"Thanks. You two look fabulous." Antonio wore a tailored navy suit, while Natasha had chosen a semi-fitted long-sleeved dress of the same shade with ruching in the midsection that artfully disguised her baby bump. "Has anybody else arrived yet?"

"Gabriel texted and said he should be here in a minute. He dropped Giana off at Ms. Della's."

"She loves her great-granddaughter. Well, I'm going to take a seat and wait for my hubby to get here." As soon as Terri sat, she heard the doorbell. Antonio excused himself to go answer it, and came back with DeAngelo and Gabriel.

The two men looked handsome in their dark suits. She greeted them, reclaimed her seat, then checked her watch, wondering when Jon would arrive. She was eager to see him.

"Well, don't you ladies look gorgeous," DeAngelo said when Serenity and Dana joined them a moment later. He gathered Dana in his arms and placed a lingering kiss on her lips.

"While we're waiting for Jon, I wanted to show you all what we did to the backyard near the lake," Natasha said. "My hubby is so amazing." She leaned against him.

They all followed Natasha and Antonio while talking about the new deck and redone sheds. When they reached the edge of the yard, Terri stopped short upon seeing Jon standing there inside a circle of roses interspersed with flameless tea light candles, his hand extended. She glanced around at all the smiling faces. "What are you all up to?"

"Step into the circle and find out," Serenity said, giving Terri a gentle push forward.

She took tentative steps toward her husband and grasped his outstretched hand. "What is all this? Aren't we going to be late for dinner? I—"

Jon cut her off with a kiss. "Relax, sweetheart. The reservation isn't for another hour." He leaned down and whispered for her ears only, "But I can't promise we'll make it, not with the way you look in this dress." He straightened and gave her a wolfish grin.

It took Terri a moment to realize that their friends had surrounded them. "Is somebody going to tell me what's going on?"

"It's simple. Tonight, I want to recommit my love and my life to you." He took her hands in his.

"Jon," she whispered as tears filled her eyes.

"When I pledged my life to you almost five years ago, I promised to love you, honor you, comfort and keep you. These last couple of years, I haven't done a good job living up to those promises." He paused, seemingly trying to gather his emotions. "But tonight, I want to make a fresh start, to reaffirm those vows. In your heart, I found my forever home. I promise to always be thankful for the love and support you've given me, to be the best partner in this relationship today and every day. To be your rock as you've been mine, to share my innermost feelings, even when it's uncomfortable."

A sob escaped Terri. Every word touched her to her very soul.

"You are my greatest gift, and I promise never again to take our love for granted. Standing here at this moment, I'm reminded of the timeless nature of true love. I promise to continue loving you with the same passion and devotion as the day we first said 'I do.' You are my forever love, and I am yours. I promise. Forever." Jon slid a diamond band on her finger, then kissed it.

She was crying so hard, she couldn't utter one word. It took a minute for her to finally pull herself together. "Jon, you are my heart, my safe space. When I'm with you, nothing else matters. My love for you deepens with each passing day, and I am *so* grateful for your presence in my life. We may not be perfect, but our love is, and together we will become the best versions of ourselves. I will always be there for you, supporting you and loving you with my whole heart. I promise. Forever." The kiss that followed was one of love, commitment, and a promise of forever.

"Oh, my goodness. That was so beautiful," Natasha said, wiping her own tears. She hugged Terri, then Jon.

"You all knew about this?" Smiles blossomed on her friends' faces as they all nodded.

Gabriel kissed her cheek and did a fist bump with Jon. "We just carried out what Jon wanted."

Terri turned back to Jon. "I love you." She threw her arms around him and held him close. "And tonight when we get home I'm going to show you how much," she whispered to him. She stepped back and accepted hugs from everyone.

Antonio held up his phone. "I videotaped it, so I'll send it to y'all later."

"Thank you so much, Antonio." She couldn't wait to send it to her mother and Candace. "I thank all of you," she said emotionally. When they'd moved here, she only hoped to find a few friends. But they had found so much more.

Serenity tapped her wrist. "We should probably head over to the restaurant."

"Before we go, DeAngelo and I have an announcement," Dana said. She waited a few seconds. "Both our mothers are driving us crazy, and we decided to elope in April. We've already booked a spot in Napa."

"We're giving you all advance notice because you're special to my baby. Whatever she wants, I'm going to do everything in my power to make it happen," DeAngelo said. He pulled Dana closer. "We'd been talking about it, but helping put this together sealed the deal. I've sworn my brothers to secrecy, and you'll get to meet them, as well."

"Oh, and I already texted Andrea, and she said she'd be here."

Serenity rubbed her hands together and grinned. "I'll be back in the kitchen, so let me know what you want to eat. The entire supper club crew will be here." She made a show of thinking. "Ooh, I know what—"

Gabriel just shook his head and gently took Serenity's hand. "Come on and let's go before you get started with menu planning and who knows what else."

Terri hooked her arm in Jon's as everyone made their way to the front of the house. "This was so amazing. And your words... I can't even describe how deeply they touched me. And you planned this whole thing." She stared at the diamond band on her finger. "This ring is absolutely beautiful. I can't stop looking at it."

"It doesn't hold a candle to you, baby. And I meant every word I said. You are my everything."

"And you are mine." *Forever.*

"By the way, I love the dress, but I gotta be honest. I'm not sure how long I'm going to last before I try to find a dark corner and take it off you. No promises on me being gentle about it, either. So be warned." Jon helped her into the car.

"We are going to dinner, right?"

"Maybe we are, maybe we aren't." Shrugging, a wicked grin curved his lips as he closed the door.

Heat thrummed through her body, and Terri seriously considered sending a text to cancel.

CHAPTER 29

Jon entered Harmony Cove center on a Friday afternoon and headed for the receptionist to ask her to let Terri know he'd arrived. She had her monthly appointment with the ob-gyn, and they would be making sure the baby's heart was still beating normally. He was admittedly nervous because Terri was almost at the same point in her pregnancy as last time.

"Jon. What a pleasant surprise."

He whirled around and saw Mama Nora approaching. "Hi, Mama Nora." She reached up and hugged him, holding on a little longer, as if she knew he needed the strength. "You here to see Papa Fred?"

Mama Nora's eyes lit up. "You'd better believe it. I've been coming every day since he moved in two months ago. Are you here to take your beautiful wife to lunch?"

"No. She has a doctor's appointment."

The receptionist waved to get Jon's attention, then said, "Terri said she'll be out in five minutes."

"Thanks."

Mama Nora hooked her arm in his. "While you're waiting, come sit with me and tell me what has you so concerned."

How in the world does this woman read me so well? His own mother had never been able to tap into his psyche this way. She led him outside to one of the benches placed along the walking path, sat, and patted the space next to her.

"Are you worried about the baby?"

Jon hesitated. She laid her hand on his and gave it a gentle squeeze of encouragement. Before he knew it, he found himself blurting out the details of the previous loss, the anguish he and Terri had felt, and their fear that it would happen again. There had to be some kind of truth serum in her comforting touch because he couldn't stop the emotional words that tumbled from his mouth. "We lost Amara, and I don't know what I'd do if we lost this baby, too."

Her hand still covered his. "That is a heavy burden, but baby, as much as we'd like to control everything around us, there are just some things that are not ours to control. The best we can do is pray and have faith that all will be well. You and Terri aren't in this alone. Your friends and family will all be here to support you both. And as I told you before, I'm always willing to lend a listening ear. I know my great-granddaughter has adopted you as her uncle, but you need a grandmother close by, so I'm just going to have to adopt you, too."

He smiled, even as his chest tightened with emotion. As he'd told himself before, he should've just canceled therapy and sat on her couch, instead. In talking with her, he realized that he'd never had these kinds of conversations with his mother or grandmothers. Jon had to wonder if he would've had fewer issues as he grew up if he'd been able to talk with one of them. "I'd like that."

Mama Nora returned his smile and patted his knee. "Good. Now, let's go meet your wife, and I can see my Fred."

Jon stood and helped her to her feet, then took her arm in his. When they went inside, he hugged her. "Thank you."

"Any time. Here she is," she said with a huge smile, reaching out to hug Terri.

"Hey, Mama Nora. Papa Fred was asking about you a little while ago."

"Well, let me go and see about him. You two take care, and remember what I told you, Jon."

He saw the curious expression on Terri's face. "I will, and thanks again."

"I think I'm going to enjoy having another grandson," she said, strutting off.

Terri stared at him. "Grandson?"

"She decided to adopt me. Can't wait to tell Antonio I've got dibs on his grandmother. I'll tell you about it on the way." Once they got in the car, he filled her in on his conversation with Mama Nora. "I swear that woman has psychic powers. She can read me like a book."

"She's got a lot of life experience and wisdom, and I think it's pretty cool. Are you uncomfortable with it?"

"Actually, no. I don't know what it is about her."

"I hear you. Mama Nora does have that effect on people. It's probably why everybody loves her."

Jon parked in the lot next to the medical building and sat for a moment. Her doctor's office was in the same place as his therapist, but on another floor. He took a moment to whisper a prayer, then grasped Terri's hand. "Mama Nora said we have to have faith that things will be different this time."

Terri nodded. "I know, and I'm trying."

"Me, too. It's going to be okay." He hopped out of the car and came around to her side. Gently pulling her to her feet, he wrapped his arms around her. "It's going to be okay," he repeated. They strolled hand-in-hand across the lot and through the doors. Inside the waiting room, only two women sat reading magazines. Terri went to check in, and Jon sat in one of the chairs. The longer it took, the more his gut swirled. Finally, the nurse called them back. Then it was another waiting game before the doctor came in.

"Hey, Terri. Jon."

"Hi, Dr. Meyers," Terri said.

Dr. Meyers asked all the typical questions about eating, resting, whether Terri was taking her prenatal vitamins, and if she was having any problems. Afterward, she had Terri lie on the table.

A look of panic crossed Terri's features, and Jon was up in a flash and at her side. He held her hand as the doctor squirted the gel on her stomach and turned on the doppler. His heart started pounding. After a few seconds of squishy sounds, he clearly heard the steady, strong beating of their baby's heart. Relief spread through him. Jon wiped away his wife's tears, and they shared a smile.

"Baby Rhodes is doing just fine. The heart rate is a hundred and forty beats per minute. Would you like to know what you're having?"

"We're still undecided," Terri said.

"If you change your mind, we can do it next month."

Jon nodded. "Thanks, Dr. Meyers."

"You can get dressed. I'll see you next month."

As soon as the doctor left, Terri placed her hand on her growing belly, "Our baby is okay."

He covered her hand with his and wrapped the other around her shoulders. "Everything is okay." She leaned her head against his chest and he sent up a prayer of thanks. *We're going to have our rainbow baby.*

***

Terri had been floating on cloud nine since finding out that their baby was doing well last week. She and Jon had come home and celebrated with dinner in the sunroom. With the April temperatures in the upper seventies, she'd been able to leave the windows open. Now they were getting ready to head to Napa for another celebration. Dana and DeAngelo would be getting married at three in the garden of a small winery and vineyard. Terri had seen photos of the place and agreed it was perfect for their elopement. Instead of taking advantage of the food services there, the group had opted to drive back and have the celebratory dinner at the Hayeses' home.

Jon came into the bathroom, where Terri stood applying the last touches to her makeup. "You almost ready?" He expertly looped his tie.

"Yep. I just need to put on my shoes." They were picking up Dana, while DeAngelo and his siblings would be riding with Gabriel and Serenity, so as not to see his bride before the ceremony.

Fifteen minutes later, they parked in front of Dana's home. "Someone's a little anxious," Jon said with a little laugh as he got out and went around to hold the rear passenger door open.

Terri smiled. Dana was out the door and striding down the walk before Terri could undo her seat belt. She shifted around in her seat to see her friend. "Oh, sis, you look absolutely stunning. I hope DeAngelo makes it through his wedding night," she added, grinning.

Jon got in on the driver's side and cracked, "I hope my brother makes it through the wedding."

They all laughed. Dana said, "Hey, what good is a wedding without a little temptation?"

Terri waved her hands in the air. "I know that's right."

"Oh, Andrea called a little while ago. Her flight got in a little late, so she said she'd just meet us in Napa."

"I thought she was planning to fly in last night."

"That was her original plan, but she mentioned having to change the flight. We didn't get into specifics, though."

"As long as she's coming. I miss having her around." They spent the remainder of the drive discussing the newlyweds' plans once they returned from their two-week honeymoon in the Caribbean. When they arrived, Terri and Dana set off to meet with the venue's coordinator, while Jon headed for the ceremony area. A few minutes later, Serenity and Natasha joined them.

"Oh, Dana," Natasha said. "How long did we dream about having our weddings when we were kids, and what kind of dress we'd get? I always wanted the Cinderella ballgown, and you kept telling me it was too much material," she added with a laugh. "Girl, you were right, and I am *so* happy for you." The two women embraced.

"You've been my sister of the heart from day one, and I don't even want to think about how my life would've been without you in it." Dana dabbed the corners of her eyes with a tissue. "Now, stop with the mushy stuff before you make me cry and mess up my makeup."

Laughing through her own tears, Natasha said, "Same."

"You all are the best friends a girl could have. I love y'all." Serenity opened her arms. "Group hug!" They laughed and linked their arms together.

"Hey, no hugs without me."

"*Andrea!*" they chorused and made room for her in the circle.

"I miss my supper club sisters so much," Andrea said.

Serenity gave Andrea's shoulders a quick squeeze. "Well, you're in luck today. The reception will be back home in full supper club style."

She placed a hand on her heart. "Bless you, my sister."

"Hold up, hold up," Terri said, grabbing Andrea's hand. "Is there something you need to tell us?"

Andrea wiggled her left hand. "Oh, this old thing. Well, I may have sort of... *gotten married*!" she screamed excitedly.

"*What?*" they all shouted and started firing questions.

She held up a hand. "I met Dalton at a New Year's Eve party. We ended up getting stranded together when the power went out, and it just went from there. He took me away for vacation in Hawaii two weeks ago and proposed. I was joking around and said we already had the perfect honeymoon spot. The next thing I know we're getting a license and standing in front of an officiant at sunset on the beach. It was so incredibly beautiful. My only regret was not having you all, Gabriel, and

Nana there. We'll be here until Monday, so I'll show you the pictures before then."

"I'm so happy for you," Terri said. "What did Gabriel and Ms. Della say when you told them?"

Andrea ducked her head sheepishly. "Let's just say this visit will have a dual purpose. And since it's already done, my big brother won't be able to use all his scare tactics like he used to do with all my boyfriends."

"Wait. Is Dalton here now?" Natasha asked.

"Yep. He's waiting for me outside. I wanted to see you all and tell you first."

"Talk about a celebration," Dana said. "Well, this sister is ready to make it official. I can't believe we'll all be married now."

"I guess that means way more supper club couples dinners. But for now," Terri said, glancing down at her watch, "it's showtime." The women filed out, and Dana hung back until the coordinator came to get her.

Jon leaned close to Terri's ear. "Who's the guy with Andrea that Gabe keeps shooting daggers at?"

"Her husband."

His eyes widened, then a grin tilted the corner of his mouth. "I take it Gabe doesn't know." When she shook her head, he said, "It's going to be an interesting evening."

"No doubt." She refocused on the ceremony and listened as Dana and DeAngelo read their individual vows. A few short minutes later, the ceremony ended with DeAngelo kissing Dana as if no one else was around. The group cheered.

While waiting for the photographer to finish, Terri laughed to herself watching the exchange between Andrea,

Dalton, and Gabriel. After a few tense moments, Gabriel smiled, shook Dalton's hand, and hugged his sister.

Once the photos were taken, they drove back to Firefly Lake. Natasha and Antonio had elegantly decorated their back deck with tulle, greenery, and lights and had placed a table with enough seating for the couples in the center.

The relaxed camaraderie Terri had felt from the first was on full display, and Dalton jumped right in as if he'd known everyone for a lifetime, instead of just a couple of hours. At the end of the meal, they offered up toasts to both new couples.

Andrea stood and said, "To Serenity's Supper Club. Good food, great friends—"

"And a whole lot of passion," Gabriel finished. A loud roar went up.

Later, as everyone stood around laughing and talking, tears blurred Terri's eyes as she thought about all they'd been through these past few years.

"You okay, baby?" Jon kissed her temple.

She leaned against him. "Yeah. Just thinking about how far we've come since moving here. It's been a blessing in so many ways."

"It has. But the greatest blessing has been us finding our way back to each other." He caressed her belly. "And our little miracle."

Terri intertwined her hand with Jon's and smiled up at him. They were blessed indeed.

EPILOGUE

Four months later

Jon tenderly wiped his wife's brow as another contraction hit her. "You're doing good, sweetheart. Just a few more minutes." She'd only been in labor for three hours, but the baby's head was already crowning.

"Mm-hmm. I can't be too mad since he or she is being gracious enough not to have me in labor for a million hours. *Ohhh*," she groaned when another pain hit, and the doctor instructed her to push.

He chuckled. Antonio and Natasha had welcomed a baby boy a month earlier after almost twenty hours of labor. Little AJ looked like a mini replica of his father. Jon continued to encourage her. They had elected not to find out the sex of the baby, and he was more than ready to find out.

"All right, Dad. Come on over here," the doctor said.

Jon moved to the other end of the bed and, following the doctor's instructions, helped deliver their baby. "We have a beautiful little girl," he whispered as tears filled his eyes. He stared down at the wailing little baby, who was a perfect mix of him and Terri, and sent up another prayer of thanks. He'd prayed more in the past year than he had in his entire life. The doctor placed her on Terri's belly.

"Hey, my sweet baby," Terri cooed as she stroked a gentle finger down her small cheek. The baby immediately stopped crying. "She's so beautiful, Jon."

"Just like her mother." He placed a soft, lingering kiss on her lips. The medical team cleaned her up, weighed and measured her, then wrapped her in a blanket and handed her back to Jon. He cradled her against his chest. "I love you, Semira Johari Rhodes." He placed a soft kiss on her brow. They'd chosen the names that meant sent from heaven and something precious and adored, respectively, because they expressed his and Terri's feelings perfectly. Transferring her carefully to his wife, Jon sat in the chair close to the bed. A few moments later, both his girls were asleep.

Jon looked forward to loving, guiding, and being there for his baby girl forever. *I promise.*

RECIPES

Terri's Slow Cooker Short Rib Tacos

- 1½ teaspoons seasoned salt
- 1 teaspoon black pepper
- 1 teaspoon light brown sugar
- ½ teaspoon smoked paprika
- ½ teaspoon onion powder
- ½ teaspoon garlic powder
- ¼ teaspoon chili powder
- ½ teaspoon cumin
- 3 lbs boneless short ribs
- 1 tablespoon olive oil
- 1½ cups beef broth
- 2 cups shredded green cabbage
- 1 lime
- Pinch salt
- Corn tortillas
- Crumbled queso fresco cheese (or your favorite cheese)

In a small bowl, combine seasoned salt, pepper, brown sugar, paprika, onion powder, garlic powder, chili powder, and cumin and mix. Season short ribs, reserving some for later. Heat olive oil in a large skillet over medium-high heat. Once hot, add short ribs and sear on all sides, 1–2 minutes, until golden brown. Remove and place in the slow cooker.

Sprinkle remaining seasoning over short ribs, then add broth. Cook for about 8 hours on low, or until meat is tender and falling apart. Rotate short ribs once or twice during cooking. Once the meat is done, shred with a fork. Place cabbage in a medium-sized bowl. Squeeze lime juice over top and add a pinch of salt. Stir with tongs to combine.

To Serve:

Fry tortillas in a small amount of vegetable oil. Assemble tacos, adding meat first, then cabbage, and topping with the cheese. Enjoy!

Dana's Coffee Liqueur
(Homemade version of Kahlúa)

- 2 cups sugar
- 1¼ cups freshly brewed coffee (strong)
- 2 vanilla beans split lengthwise and cut into thirds
- 1¼ cups white rum
- Large canning jar (or other lidded glass container)

Place sugar in a large mixing bowl. Add hot coffee and whisk until sugar is completely dissolved. Allow mixture to cool completely. Once cool, stir in vanilla beans and rum. Transfer mixture to a large canning jar and allow it to sit in a cool, dark place for 2–3 weeks. Once ready, strain and remove vanilla beans. Store in airtight glass bottles you can pour from and enjoy!

ACKNOWLEDGMENTS

My Heavenly Father, thank You for my life and for loving me better than I can love myself.

To my husband, Lance, you remind me every day why you will always be my #1 hero!

To my children, family, and friends, thank you for your continued support. I appreciate and love you!

To all my readers, thank you for your continued support and encouragement. You keep me going!

ABOUT THE AUTHOR

Sheryl Lister is a multi-award-winning author who writes sweet, sensual contemporary romance featuring intelligent and slightly flawed characters who always find love. She is a former pediatric occupational therapist with over twenty years of experience and often says she "played" for a living. A California native, Sheryl is a wife, mother of three daughters and a son-in-love, and grandmother to two special little boys. When she's not writing, Sheryl can be found on a date with her husband or in the kitchen creating appetizers.

Find out more at:
   SherylLister.com
   Facebook.com/SherylListerAuthor
   X @SherylLister
   Instagram @SherylLister